A NORTH SHORE BUDDHIST

a novel by
Millie Jackson

Printed in Sydney, Australia
Published by Sue Kennedy Publishing

Dedication

I dedicate this book to my wonderful children, my loving family and my supportive friends who have all encouraged me to write this story.

I would also like to thank the Open Genre Writers' group at the N.S.W Writers' Centre for their respectful and insightful critiquing.

Finally, I would particularly like to acknowledge Sue of the Author Academy and Sue Kennedy Publishing as well as Emma from Emma's Edit for helping me bring this to life, to help me shine the light for so many women who battle on in the darkness.

Prologue

As I reach for another cigarette, I wonder how many times have I tried to quit now and what keeps leading me to my last cigarette again and again. Would it be easier to simply not quit, blow the consequences, love myself as I am, addictions, issues and all? There's a question to challenge all the new age, self-improvement books gathering dust in my bookcase, next to every known diet and my precious T.S. Eliot poetry.

We are the hollow men
We are the stuffed men
Leaning together
Headpiece filled with straw

The Hollow Men is my favourite poem of his. I often identify with these words and have frequently felt throughout my life that my head is full of straw or rocks or hot air and that my brain operates in a smoky haze of confusion and indecision. I remember studying this poem at university and having in depth philosophical discussions in tutorials with fellow students about its meaning, more often than not under the influence of some mind-altering substance.

My life certainly has been a life with very little boring beige to disturb the vast kaleidoscope of colour, with experiences full of shape and substance, a glorious rollercoaster of love, loss, pain and lots of laughter.

Most of the time, I feel like I'm twenty-five rather than rapidly approaching sixty, and yet my body is a dead giveaway, a few aches and pains that don't belong to a twenty-five-year-old, a saggy behind and arms that tend to sway annoyingly whenever I'm waving. I try to keep them by my side and just wave the forearm but often I forget and away they sway. As for my mirror, it tells me that only huge amounts of Botox, expensive facials or surgery could change what is; gravity and the inescapable evidence of time.

I had often thought about telling the story of my life, but had worried that it would sound like a B-grade novel, one that you would buy at any airport, read on the plane and throw it out upon arrival, without a second thought. Who would be interested? Would people laugh and cry in the right places or laugh at me?

I also wondered whether the regular soap opera viewer would be disappointed about the lack of artificial beauty and glamour. Would the reader who is looking for depth of meaning in addition to stimulation of the mind find the pages full of shallow pointless experiences? The truth can sometimes be like that.

I have often felt challenged by the need to go on, to look back with mystery, confusion and wonder, to look forward with anxiety and excitement. Remembering the dear friend who lost her battle and the dear friend who could not face another day, I often think about death and why her and why her? Two such amazing, sparkling souls gone from my world and yet never totally far gone from my heart. They would have loved to read these words and have a laugh and a cry in exactly the right places.

I can't help but think about the multi- generational melting pot of personalities from whom I have inherited, among other things, my peculiar sense of humour and my intense love of music. I have always tried to see the bright side among the drama, the sense of the ridiculous in situations where others are being too damn serious. Often that has been a challenge. Perhaps I am too bawdy for some, too dry for others, too quick for others, but for some, not too many, maybe I am just right.

Having arrived at this frighteningly grown up point in my life, I feel the need to reflect on the belief systems and values that have shaped me, my thirst to know more and to share the story of my life along with the learning that has led me to my last cigarette again and again.

Chapter One
A Lapsed Anglican

At the age of twelve, I knew three things for sure:

1) Boys must be better than girls;

2) Flirting was fun, and I was already getting very good at it;

3) God was there on Sundays to fix all the bad stuff you'd ever done, so I could pretty much do what I wanted the rest of the week.

Well, apparently God couldn't fix everything, according to Mum.

My family had recently moved to a new house, the fourth since I was born. My Dad, Carl, used to get moved every couple of years in his job in the bank.

"No point whingeing," my Mum, Marg, would say. "It is what it is." God, I hated that expression. It had just started becoming popular at the time, and people loved saying it. Little did we know that it would continue to be an annoying saying for many years to come. I still can't stand it! My Dad agreed that 'it is what it is', so, as kids, we all had no choice but to go along with it.

This new house in far west NSW was so different to our other houses on the mid-north coast, in Newcastle, and our previous one in the Blue Mountains. The house was bigger and made from timber. It had a huge back yard and I finally had my own room, even though I hadn't really minded sharing with my sister Annie before. She always wanted to tell scary stories before we went to bed. My brother, Tom, would join us sometimes and make fun of me when I got scared and wanted to sleep in my sister's bed for comfort. He could be such a jerk at times. My sister was okay, though; she didn't ever tease me or pick on me. She was into books, and didn't like all the girly stuff that I did. She kept to herself, and Tom didn't make fun of her for some reason that I couldn't fathom. Or, at least, that was how it seemed to me as a young, self-absorbed twelve-year old.

I always thought that boys must be better than girls because Tom appeared to be the favourite child in my eyes, and I mostly couldn't stand the way he treated me when I was younger. He was three years older than I was, and Annie was five years older. He teased me a lot, and a great deal of the time he tended to get away with murder.

"Jacq's a sooky baby," he'd often say in his sing-song voice. I wanted to punch him in the face!

"Stop tormenting your sister," Mum would say, with little or no conviction.

Another favourite was, "You're a fatty boom bah. You can't even fit through the door!"

This one had been going on for years, with more of the "Stop it, Tom. Just ignore him, Jacquie," from Mum, still with the same attitude. Again, the desire to cause him some serious harm, but, due to my burgeoning expertise at flirting, I was starting to doubt the accuracy of this statement. So I was thinking *Piss off, Tom. The boys at school don't seem to think that I'm fat.*

Dad was pretty good at giving me a hard time as well. "I wish I could get the fish to bite like you, bubs," he'd often say. He loved fishing, smoking, whistling really old tunes, and beer. The difference with him, though, was that he was a big softie and would always give me a hug after the smart comments. He had quite a quick wit, which I like to think was one of the best things that I inherited from him. He also enjoyed teasing Mum a lot but, judging by the look of impending thunder which was on her face whenever he did, I don't think she ever thought he was as funny as he did.

As she was very good at being invisible and ignoring Tom and Dad, Annie appeared to miss out on all this 'you can't take a joke' stuff that Tom and Dad thought I should be able to do. I used to wish that I could be more like Annie, calmly confident, but that was never going to happen. I think even back then, in my own warped little way, I just enjoyed the drama too much. Annie was always there for me whenever Tom would go too far – she never pushed me away or told me to get out of her room, like Tom did. Mum and Dad used to say things to Tom and me like "Why can't you two just be nice and quiet like your sister?"

When it rained, we would join many of the local kids and ride our bikes down the road to a street one block away. It had a dip down the middle and all the water would gather there, sometimes becoming quite deep. So we would ride our bikes as fast as we could from one end to the other, splashing ourselves and each other. Mum would go off her brain when we came home saturated and muddy, but we didn't care. It was the best fun in a town where not a lot happened. Most of the time it was stinking hot, raining torrentially or crazy and wild when the winds would come up. We had the local pool, one milk bar (where I wasn't allowed to go), and a rundown park just outside of town. The town was very spread out and quite tired looking, like a lot of the people in it. I think they must have been sick of the heat, sick of the rain and sick of the red dirt.

When the wild winds would hit, the washing and the back verandah used to get covered in red, powdery dust from the dry western countryside where we lived. It drove my mum crazy. We thought it was funny, and we used to love sleeping on the verandah on the old lounge when it was too hot to be inside. We would wake up with red faces and play games of Cowboys and Indians in the yard. It was so much fun when Tom didn't play too rough. One time, when we were playing, he tied me to the clothesline and threw fake (I'm pleased to say they were plastic!) knives at me, while Mum was out at the shops. This was one time where he really copped it from her. She could see that I was extremely upset and sent him to his room for hours. That brought a huge smile of vindication to my face.

I had my best friend, Denise, who lived very close to my house. We used to play a game of paper fortune-teller, where we'd write things like boy's names, where you were going for your honeymoon and how many kids you were going to have on a piece of paper. We'd then fold it in such a way that when you opened up the answer, it was supposed to be a huge and factual revelation. We loved it and believed these paper prophecies at the time.

She always used to tell me how pretty I was, which was something that I didn't often get told at home by anyone. She thought that she was terribly plain because she had red hair and really pale skin. I just thought she was the coolest person that I knew. She didn't have to try to be; she just was. Mum used to say that she was 'self-contained', but I had no idea what that meant. I preferred to think of her as just cool, a word I normally reserved for the boys at school that I liked. I didn't like girls very much, but she was different, not a princess like so many of them at school. Apart from Denise, I much preferred boys.

To look at the three of us, we were like chalk and cheese. Annie had inherited Dad's curly hair, although hers was blonde while his was almost black; she had piercing, bright blue eyes, and she was short like both my parents. Tom had Mum's huge green eyes, prominent nose and straight brown hair, but was very tall. We used to joke over the years that Mum had had an affair with the milkman – not that any of us knew if the milkman was tall. It was an expression that was quite common back in the fifties and sixties, when people still had their milk delivered to their front door by a man in a milk van. I was a total mixture of the two of them; my face was more Dad's shape, with a smaller nose, my eyes were big, round and hazel, and my hair was a lighter, more golden brown than Tom's. I was also, as Dad used to say, a 'short-arse', which of course meant small in stature.

So, back to the God thing. We used to go to church every Sunday, and I even went to confirmation classes after school twice a week for a while. I actually liked it, because after we all sat and listened (or at least tried to listen) to the many Bible readings and lessons to supposedly make us better people, we were given red or green cordial and cream biscuits. At the actual confirmation, I wore a lacy white dress and looked, for a change, pure and so innocent. Even back then, I favoured darker clothes and tried my absolute best to look as appealing to the boys as I could. Mum made most of our clothes, and she had really outdone herself with this dress. It felt so weird wearing white, but that was the expectation of the church for this ceremony. I used to dream about store-bought clothes, but money was tight, and Mum was pretty clever with her creations.

One Sunday, we were walking out of church in the line to shake hands with the minister. When it came to my family's turn, he was so keen to talk to the people behind us that he didn't pay much attention to us and didn't even bother to make eye contact with any of us as we moved down the line. Mum was furious; she reckoned that "if this is Christianity, we're not having a bar of it". She said that he had a bad attitude and we weren't going back. She thought he should have been nicer to new people in town. She could be a bit like that – one strike and you're out – although she did tell us afterwards that it had been building for quite some time.

Dad, having been raised to be a good Anglican boy, wasn't impressed at first but thought he'd keep the peace, which was always the best thing with my mum. Also, staying at home on Sundays had its benefits. He could have his first beer earlier; he could hang out in the garden smoking. I can imagine that he must have been thinking, *Yep, maybe she has a valid point on this one.*

Well, if God wasn't going to fix everything, what next?

Maybe boys, then? I became quite skilled at flirting with the boys at school. I met my first of many, many boyfriends – started a bit of playing around, kissing and stuff at his house, so that Tom wouldn't bother me – and I soon forgot all about God.

Chapter Two
Throwing Out the Lunch

Just as I was having the best time moving from boy to boy at school and becoming quite good at kissing, I thought, once again Mum and Dad told us that we were moving to a new house. I really didn't want to leave Denise and the boys and the red dirt house, but 'It is what it is!'. Thanks, Mum. I could tell she wasn't too happy about this either, even after we had officially left God and upset the good Christians in the community. But she put on her best brave face, and we started with the packing of the boxes once again.

I overheard Mum and Dad having a big talk about Annie and the impact that it would have on her moving again. She was in the middle of her last year of school, and they didn't want to upset where she was in terms of her education. The bank manager and his wife were very good friends of Mum and Dad's. They used to come over with their kids sometimes for meals, or we'd go to their place, which was big and posh. Their daughter was in the same year as Annie and they got on very well. They had said that she could stay with them, apparently, and assured Mum and Dad that they'd look after her until the end of the year. There was a lot of other chat going on that I couldn't hear, but the difficult decision was made; we were going, and Annie was staying.

When they told her, she didn't cause any drama, like I would have. She just accepted the decision without a fuss – but she also was very 'self-contained', according to Mum. I used to wonder what not being self-contained must mean. I guess that was just how I was, the opposite of Annie in many ways – and yet, despite that, we had some kind of bond that was solid and unbreakable. She was always there; not as a playmate so much, but as a big sister who would never give me a hard time or tease me for being fat or a sook or a drama queen.

We watched the removal truck leave the house. I said very teary goodbyes to Annie and to Denise, and we piled into the old white Holden, which Dad loved so much. We set off to make the eight-hour trip to our new house, in a small township on the outskirts of Sydney. For once, I had a window seat – I was usually in the middle of Tom and Annie on all our other trips, conveniently close enough so that Tom could pinch or poke me. As there was no aircon in the car, a window seat was always a highly desirable spot.

Mum mostly sang very loudly, chattering about everything that she noticed as we drove, while Dad smoked and whistled. The window was usually down, but we still managed to cop a lot of secondhand smoke in the back seat. We all loved to join in singing songs from decades before we had been born. Music was the one thing that we all loved as a family and we all thought that we were fabulous singers, especially me; I had already decided that I would be a famous singer or an actress when I grew up.

Mum and Dad loved songs like *Now and Then There's a Fool Such As I*, by Hank Snow, and many other favourites from their younger years, while we all loved anything modern by The Beatles, The Rolling Stones and The Supremes, amongst others. We all knew the words to every song, and nobody cared how out of tune you were, as long you sang loudly with a great deal of passion. This is one family trait that has remained with me my whole life and has been passed on to my children – with some mockery of the old stuff, of course. "Oh God, Mum, do you actually like this stuff?" my kids still say to me. However, some of it, I'm pleased to say, has actually made it to their playlists!

Even though it was great to have a break from the old songs, the chattering and whistling for once, this trip was far too quiet for my liking. The only sounds were Mum sighing, Dad inhaling deeply on his many cigarettes, and the thump thumping of the wheels on the never-ending road to our new life. I almost, only almost, hoped for a dig from Tom to break the silence, but for once he was lost in his own thoughts, staring out the window as we moved inevitably onwards to another town, another strange place to call home.

From what we could see as we were finally driving into the new town, there were a lot of pretty red brick houses, some of which, Mum told us with some authority, were very 'historical'. There were neat, colourful gardens in all of the houses, huge trees lining the streets and no red dirt. Before we turned into our new street, I noticed an enormous park with massive flower beds full of all sorts of beautiful plants, totally different to what we had had out west. Dad was telling us all the plant names as we drove, as if we should be fascinated – I wasn't. We arrived before the moving truck after what felt like a year and a half of driving. The new house was much like many of the others that we'd seen driving in, the same neat, colourful garden out the front. It was a lot smaller, made of red brick, and a lot darker inside than the red dirt house, which had been very open and airy. As we walked through the rooms, familiarising ourselves with a new environment, it felt so different. There was a slight pain in my stomach, a familiar fear of the unknown yet again. Without anyone having to say anything, I knew that we all missed Annie. She was such a calming influence within our often feisty family unit. I wondered if she could teach me how to be 'self-contained'.

Once the removal truck arrived, we began unpacking and started to get ourselves ready for another town, another school, new neighbours, hopefully new friends, and maybe even some more boys whom I could flirt with. I could tell that everyone was getting fed up with this constant readjustment, especially poor Mum, who looked completely worn out and worn down. She had been on the phone to Annie not long after we arrived, and I could now hear her in her room, softly crying. I hated hearing her crying. She was always so in control and stoic as we packed, moved and resettled into our new homes. Not knowing how to help her, I tried to entertain her by making jokes and being silly whenever I was around her. She pretended to be amused, but I didn't think she was in the mood for cheering up, so after trying a few of my best standup comedy routines, I let her be and stayed out of her way.

It took a few weeks to completely finish the unpacking, finding just the right spot for everything, and setting up another garden for Dad. Finally we all felt that we were settling in. Mum appeared to be a bit more cheerful, Tom and I were going to the local school, and Dad was working hard, whistling in his new garden, smoking and drinking beer. Everything was a lot more normal, but Annie's absence still felt like a gaping hole within our family unit. We were used to being a family of five, not four, and it just wasn't right.

I started to notice that Mum was drinking a lot more coffee than usual. It had always been her favourite drink with a couple of spoonfuls of sugar, but she seemed to have doubled her normal intake as far as I could see. She was using this artificial sweetener which was really popular at the time, and eating biscuits and all sorts of sweet treats with every cup. She reckoned that she could have something a bit sweet because she had given up the sugar. She was rapidly gaining weight – her clothes were becoming much tighter – but she just didn't seem to care a bit, at least initially. She definitely appeared to be at her happiest with her coffee, something sweet to go with it, her magazines and her book of crosswords.

She hadn't worked since us kids had been born because we were too little, or we were moving, or the only jobs in each place that we lived 'went to the locals', as Mum said, clearly not very impressed. Dad didn't care, as long as there was food on the table, beer in the fridge and a starched white shirt to wear to work. He was only ever in a really bad mood when it was raining and he couldn't go outside to the garden and smoke.

He was an avid gardener, and always grew some vegetables for the family as well. He would often walk in whistling and deposit something covered in dirt, with a flourish, a huge grin and a "There you go, darl". It was then up to Mum to clean and apparently find a use for this precious gift in our next meal. I did notice quite a bit of eye-rolling from her when he walked out the door. He was oblivious to the fact that quite often she had already scrubbed, peeled, chopped and diced whatever we were going to eat. She would often look at me and, with a wink, say something like, "Well, at least it makes him happy." I guess she didn't want to deflate such obvious enthusiasm.

School was okay, once I'd managed to make a couple of friends and had started flirting again. There was no doubt that the girls at this school were a lot more into looks and fashion than at my last school, wearing their hair like the stars I saw on the TV (which we'd only had for a few years now), and the clothes that I'd seen them wear outside of school were a lot more modern than anything that I ever wore from my homemade wardrobe. Maybe it was because this new town was reasonably close to Sydney, where all the fabulous big shops were. I'd never been shopping for clothes or makeup or anything for myself apart from sensible underwear, school clothes and groceries; fortunately, though, Mum was very good at copying some of the latest styles.

The girls brought fashion magazines to school, along with makeup, various hair products and accessories. It was definitely a lot more competitive here, and I used to take extra care with my hair each morning. I would hitch up my school uniform to make it shorter before I walked into the school gates to make sure that everyone could get a good look at my now rather shapely legs. I also started borrowing a bit of Mum's makeup when she wasn't looking for when I met up with any of the girls at the weekend. I'd been looking through her magazines to get some ideas and copying the popular girls at school. I thought that I was slowly but surely beginning to look so much more glamorous and grown-up.

One day I came home from school to find Mum so intently gazing at a magazine that she didn't even look up when I walked in. When she finally noticed me, her eyes were bright with excitement.

"Hey, bubs," (this has stayed with me most of my life!) "I think we should try this new diet," she said. "You just eat no bread or potatoes or biscuits or cakes. You can have as much coffee and diet soft drink as you like, as long as you only use artificial sweetener."

In the late sixties, we didn't follow the Paleo diet or the food pyramid, but we still did love a good fad diet. We all thought that lowering our calorie intake the artificial way was definitely the way to go. There were no labels or scary numbers to warn us about the dangers of colour or flavour enhancers. Apparently, Dad and Tom would be able to have whatever they wanted – but for me, I decided that it would be solidarity with Mum. Anyway, I could do with making sure that I didn't ever put on any weight, not at this school with those girls and the competition for the best-looking boys. The most popular international models in the magazines were really, really skinny and that was exactly what I wanted to look like.

After a few weeks of this, Mum hadn't lost any weight, but I sure had. I was looking much slimmer than usual, according to what I saw in the mirror. Poor Mum; I think she was missing Annie and didn't have enough to do with her time around the house, so she had probably been sneaking the sweet treats that she loved so much while I was at school. Also, because I was so good at this weight thing and looking, in my opinion, damn good, I reckoned that it might be a great idea to throw out my lunch every day to help further the cause. A lot of the other girls were doing it too. Of course, I didn't tell Mum that this was my unfair advantage. I did get a bit hungry, but didn't care too much, as I was enjoying having my clothes get looser and looser.

Never despondent for too long, Mum discovered these dehydrated meals in a box, which were 'low fat and delicious', according to the box. Thinking back, they sure as hell couldn't have been too low in salt, sugar and a million unpronounceable artificial sweeteners and preservatives. But Mum reckoned it would be good, and she thought she wouldn't mind losing a bit of weight (again). Annie, who had by this stage come home after finishing school out west, escaped this fad as she headed off to the city almost straight away to live on campus at Sydney University and become educated, something that Mum couldn't really fathom.

"What's the point of all that education? You could stay home and learn to cook and sew!"

What? Meals in a box, Mum? I said under my breath.

The meals involved adding water to the contents in a saucepan and stirring until it thickened. Fortunately for our arteries, we always had some fresh vegetables, often from Dad's garden, with this gourmet meal as well. We actually thought that we were being healthy because we believed what the box told us.

Mum and I used to cheat sometimes when we were shopping for material to make our own clothes. There was a local cake shop where we would buy this amazing new coffee called cappuccino and an iced doughnut as our occasional treat. I had recently joined Mum in her coffee addiction, and we loved spending this time together. I particularly enjoyed it as the coffee tasted a whole lot better than the cheap instant stuff we drank at home.

Money was still pretty tight. Mum was always trying to please me by creating garments as close as possible to the latest in fashion, and I was lucky enough to be able to wear clothes that looked a lot like the most popular designs of the time. We would pore over all the patterns, choosing the most current ones, and then find some material that would best suit the style and my colouring – which brings me to another of our favourite pastimes.

We had also discovered this cheap hair dye in the supermarket and decided that we would change our hair colour. The box promised us 'natural highlights and a radiant new glow'. The colour that I chose was a reddish brown, to brighten up my naturally highlighted light golden brown, while Mum chose natural brown despite my trying to convince her to be a bit more daring. With our new hair and never-ending diets, we really felt like we were keeping up with the latest that the magazines were dishing out for us to follow. Mum was still struggling with her weight, always trying a new fad, but she was happy enough and had sewn herself a whole lot of bigger clothes to wear. I had stopped throwing out my lunch by then, as I was starting to get a bit dizzy at school. My mission was accomplished. I had a great figure and loads of boys who were interested in hanging out and flirting with me.

You may have noticed the lack of mention of Tom. Well miraculously, he'd decided that I was now no longer in need of constant teasing. He had taught himself the guitar and was pretty good at it. Because I considered myself to be the best singer ever and had a better voice than he did, I used to sing while he worked out the chords to play to all the newest songs that we would listen to on our transistor radios. We thought that we were amazing and destined to be famous. We used to go into his room and practice most days after school. It was like we were finally equals. His friends used to pay a lot of attention to me too, so I guess he thought that I wasn't his annoying little sister anymore. We were actually really enjoying each other's company at last. He used to ask me (politely!):

"Hey, Jacq," – not sooky baby, or fatty boom bah – "I wanna figure out the chords to some songs this arvo. Wanna help?"

How can I resist? I thought. No fake knives or nasty names, so of course I agreed.

But then Tom also went off to become educated and I was left with my transistor radio, Dad's whistling and Mum's latest diet. I missed him now that we had become so much closer and we were so talented. I also missed hanging out with Annie, but she'd been gone a lot longer and I had had more time to get used to her not being around. It was lonely, but also it had its advantages, as both of my parents only had me to fuss over and focus on.

Mum and I developed a special closeness when Annie and Tom were away at uni. We started to do everything together, when I wasn't at school and the others weren't home for their holidays. As much as I did love my siblings, even Tom by this time, I almost resented the intrusion into our private time when they were back. Dad was either at work or in the garden doing what he did best, keeping the tobacco industry and the breweries in business.

Mum was getting on really well with all the neighbours, many of whom were much younger and with younger kids, but she still seemed to want to eat cardboard meals and read magazines with me whenever I was home. I was asked to do quite a bit of babysitting for a few of the people that Mum had become closest to, giving me the opportunity to earn my own money for the first time. It was exciting to be able to spend it on things like cheap makeup and all sorts of stuff for my hair.

The more I read the magazines and the more I flirted with the boys, the more I became obsessed with looks and fashion. Poor Mum would struggle sometimes to make exactly the outfit that I just had to have. I remember one time she had made me the most amazing mini-skirt in navy-blue corduroy (yes, really!). I kept asking her to make it shorter, and she kept pinning up the hem for me to keep the peace. When I was finally happy with it, I was going out to meet 'friends' (probably code for the boyfriend of the moment), and Mum called out to me, "You're not going out in that. I can see your knickers!"

"Mum, for God's sake, it's the fashion. I'm not changing it!" I screamed back at her.

We argued for ages, which was unusual for us, and eventually I had to reach a compromise of half an inch longer. I was not happy! This was our first real argument, but I had to give in or not go out, so it was a relatively small price to pay after all.

This was also around the time that I noticed that my hips were starting to get a bit rounded. Mum had quite wide hips, inherited from my eccentric grandmother, who had exactly the same body shape. She used to call them her 'childbearing hips'.

"Bubs, it looks like you've inherited the hips," she said to me one day with a smile.

Is she happy about this? I wondered. She seemed like she was quite thrilled, but I sure wasn't. There was no way that I was going to be a 'fatty boom bah'! As much as I was excelling in my schoolwork, how I looked was way more important to me and became my top priority. I cut down on my food intake immediately and discovered, in one of Mum's magazines, some apparently miraculous exercises that I could do in private on my bedroom floor. As much as I had always been conscious of having a great figure, I was now to begin my ongoing obsession with diets and body image in earnest. I was to become one of the best yo-yo dieters on the planet, losing it and putting it back on, over and over again.

Chapter Three
Show Me Your Knickers

At this time, some crazy person invented witches' britches (it's worth a Google. Seriously, what were we all thinking?). They were these disgusting, often brightly-coloured long knickers that had rows of lace along the bottom. My friends at school and I saved our pocket money; we just had to have at least one pair. When we thought that we had enough, rather than go straight home after school, we went to the shops together to try them on, buying whichever ones we were able to afford.

"Sorry, I missed the bus, Mum," was my excuse as I smiled happily to myself, so excited with my new purchase. It had taken me ages to save enough for mine, which were bright red with three rows of very cheap-looking lace. We all thought that we were so sexy when we put them on.

The trick was to have the lace showing just enough under your ugly navy-blue serge school uniform. The teachers were furious. There'd be a constant "Pull up your knickers!" from whoever in authority saw us, which we'd do until they weren't looking, and then we'd pull them down so that the boys could see them again. I'd like to know why boys would actually think that cheap, stretchy lace and nylon under such an unattractive uniform could possibly be considered a turn-on. At least they covered up the stockings and suspenders (not the appealing lingerie kind) which we were still wearing at that stage, before someone had the good sense to invent pantyhose.

Mum and I gradually stopped spending quite as much time together, as I had a great group of friends which included Di, the friend I had made not long after moving to the red brick house. She quickly became my best friend for the whole time that we were at school. She had a wild mane of pale blonde hair that sat around her open, smiling face like a halo. The girls in our little group seemed to get my humour, which was always important for me, and they laughed with me whenever I cracked a joke. I never could figure out those people who didn't think I was funny and shared my sense of the ridiculous, but there were enough who did, so I kept being the clown whenever I had a chance. Having Tom as an older brother and Carl as my Dad had greatly helped me to cultivate this. Without them, I wouldn't have learned to roll with the punches and give as good as I got. It was almost like a competition at times, growing up, seeing who could be the funniest and who would be the quickest to be offended – usually me. I did, however, have a very quick bounce-back reflex; I had to if I wanted the teasing to stop. I learned about points of vulnerability that could be used for comedy, and I learned where the line was that you couldn't cross.

Di and I became closer and closer, even more so than Denise from the red dirt days. She was smart and funny, and we did mostly the same subjects together, much to the ongoing frustration of many of our teachers. We would find ourselves laughing at the craziest of things that many people didn't find the slightest bit amusing. Fortunately, the rest of our group knew to laugh along with us – or perhaps it may at times have been at us. She also liked to sneak cigarettes from her father, just like I had recently started doing. Unlike many first timers who are put off by the taste and feel of it, we loved smoking. We had both just turned fifteen, and usually enjoyed copying the dramatic style of the movie stars that we had seen when they smoked on the big screen.

I also now had my first ever serious boyfriend. We were so in love; my flirting days were over. This was one hundred percent the boy for me. He was the year above me at the Catholic school across the bridge from our school. He was unbelievably handsome, tall with dark wavy hair, and eyes the same colour hazel as mine. We spent many moments gazing into each other's eyes, the young love blossoming so strongly that it felt like we were going to be together forever.

Dad didn't really approve of him – a carryover from being the good Anglican boy that surfaced from time to time. He had never been a fan of Catholics, or any other form of religion for that matter. You were either an Anglican or a heathen – funny, as we didn't go to church anymore anyway. He didn't, however, try to stop me seeing him, as he could see how happy and besotted I was. I guess he would have known that my first love would run its course eventually, and then maybe I would meet an Anglican boy.

Harry (that was the name of the love of my life) and I mostly met at the record shop – no CDs or downloads yet – which was just down the hill from my house. Most of the kids around town had started hanging out there after school, smoking cigarettes and generally trying to look as cool as possible. The girls used to hitch up their uniforms even higher and the boys tried to blow smoke rings. The things that used to impress me! He was the coolest of all the boys, and I considered myself lucky to have been picked to be his girlfriend. There was another girl from his school who used to look at him a lot, obviously flirting even though he was with me. An insecure little knot was forming in my stomach. *She better keep her distance!* I muttered under my breath more than once.

Mum really didn't appear to mind that we weren't together as much as we used to be; apparently things with the neighbours were really hotting up. I suspected that Mum was doing a bit of daytime drinking, judging by the smell on her breath some days, but she seemed happy and couldn't wait to share the latest gossip with me when we did see each other. She told me that two of the couples were wife-swapping: a regular soap opera in the suburbs. We used to sit and giggle about it all when she told me the secrets that they shared with her. I loved seeing how happy she was. For the first time since I could remember, she acted as if she was settled and had told me that she hoped that we could stay here.

"I never want to pack another box as long as I live, bubs! I've had enough," she told me one day.

"Me either. I want to stay here," I agreed.

After discussing it at length with Dad, he told the bank that we wouldn't move again, even if it meant that there would be no further promotion. In his mind, he had had enough, as we all had, and he wanted to have his family happy and stable. Annie and Tom could come home to the same house in university holidays, I could finish school in the same place, and Mum could keep having fun with the neighbours. We were going to be able to stay in the red brick house until Dad retired.

Mum had recently discovered these amazing headache powders, which were popular at the time, called *Bex*. Rather than pills, they were in a paper packet that you'd unwrap and you'd swallow the powder with a glass of water. The advert on TV said that you should have 'a cup of tea, a *Bex* and a good lie-down'. She took this quite literally for a while, and I'd often find her having a lie-down when I came home from school. I think this may have been a result of the odd hangover from the increased daytime drinking. As long as Harry and I had time to fool around without being bothered, I would just let her be. She was making friends and enjoying herself as a non-Christian living in the red brick house that felt like home.

While Mum was still struggling with her weight, mine was perfect, and I had a confidence that I wouldn't put on any weight while I was with Harry. I simply wouldn't let myself. I used to jump on Mum's bathroom scales every day and if there was even a quarter of a kilo extra, the lunch would be thrown out once again for a while until the scales read what I wanted them to. Even though I was quite smart at school, especially in French and English, the area where I continued to excel was my never-ending fight against any weight gain.

Ever since I had been very young, I had always loved reading – often well past my bedtime, with Mum screaming out, "Go to bed, Jacq! You'll never get up in the morning."

As she would always make sure that we were up and ready for school every day like clockwork, I didn't take too much notice, and would turn the light back on after she left.

"Ok, Mum. Five more minutes," I'd reply, knowing that this was a big fat lie.

I often borrowed books from the school library, but found that there wasn't enough variety for my tastes. I loved fantasy and romance – not the favourite genres at school. Some were okay, but I needed something more grown-up; I wanted to read every night that I possibly could, and to become totally lost in another world.

And so I decided to join the local library in the main street of our town. It was enormous compared to the school one. As I was devouring all the delicious titles one day, I noticed a book on the occult and some more on fortune-telling. Something in me was fascinated by these topics, especially now that we weren't Christians. I borrowed four books and went home excited to discover more. I loved reading them all, from the ones about black magic with satanic rituals to astrology and predictions for the future. I was totally enthralled by it all and was drawn back to the library, hungry for more and more.

When I wasn't with Harry, my girlfriends would come over and sometimes we'd all pretend that we were totally spiritual (although for me, it wasn't too much pretending now). One of the girls had been given a Ouija board for her birthday – a rather interesting present! We used to all sit around the dining table when my parents were out and ask questions, then we'd all put one finger on a glass, and watch to see if the glass would move to yes or no or even spell out somebody's name. As much as I wanted to believe it, I used to swear that someone would move the glass, but everyone would always play innocent and say that they hadn't. We would often get totally spooked when the answers were accurate; we drank really cheap alcohol and snuck outside for cigarettes so that my parents wouldn't smell it in the house. I reckon that they probably knew anyway, but they always turned a blind eye to it all. They didn't like too much drama or confrontation; they weren't the toughest of disciplinarians, being quite easy-going and preferring to just let things go.

This was to be my first dabbling into the spirit world, and I noticed that I was taking it way more seriously than the rest of my friends. I wasn't interested in the complete witch look, but I did love reading about witchcraft and wearing a lot of black clothes and heavy, black eye makeup. It was the time when Mary Quant make up was popular and the look was all about thick black lines all around your eyes. I became quite an expert at drawing the lines, often helping my friends who were not as good at it as I was.

At one of our many séances, I was wearing a black miniskirt, a flowy black blouse and a pair of high black boots, with my usual makeup.

"You look like a sexy witch!" Di giggled. I was delighted, and definitely took it as a compliment – a combination of two things that I loved.

As I had read as much as I could get my hands on at the library about all things spiritual, my friends elevated me to the position of the queen of spirituality, and I must say that I did enjoy this position among my peers. I was absolutely fascinated by magic and fortune-telling in particular, but Harry came first in my world and he wasn't into it at all. So I decided to keep it between myself and my friends, at least for the moment, and I toned down the 'sexy witch' look more when I was with him.

When I turned sixteen, Harry and I decided that it was time to have sex. We'd been doing a lot of fooling around, but now he told me that he wanted to 'go all the way'. He was so good-looking, and I'd noticed a lot of other girls staring at him with dreamy looks in their eyes. I even thought that a couple of times he might have been flirting back, so I thought I'd give him what he wanted (and, let's face it, what I wanted too). It was amazing; I absolutely loved it from the very first time that we did it. We were both so inexperienced and yet remarkably good at it, from what I could tell. We had sex in Harry's car, in my room when Mum and Dad weren't around, and once in the park in broad daylight, hidden by huge trees and flower beds, the thrill of potential discovery heightening the excitement for us.

So, at this point in my life, I knew that God didn't fix everything, that flirting was fun (not that I was doing any more of that now!), that having the perfect body was imperative, and that I loved cigarettes. My new addiction, however, was definitely sex. If I was writing a book, I would have called it *The Joy of Sex*. I was, however, into reading at that point, not writing – and very soon afterwards, someone beat me to that idea anyway.

One day, I was yet again asking Harry if he loved me. He always said 'Yes', so God knows why I was asking him. Perhaps it was just a bit of my occasional insecurity and doubt creeping in, or maybe I was just becoming psychic. Anyway, he took just a bit too long to answer this time, I thought, so after a lot of pushing and prodding him to tell me the truth, he finally admitted to having a thing for Julie.

"Why would you do that to me? Julie? She has sex with everyone!" I sounded so whiny and pathetic, but it hurt like hell.

"Don't be like that, Jacq. We've been together a long time. We just need a break, that's all. It's not serious with Julie anyway," he replied, pathetically, not able to even look me in the eye.

"So, you actually think that it's okay what you're doing?" I asked, feeling like someone had taken a huge sledgehammer to my stomach.

And just like that, he decided that we should stop seeing each other for a while and that 'maybe we would get back together at some point'. *Sure thing,* I thought, *I'd love to have you back once you've been with Julie – not!* Talk about having your cake and eating it too. I ran away from him as soon as he had finished speaking to find Di, completely and utterly heartbroken.

That was my first experience of rejection, and I was devastated. I had thought that this was the true, forever kind of love. Poor Mum didn't know what to do to help (she was always a bit awkward around big emotions), so I lay on my bed sobbing for what seemed like an eternity, refusing to talk to anyone but Di. I didn't go anywhere near the record shop after school anymore; I didn't want to see him with 'I have sex with anyone' Julie.

When I had finally calmed down and the tears had stopped, I was more pissed off than hurt, utterly furious and ready to exact my revenge.

How dare he do this to me? I asked myself. *I'll show him.*

I started to think of some ideas to pay him back and to get him back. The problem was that I thought that I did still love him deep down, no matter how upset and angry I was. After a bit of plotting and planning, I came up with an excellent idea.

Chapter Four
Getting Even and Getting Educated

I did what any heartbroken high-school girl would do, and hooked up with his best friend.

Looking back on it, I feel kind of bad, as the friend, Mike, really was keen on me; I guess I wasn't thinking at all clearly, logically or, in fact, morally. I wanted Harry to feel some of the pain that I had felt, and I wanted him to love me again. Mike and I went to the school formal together in my final year of high school, and Harry was there with bloody Julie. All the fake giggling I did at everything that Mike said and the gazing into his eyes flirtatiously must have worked really well as after a few days, Harry came running back and wanted us to be together again.

"I miss you, Jacq," he whined. "Can't we get back together? I made a huge mistake. It's over with Julie. Please," he begged me. My dramatic sigh must have given my true feelings away, and he knew he had me.

Poor Mike. I dumped him and went back to Harry, a little more in control and a whole lot more wary. We stayed together right up until my best friend Di and I went off to become educated at a university in Canberra, which was about three hours away. We said that we'd see each other in the holidays because he hadn't managed to get a university offer and was staying in town to work in his Dad's business. Well, that was our plan.

Mike and I sorted things out, after a grovelling apology from me, and I left the red brick house feeling rather optimistic about my future. I wasn't really a bad person back then. I had just wanted Harry back, and hadn't thought about the consequences to anyone of my rather cruel behaviour.

"Love you, babe," Harry had the good sense to say as I was about to leave. "I'm going to miss you heaps."

"You too," I replied, secretly wondering if I would. The hurt that I had felt over the breakup had toughened me up, and I was keen to try a new adventure. The power over me going and him staying had created a balance in my favour for the first time in our relationship.

Once I arrived at uni, and after a great many tears and waving of the handkerchief by a very confused Mum ("I thought at least you might stay home and cook and sew with me!"), I went out and bought myself a packet of cigarettes and went walking around campus with Di, both of us puffing away, to see what the guys were like here. You couldn't call them boys anymore; they were much more grown-up, and many of them were so much better-looking than the boys I'd been used to at school. As they were mostly older than us, we were very impressed entering this new, independent world destined to be full of a new brand of excitement. Of course, there was the education side of things as well, but in my head that was going to have to play a poor second to the social life that we were bound to be having.

Di was as crazy about boys as I was, and she was just as into having fun and pushing the boundaries. We had always made a good team, and I was happy to have her by my side for this next chapter in our lives. We smoked and laughed and started to settle into our tiny rooms with a feeling of optimism and a freedom that we had never known before now.

There were two guys who lived in the same college as us on campus, and when we met them in the cafeteria at dinner within the first few days of our arrival, one of them asked, "Do you want to come smoke a joint with us?"

"Sure, why not?" I said, the new queen of cool, even though I was rather nervous, to say the least.

Classes weren't due to start for another week, and we were both keen to try anything and everything new. Neither of us had ever smoked pot before, and I wanted to live my life a bit more on the edge compared to the school life that I had now left behind. So far I'd done quite a lot of drinking and smoking in secret, but here I was free to do whatever I wanted without any fear of being caught.

I laughed more than I ever had in my life that night, delighted by the instant effects that the pot had on me. Di and I were thoroughly enjoying ourselves already, with not even the slightest feelings of homesickness, and I didn't miss Harry one bit. The guys we were with came from Sydney, or 'the big smoke', as Dad used to call it. We were a bit awestruck by them; our little town didn't offer anything like the allure of the city.

Sometimes, on the weekends and in school holidays, my school friends and I had been used to catching a train to the city centre, where we would smoke and look at all the big, dazzling clothes shops.

It was like a whole new world to us, big, bright and shiny. We would go back to our town elated by our day out and yet equally frustrated that we didn't live somewhere more glamorous. These guys at uni represented a world that we had always envied and admired. Now we were becoming part of their world, and we loved it.

I met so many people in the first few weeks that I kept forgetting to call my parents or Harry. In fairness, there were only two pay phones in the college – this was many years before mobile phones were invented. I still could have made more of an effort if I wasn't having so much fun drinking, smoking and getting high. One of the guys that we'd met, Paul, was so good-looking and I really fancied him, but he came from a rich family and that was a bit like going out with a Catholic, according to Mum and Dad. So I just used to stare at him in awe and have wild dreams about living with him in a posh house in Sydney that his family owned, instead of our red brick house in our little town, owned by the bank.

One of the things about pot smoking was that we always had the munchies, so virtually everyone started to put on weight. For the first time in a long time, I couldn't care less, funnily enough. As long as I fitted in and everybody liked me, that was fine with me. We used to eat chocolate and pizza, smoke more pot, and then eat more chocolate and pizza. I was mostly laughing too much or too out of it to even think about the fact that all I was now wearing were my stretchy pants or my new hippy Indian dresses that would fit any size that I became. We did almost no exercise and sat around acting like we knew absolutely everything about everything, having intense debates on the meaning of life, which I'm very sure made no sense at all to anyone but ourselves.

During my three years at uni, I did manage to have sex with Paul and a countless number of other guys. I broke up with Harry, who was already moving on anyway, I suspected. He certainly didn't seem too fazed or hurt by my decision. I didn't have any serious boyfriends, because I didn't want to be too serious. It was one huge exciting blur of parties, drugs and booze. Still to this day, it is of great amazement to me that I actually managed to get my degree (all passes, not even one credit or distinction) at all. I was one of the smartest people at my school, but study just seemed to get in the way of a good time at uni.

I again dabbled a bit with my interest in spirituality during this time, going to the occasional séance and even to a tarot reader a couple of times. My new friend Meg, whom I had met in my first year of uni at our English Poetry tutorial, used to come with me sometimes. We discovered that we both loved T.S. Eliot poetry, dressing like hippies, and wearing heavy makeup, platform shoes and Indian dresses or super flared jeans.

I didn't go too deeply into the whole spirituality thing at that time, though, as I was having so much fun doing other things. While I did want to know more about what or who God was and the meaning of life, it was just a bit too serious at this stage, so I decided that it would be pushed to one side for the moment. It appeared to me that I was the only person I knew, apart from Meg, who really was interested in questioning everything, with everyone else being content to just party and not get too heavy about anything from a spiritual perspective. It was an itch and an interest that could wait for the time being.

I'd moved out of college after my second year of uni and was living in a group house with six other people, including Meg. We both managed to find some waitressing at a local restaurant so that we could afford the rent. Mum and Dad also continued to send me the small amount of money they had done while I was in college. I was able to pay the rent and have a little bit left over for pot, ciggies and alcohol. Somehow, while living this crazy lifestyle, we both managed to finish our degrees and keep our waitressing jobs. Serious jobs could wait. Life was too damn good to spoil it by growing up any further.

Di had stayed in college and was mixing with a different crowd by this stage. We still saw each other, but not as much as we had in our first year. She had lost interest in pot smoking and was more focused on her studies and the people she met who were also studying Law with her. We'd catch up for the occasional drink and laugh about old times; we shared a past, but we just didn't share the same present. I thought I was the one who had it all together and that nothing could ever bring me down, so while I still loved her and respected her choices, I felt that I was living the better life out of the two of us.

Sometime during my final year at uni, a lot of our friends and housemates started experimenting with harder drugs like LSD and heroin. I'd really always been happy with just smoking pot and didn't like the effect that I witnessed on my friends of anything heavier. There was gradually starting to be nowhere near as much fun and laughter as there had been; people would sit around, not talking, for hours. I was beginning to feel somewhat paranoid about this new, serious, totally-out-of-it behaviour that I hadn't been used to up until this point. Then the drug-taking went way too far.

One night, one of our housemates, Peter, was rushed into hospital after another of our many all-night parties, having taken God knows how many different drugs. He had always been so much fun to be around before the hard drugs. We used to love having a whinge to each other over our latest break-ups, often sitting curled up in each other's arms, listening to very loud, very heavy rock music. We'd never had sex; we enjoyed our comfortable friendship too much to spoil it. His family was by his side as we all waited for what we were sure would be good news. We were young and we were bulletproof – surely we could get away with anything.

He didn't survive. His sister, sad beyond imagination, called our home phone the next day to tell us that he had gone into a coma and hadn't made it through the night.

This was such a shock and a huge wake-up call for some of us: way too much reality in the midst of a fog of invincibility and immortality. We were all stunned, and the laughter stopped. Sadly, many of my friends kept taking drugs, even the harder ones – especially heroin – unable or unwilling to make any changes to the lifestyle to which they had become accustomed. Meg and I stopped completely, shattered by the loss. I didn't want to speak to anyone but Meg, and she felt the same. This wasn't supposed to happen to one of us. I wasn't ready to grow up and to feel this much pain.

I found that I didn't want to stay in Canberra anymore after we attended Peter's funeral. We weren't immortal; I knew that now, even if others were still going to keep doing drugs. As we all started to recover from this tragic dose of reality, I started to make plans to move to Sydney with Meg. She said to me one day, "I think it's time we got out of this place before this happens to someone else. It's not fun anymore. Nobody's laughing. Peter is not coming back."

"I agree. I reckon we should go to Sydney, find our own place and get jobs. I'm done with the drugs, and I can't be around all the people who won't stop. I miss Peter; it's too sad being here," I replied.

With that, we agreed on a very loose plan at least, then gave notice to our housemates and started saying our goodbyes to all our friends.

The hardest goodbye was going to be Di. She was still drinking and smoking a lot, but as she preferred to stay away from drugs, it had caused a slight distance in our friendship. I guess that she didn't share the delusion of immortality to drug-taking that my current group of friends had. It turned out that she was right. I felt sad leaving her, but just had to make a break, a fresh start. We hugged and cried and knew that we would always be friends – but for now, we had to go our own separate ways.

"I'll come and visit you in the Christmas break. I promise," she said.

"And I promise we'll go shopping and to bars and dancing. I'm going to miss you so much," I answered her, wondering if we would actually keep our promise to each other. It wasn't like they didn't have bars and shops and dancing in Canberra. It was just that everything we did was on campus with uni friends. This was going to be a very different and an even more grown-up lifestyle, I thought; one that didn't include drugs. I did feel a small buzz of excitement and relief along with the heaviness of my sorrow.

Meg and I packed up our few possessions and caught the bus to Sydney. Neither of us could afford a car, and we were accustomed to catching public transport. She was also from a small town, about two hours west of my family home, and not used to having a lot of money. We got on so well and had a great deal in common. She knew what it was like to not be a part of the city life, and she also loved flirting and partying – as well as T.S. Eliot and heavy makeup, of course. We knew that we were going to have a ball in 'the big smoke'. We both thought that we'd make heaps of money, buy a car and wear fabulous clothes when we started working.

The sadness sat with us for most of the trip, but the closer we were to arriving in Sydney, the more our spirits lifted, and we felt the dawn of new beginnings and possibilities. We smiled at each other, full of hope and giddy with the prospect of whatever lay ahead for us. We were both so pleased that we had each other to start our new chapter with, rather than having to face it alone.

When the bus stopped, we headed straight to the YWCA, about a ten-minute walk away, which would be our temporary home until we could find an apartment that we would be able to afford on our rather limited budget. It smelled of dirty socks and undried washing. Our first meal there was virtually inedible, and we knew that we needed to find somewhere as quickly as possible.

After a solid week of looking around, Meg and I found a fantastic apartment right near the harbour on the lower North Shore of Sydney in a place called Neutral Bay. It was fantastic particularly because we couldn't wait to get out of the Y. Back in the mid-seventies, rent was reasonable and rental properties weren't too hard to find. The place we had was in an enormous, rambling old house that had been converted into tiny apartments with two single beds in the one room. It wasn't in the best condition, with an ugly green floral carpet and even uglier green chipped paintwork, but we were able to move in straight away. The view from our place was spectacular, looking right over the Harbour Bridge, and the rent was unbelievably cheap compared to today's exorbitant prices.

"Oh my God, oh my God, oh my God!" I kept saying. I was so excited to be here in this city that I'd never thought I would do more than visit.

"Let's go buy some stuff to see if we can make the place look posher." Meg grinned at me, equally happy that we would be settled.

So we went to a really cheap import shop (our version of posh at the time) and bought some kitchen stuff and a few cushions to brighten up the place as best we could, making it look less drab and run-down. After our tiny college rooms, we thought we were living in a paradise once we were finished with our simple interior decorating. We bought a bottle of very cheap wine and raised our glasses to Peter. We weren't going to forget him. We were just going to live our lives in the city, away from all the sad memories.

Now that we had a place to live, next we would have to face the huge task of job hunting.

Chapter Five
The Working World

We were starting to build our new lives and to leave the sadness and madness of our uni days behind us. It was time for me to get my first serious job. I had had my waitressing experience while at uni, when I wasn't too tired or stoned to actually turn up for my shifts, but I'd never really thought of getting a proper job until now. I had been just trying to get through my degree and party as much as I possibly could. There was now going to be rent to pay and all the ongoing living expenses to consider.

The main subjects that I'd studied, French and English, were good for teaching, and Philosophy was good for discussing a wide range of theories and viewpoints (something that went well with the pot). We all had thought that we were so wise about everything and that we had it all sorted out. *But how will that be able to help me now?* I wondered.

I had tried to get my teaching qualification after uni at a college near the university in Canberra, but that hadn't ended well for me. One of my main tutors had asked me to stay back after class one day. I had really thought that I got on famously with him, and I was about to find out just why, in fact, that was. When I had knocked on his door and been asked to enter, he closed the door behind me and told me to come and sit down beside him. The room was stuffy, full of dusty books, and I felt a sense of discomfort coming over me.

There was a bit of light banter about my studies, and then his voice took on a different tone altogether.

"Now, Jacquie, you must know that I've always fancied you, and I can feel the same vibe coming from you." No preamble, just straight to the point. "I really want to have sex with you, and I'm guessing that you want it too," he said, smug, self-assured, and obviously used to getting his own way.

Now, you may think that I was pretty easy when it came to sleeping with everyone at uni, but this guy was married and a lot older. Apart from that, I definitely did not fancy him, and in my opinion had done nothing to intimate that I was at all interested in him physically.

I absorbed what he had said, realising that he was in fact serious.

"No way. I'm not going to do that. Why would you think that I'd even want to?" My tone of voice made it abundantly clear to him in no uncertain terms that I was absolutely disgusted. He looked shocked and angry; I, on the other hand, was frightened. The door was closed, and he was way too close to me.

"Then get out of my office, you little prick-tease!" he spat at me, standing up and towering over me.

I ran out of the room, saying nothing further. Shaking uncontrollably and sobbing, I went straight home. I didn't complain to anyone, because I felt that he had all the power and that no one would listen to me anyway. I never went back, and as far as I know, he probably moved onto the next victim. I so wish that I had had the confidence and maturity to stand up to him even further and to report him, as I'm sure a lot of people who have ever been in my situation would agree.

No longer considering teaching as my career, I had taken on more hours in my waitressing job until I could figure out what to do next. Before I could do just that, Peter died, and Meg and I made our decision to come to Sydney.

Looking back, I wonder just how many young women might have faced what I did and felt that they had to give up without a fight. What a jerk! I'd met his wife once at a college drinks thing, and she had been really nice and really pregnant. I was so upset, but felt that I just had to move past it. I still regret not making him more accountable for his actions, though.

Back in those days, when you wanted a job, you'd have to buy a newspaper and if you were female, you'd look at the Women and Girls section. There was a Men and Boys section (the largest!) for the males and a General section for those few employers who felt that the job could be done by either gender. Even though we were supposedly experiencing a more liberated time for women, the feminist movement still hadn't been able to break the workplace stereotypes sufficiently for an even close to equitable job market.

Before I could even think of going for any interviews, however, the dieting had to start again. I only had a couple of things that I could wear, and they definitely weren't going to fit this new body of mine, probably a whole three or four kilos over my pre-uni weight! Meg and I tried the *Israeli Army Diet,* which was popular at the time. It consisted of apples for two days, cheese for two days, chicken for two days, then salad for two days. Boring as hell, but it worked pretty well, and I could squeeze into my very tight skirt to head off for my first experience in the business world. I had made a few calls; there was one job as a Sales Representative which was offering good money, and it was close to Circular Quay wharf. There was a ferry that left from really close to our apartment that would be able to take me to work each morning, if I was successful in securing the job.

I was a bit nervous, I must say, but also feeling extremely positive. With my flair for the dramatic, my (I'm ashamed to say) provocative way of dressing, helped by the extreme tightness of my skirt, and my 'gift of the gab' (according to my parents), I was able to talk my way into the job interview fairly easily and then to ultimately be offered the job.

I only had one other outfit that was sort of decent for work apart from my interview outfit, although it was a bit too low-cut probably to be appropriate. I knew that I would have to borrow some money from Mum and Dad to get by temporarily. As they'd already given me some money for the first month's rent, I felt bad, but I knew I'd be able to pay them back. Meg had to do the same thing, and while neither of our families could really afford it, they were happy to see us becoming so responsible.

I knew nothing about sales but the sleazy Sales Manager, Pat, in his brown safari suit (a disgusting fashion trend and, again, worth a Google if you don't know what that is!), thought that I would be a natural. I did feel that his eyes were wandering a bit lower than my face during the interview, but I needed a job and this one seemed like it would be perfect. He said that he didn't need experience – just the right look and attitude.

"You'll go out with Carole for the first few days to see how it's done, and then you'll have your own territory and be able to work by yourself," said Pat the Perv.

"Absolutely, Pat. I'm a really fast learner. I know I'll pick it up quickly. You won't be sorry," I replied, Little Miss Perky, keen to impress and hoping that I wouldn't have to be alone with him in his office too often.

Pat's teeth matched the colour of his suit and he smelled like stale cigarettes. My dad, who, as you know, loved to smoke, never smelled this bad. Pat had tried to cover up the smell with a lot of Brut 33 cologne. Again, you might have to look that up, as I'm hoping that no one would dream of wearing that anymore. No judgement on the nicotine addiction, though, as I was still puffing away whenever I had the chance. I was probably at around a pack a day most days, but I did discover breath freshener at the chemists. It wasn't hard – it was on the shelf; it's not like they were trying to hide it from everyone.

The job involved walking around to office buildings in the city and trying to sell people stationary supplies; I learned quickly and came to really love it from the moment that I started.

What I loved more, though, was drinking huge amounts of alcohol at the Customs House bar every Friday afternoon with my workmates: two slightly older women, Carole and Wendy, who were fabulous to work with. They taught me how to do my hair and makeup to look a lot classier and more modern. I'd been dressing like a hippy – a trendy one, of course – with lots of black eyeliner (a hangover from my semi-witch days) and huge, chunky platform shoes. Seventies fashion was really something else. Office-wear was more about the stilettos, short skirts and bright lipstick, which I hadn't mastered yet. We became great friends, and they also really liked Meg, who had managed to get a job in a small bookshop quite near our office. She would almost always join us on Friday nights after work for a drink and a good laugh with the girls. We would often all move on to dance clubs and pick up a man to dance with, and maybe even go home with for the night if the mood took us there.

This was definitely a lot better than the uni drug scene, and making lots of money was an addiction that I wasn't going to give up. I became very good at sales and made a huge amount of commission quite quickly, which meant I was able to pay Mum and Dad back and to start to augment my very limited wardrobe. Finally, I could buy some more expensive clothes from proper dress shops and better-quality makeup, and I didn't have to ask poor old Mum and Dad for a helping hand with the rent. Shopping in 'the big smoke' was so much fun; no more dressing like a hippie for the rapidly-becoming-successful salesgirl.

"We're so proud of you, bubs," (still!) Mum said when I called to tell her how I was doing. I wasn't in contact enough, but they seemed happy whenever I made the effort. This was a whole new experience for the girl from the red dirt house and the red brick house in the small town that was not quite close enough to be called a part of Sydney. If I'd felt independent before, this was on a whole new level.

There was a series of short-term boyfriends over the next six months that never lasted more than a few weeks. I was enjoying playing the field too much. That was until one night, when I met a guy called Nick at one of my favourite nightclubs – a place that I used to frequent with Carole and Wendy and sometimes Meg. He was a real estate salesman and he told me that he drove a Mercedes Benz. The most expensive car I'd ever been in up to this point was my Uncle Bob's new Holden last year, when we had gone to visit him at Christmas time. Nick had come straight up to me, full of confidence, and asked me to dance. After a lot of pashing on the dance floor, he asked, "Hey, babe, want to come home with me?"

Very smooth and no beating around the bush, but I happily agreed. He was unbelievably hot, after all, and he laughed at my jokes, which was always a plus in my books.

Nick and I saw each other every moment we could from that first night, and ended up moving in together after only going out for six weeks of nonstop dating. We went out every weekend and some weeknights, speaking on our home or work phones every day. He also lived on the lower North Shore, but in a really modern, huge apartment with all-new furniture and appliances – a lot posher than the cheap imports that Meg and I had thought were posh enough for us.

These days, I was becoming more and more impressed with what money could buy. I'd found my new religion – materialism – and Nick was like a kindred spirit. He loved nothing better than to go to a trendy new restaurant and then on to a club for French champagne and dancing. With both of us earning good money, we felt like we had it all. We had the craziest, wildest time together, always at glamorous parties, with glamorous friends – some I'd met through work, but mostly they were his circle of friends and work colleagues. We never stopped rushing around from work to dinner, to a party, to a club. It was one hell of a buzz living like that.

Meg decided to stay in our little place when I announced that I was moving out to live with Nick, as she was also working and could now afford the rent by herself. She wasn't earning anything like as much as I was, but she was happy, and she'd met new people through work and in the other apartments where we'd been living. We now needed our own space but would always remain good friends, already promising each other that we would catch up in the city for lunch a couple of times a week. Our social circles had rapidly become quite different, but it didn't stop the strong bond between us. Now that I'd met Nick, my nights and weekends were super busy and our scene was not really Meg's scene. I hadn't been properly in love since Heartbreaker Harry, but it felt like Nick could be the one – or the second one, at least.

Not long after I moved out, Meg started seeing Sean, a guy who worked in the café next to her bookshop. I met him a few times and he was such a sweet person, and absolutely besotted with Meg. Nick and I didn't ever see them socially, as our interests, pace and types of friends were worlds apart. Neither Meg nor I minded this separation too much; we had been in each other's pockets ever since arriving in Sydney and we both knew that we'd always be there in a time of need. We'd shared a time of outrageous fun and laughter, mixed with incredible sadness and confusion. Neither of us would ever forget that.

"I'll always love you, babe," Meg said to me at one of our regular lunches. "I know things are different for us in our lives, but just remember I'm always here whenever you need a friend, anytime – day or night."

"Ditto, sweetheart," I said, and hugged her warmly before I rushed off, as always, to get back to the money-making machine as fast as I possibly could without appearing too rude.

It was at one of our many parties with Nick on a Saturday night that I was approached by a friend of his called Johnno, who apparently knew from Nick that I was doing really well with my Sales Rep job. He told me that a business acquaintance of his, Derek, had his own recruitment consulting company and that I could make huge amounts of money if I went to work for him – much more than I was currently earning. He said that he could set up a meeting for the following week if I was interested. After mulling it over, I thought *Why not at least meet the guy and see what he has to say?* Nick and I were talking about buying our own place as soon as we could, and he thought it would be great for us to have more money to pay the mortgage. Johnno called a few days later.

Well, if I had thought that Pat was a sleaze, Derek was a whole new ballgame. He was really short — not much taller than me (I'm only five foot three inches, or one hundred and sixty-one centimetres if you're more metrically inclined). He had the most piercing, steely blue eyes that seemed to look straight through me. He shook my hand and stood incredibly close for a long time before he finally asked me to sit down next to him in his office.

"So, I hear that you're quite the successful little salesgirl," he said, accompanied by a lascivious wink. "I can show you what real money's like, if you're prepared to learn from the man."

'The man' was, of course, him. I still wonder why I didn't run out of there, but remember that my new religion was all about the dollars, and Nick encouraged me to give it a go. So I accepted the job, sadly told Pat, Wendy and Carole the next day that I was leaving, and, with more than a little trepidation about my new boss, started my training two weeks later.

Rapidly, I learned all about the recruitment of office and junior accounts and office staff, getting along really well with the large number of clients and the staff members, who were all extremely supportive and encouraging of the new girl. Derek mostly left me to it, happy to have me under the wing of his senior recruiter, Neil. I soon became successful, doubling what I had been earning selling stationary within the first month.

Derek moved me on to work on recruitment for more senior positions after a few months. The challenges and the excitement of this new job kept growing, making it easier to ignore the winks and innuendos that Derek would make when no one could see or hear him.

One night, we'd all gone out for work drinks and Derek kept trying to put his hand up my skirt when no one was looking. I told him to stop it, but he whispered in my ear.

"You do know that to be the best in this job, you have to learn from the man, and to know the man, you have to sleep with the man."

Oh my God, what a total sleazebag — and he was dead serious! His wife was our receptionist, and she had gone home to look after their kids. Talk about déjà vu after my college experience. I really didn't want to leave the job, now that I was becoming so good at it — but I told him that I wouldn't sleep with him and I was going home.

He told me that if I wasn't prepared to 'sleep with the man' then

I was fired. This really upset me, understandably, because I liked all the other people in the office, especially his wife! Also, there was the enjoyment of earning that much money; but I was not going to give in to his disgusting, inappropriate proposal, so sadly that was that.

"I can't believe that people like that are allowed to run a business," I cried to Nick when he came home that night. "What a total scumbag!"

"Well, Jacq, you know we really need the money. Do you think that he might have just had too much to drink and he'll forget about it?" replied a very unsupportive Nick, thinking he was being sensible.

"You have got to be kidding me! I thought you'd be on my side," I yelled. I climbed into bed and refused to speak to him, finally falling asleep in the early hours of the morning. By the time I was out of the shower the next morning, he'd already gone to work, and we hadn't spoken.

I went in on the Monday wearing a pair of jeans and a sweatshirt, instead of my usual office glam, and started packing up my desk. When Derek swanned in, late as usual, he took one look at me and yelled at me to get into his office immediately. Once he'd slammed his office door, he looked down his nose at me (not very far to look).

"What the hell do you think you're doing, dressing like that for the office?" he said, sneering sarcastically, with spit unattractively forming at the corner of his mouth.

I replied, confused, "Well, you fired me, didn't you?"

"Oh, for God's sake, we were just drinking and mucking around. Go home and get changed and get back here ASAP – do you hear me?" He was seething. I guess he must have been used to getting his own way. Arsehole! I had just turned twenty-three and was still quite inexperienced with the business world, so I did as I was told. I didn't have another job to go to and I needed the income. I went home, changed, went back to work and tried my best to pretend that I wasn't working for the devil.

At least Nick had the good sense to come home with flowers and a huge apology that night. I told him what had happened and that I'd stay for the moment, but I was definitely going to be seriously looking around for something else.

Sadly, not long after I'd rejected his advances, Derek moved onto someone more vulnerable: Penny, the new girl from London who had started working with us recently. She was such a sweet, innocent, trusting person and fell for him completely, for some gross reason. I did try to warn her, but she reckoned that she loved him and that I didn't understand him like she did. She said that his wife was such a bitch to him when no one was around. I guess that's the first time a married man has told that story! He would take her out to 'meetings' with him sometimes, glaring smugly at me as he walked, chest puffed out, past my desk.

After a couple of months of their 'meetings', she came into work one day looking pale and shaken. I went to the break room with her to find out what was wrong. Her eyes were red-rimmed as she told me that she had just found out that she was pregnant and wanted to talk to me in the lunch break.

"He said that he'd leave his wife for me and now he has told me that I have to have an abortion," she sobbed when we were out of the office and earshot of any of our workmates. We sat down at a small café, close by the office, where we could talk in private.

I didn't want to make any judgement; she was shattered enough. I asked her what she wanted to do, and she felt that she had no choice but to do as he said. He clearly was not going to support her in any way – big surprise. I offered to go with her to get the abortion if that was the choice that she wanted to make, but she said that he was going to go with her. (To make sure that she went ahead with it, I guessed!)

"It's for the best – you'll see," he had told her, apparently convincingly. "We can then go back to the way things were, only we'll be more careful."

When she told me this, I wanted to confront him, but she begged me to accept that she trusted him and believed in him.

Penny held on to this glimmer of hope that he was a decent guy until after the abortion, when he started to completely ignore her at work. I could see that it was almost impossible for her to concentrate; she was distracted, and there were often tears in her eyes threatening to brim over at any moment. She was totally devastated and felt that she had no choice but to leave the company very soon afterwards. I kept in touch for a while, but she ended up going back to her family in London. We didn't stay in contact after that.

Derek, the arsehole, was still strutting around the office with his chest poked out like he hadn't done anything wrong – like he couldn't care less. I hated him, but unfortunately, I still loved and needed the money. In those days, sexual harassment wasn't really policed or reported very often. Most girls and women just shut up, put up with it or left their jobs. I wish that I'd had the courage to do more for Penny, but as we were saving for a house, I kept quiet and tried my best to concentrate on my job. My loathing of him built to a whole new level, but there was the rent and the lifestyle to consider. Still, I didn't think that I'd be able to look at his smug face for much longer.

Chapter Six
A New Opportunity

I was building a strong reputation in the recruitment world and was rapidly becoming quite well-known by a large number of clients and other recruiters. So it was a wonderful boost to my ego when I was head-hunted by a larger, more successful company than Derek's to discuss the possibility of managing one of their divisions.

I'd been recruiting mostly accounting staff at Derek's company, which was weird, seeing that I had started off knowing nothing about it, and this suited the requirements of the role. I'd picked it up relatively easy and felt comfortable with all the accounting terminology. The new job would give me an opportunity to continue working on senior roles and offered a higher base rate with a better commission structure. It couldn't have come at a better time, as I wanted to get away from Derek, and so I readily agreed to go for an interview.

When I met Jack, my new boss-to-be, he didn't look at my boobs, he was very professional, and he had a crucifix on his wall. (Mum wouldn't have been impressed by the latter, still firm in her belief that Christianity was not to be encouraged.)

"We'd be so excited to have you on board. The team are all really close and I think you'll be a great asset to the business," he said at my interview with him. Very businesslike; no inappropriate flirting. "You probably want some time to think about it, but based on our meeting, I'd love to offer you the position now."

It felt right, and the timing was perfect. I was more than happy to say yes straight away.

"No need to think about it, Jack," I relied confidently, thinking, *Get me away from Derek now!* "I'd love to accept."

"Excellent news." No dirty look or wink – just a genuine, honest smile. I felt instantly confident, and knew that I was doing the right thing.

Having accepted the job, I went into work the next day and when Derek arrived, I asked to meet with him in the conference room immediately. He gave me one of his 'I'm the boss. Don't tell me what to do' looks but agreed anyway.

As soon as we were both in the room, I gave him my notice. His eyes started twitching and his face turned scarlet. He wasn't at all happy about me leaving, but I sure as hell was.

"You'll be sorry. I can't wait for you to come crawling back," said a very pissed-off Derek to my rapidly departing back as I stood to leave him in the conference room.

"Not bloody likely! You're nothing but a bully who will one day end up getting exactly what's coming to him," I told him before opening the door, finally having said what had been on my mind for so long.

It was an uncomfortable two weeks serving out my notice period, with nasty glares flying back and forward between Derek and me. The staff looked at us suspiciously, but nobody said anything for fear of being on the receiving end of the bad mood that was escalating daily.

An appropriate kick below the belt would have felt great, but on my last day I settled for a hair flick and a disdainful look as I sailed out of the office for the very last time. I felt like telling everyone what he'd done, but they all loved their jobs and I cared enough about them to just let it be. I couldn't help wondering why his wife stayed with him. Did she really not see what he was doing? Maybe she knowingly turned a blind eye to his behaviour.

The new job was going to be a huge challenge, so I took a few days off in between finishing with Derek and starting with Jack. There was time to sit on beautiful Balmoral beach, which I still call my 'spiritual home', and just relax, pleased to be away from that smug, smirking face. As I wasn't a fan of huge waves, the stillness and calm of the water had always appealed to me on this beach compared to others, ever since I had first arrived in Sydney. The peacefulness of a weekday compared to my usual weekend visits was just the tonic I needed. Rather than the usual desperation to find the ideal, towel-sized patch of sand away from overly-excited kids and overly-loud boomboxes, I had my choice with plenty of space all around me. The seagulls squawked happily; the soft ebb and flow of the water lulled me to sleep in the warm late summer sun.

There were new, exciting times ahead and after this brief time to unwind, I would be ready to do my absolute best to prove myself worthy of Jack's apparent faith in me.

I started on the following Monday with two staff members reporting to me: Kellie and Rob. Jack said that he wanted me to build the team over time to five recruiters. I hadn't been a manager in my last role, but had trained a few new people, including Penny, when they first started.

Fortunately, we all quickly developed good, solid working relationships. I didn't want to be too social with them, preferring to keep things on a professional level. My job was too important to me to jeopardise it. It was a step up the ladder, and I was so grateful to Jack for the opportunity to leave Derek and build my career even further.

When anyone managed to place a candidate in a new position, the company had a habit of ringing a large bell situated behind the reception area, and everyone would stop what they were doing to take the time to cheer and congratulate the successful recruiter. It created a buzz around the whole office, which was refreshing and fun. I worked hard with my staff, teaching them all that I had learned during my time with Derek. As much as I still hated him, there was a measure of gratitude for the opportunity that I had been given to establish myself in an area that I had come to love with a passion. When Kellie made her first placement with me as her manager, she rang the bell and came up to hug me.

"It's all because of you," she said. "I feel like I'm learning so much. You're the best manager."

Wow – me, 'the best manager'? I smiled at her enthusiasm with pride. This was a new high for me, and one that I would come to love more and more with every passing day.

I continued my Friday night drinking and heavy smoking, sometimes with Wendy and Carole from my Pat-the-Perv days, but I avoided the people from my last job because I didn't want to talk about Derek or risk him ever joining us. I didn't think that I would be able to keep my mouth shut if I ever saw him again. I was way too happy with the money rolling in, and Nick and I had found a small, semi-detached house that we wanted to make an offer on quite close to our beautiful Balmoral beach.

"With the extra money that you're earning, we could have that place we like paid off in no time," he beamed.

Money, money, money. It was 1981; everyone around me seemed to have an expense account, and it was definitely a material world. Every once in a while, there was a nagging twist in my stomach and the thought that surely there had to be more to life than money and power. *Squash it down,* I said to myself. *You have it all!* I was a star, I had the perfect boyfriend, and my life was on track, wasn't it?

I was slowly losing touch with Meg, who was still in our old apartment and now living with Sean. Our lives had become so radically different in such a short amount of time. Di was still living in Canberra, working for a small legal practice to gain experience, and we hadn't spoken in ages. There were a few old friends from uni who had also moved to Sydney, but they were all still smoking pot and I wasn't interested in drugs anymore at all; I felt like a completely different person to the hippy I had been.

So it was just as well that I made friends so easily and always had a drinking buddy, if not the sort of friends that knew me and my past as well as Meg and Di did. I didn't have time for too much deep and meaningful stuff anyway with my new status and power; light, frivolous friendships were just fine and suited this new lifestyle that had become my new norm rather rapidly. My only close friend these days was Karen, whom I'd met through Nick's circle of friends. She was great fun to be with, and we were becoming closer as time went on. She loved drinking, which of course in my eyes was not a drug, and any new diet that we both discovered. One of her favourite expressions was "I'd rather drink my calories than eat them, honey", so that's what we did, except for the occasional food binge when we were just too hungover to care about what food we put into our mouths.

There was no talk or thought about witches or fortune-telling at this time and no real interest in any type of religion, spirituality or philosophical viewpoints. I was more interested in the spirits that came out of a bottle of a high-end brand of alcohol, my latest favourite being Johnny Walker Black Label scotch with a splash of soda water. This was my everyday and out-at-bars drink, or I had French champagne whenever we were celebrating. I was surrounded by people who were just as seemingly shallow. If ever I felt empty, I pushed any thoughts of the meaning of life deeper to the back of my mind. The meaning of my life for the moment was 'work hard, play hard and always look fabulous'.

However, with the ongoing party scene also came new drugs. Most people that I mixed with thought they were way too cool to smoke pot; that was for hippies, they reckoned. Cocaine and the very best alcohol were more for the fast-paced businesspeople. I told Nick that

I wasn't into drugs anymore, but he could be quite persuasive.

"Come on, Jacq. This stuff is pure, not like the shit that you had at uni," he assured me.

Reluctantly at first, I gave it a go and became very quickly addicted to how it made me feel and the lifestyle that it represented. Often the next day we'd be grumpy, with hammering headaches. The party and the instant buzz, however, were way more important than the aftermath. It was ridiculously expensive, but to us, money was no object anyway. The coke was also great for keeping my weight down, as I was never hungry at all when I used it and even the day after, food didn't interest me.

It was during this wildly hedonistic time that Di came to visit me for the first time since I'd left Canberra. I was so excited to see her, and we went out for an expensive dinner – my treat, of course – and chatted nonstop for hours. She told me that it looked like she might be offered a job in Legal Aid in Sydney and, if she did get it, she would be moving here permanently. It was so good to see her and reconnect with someone who had known me so well from the red-brick-house days. However, like Meg, we did have some differing goals and values.

Di was committed to helping people who really needed legal advice and weren't in a financial position to be able to afford the services of an overpaid solicitor. I was into living in a beautiful house in a beautiful suburb, surrounded by beautiful people who were just as materialistic as I had become. And yet, deep, deep at my very core, if I allowed myself to go there, I knew that her life had more real meaning than mine did. So I simply didn't go there!

"Hey, do you want to go meet up with Nick and his friends and try some coke and have more drinks?" I suggested. "It's pure, Nick told me."

"I don't do drugs, Jacq, but thanks anyway," she replied very quickly. "But it's so damn good to see you. Let's make sure that we see each other more often – and be careful," she added as she stood up to leave, unable to hide a concerned and perhaps even slightly judgmental tone to her voice. As much as there was a chilly edge to her answer, but I wasn't going to let that ruin the great catch-up that we'd had.

"Absolutely, and you're right. The drugs are pretty stupid. I'm thinking of giving them up myself," I lied, knowing that nothing was going to change the way I was currently living my life. We hugged each other for ages, with sincere promises and a few tears. She was my past, and I still wanted her to be in my future, that was for sure.

Nick and I bought the little semi-detached house that we had been looking at and started some renovations and decorating – in the latest colours and trends, of course, lots of glitz and glamour, with gold swirly wallpaper in the kitchen and bathrooms and different brightly-coloured feature walls in every room. Everything was perfect – the job, the man, the friends, the house; just perfect. Shopping for furniture was so exciting, as we didn't have to impose strict limits on what we could buy. We bought the biggest glass and chrome coffee table that I'd ever seen, and the expensive foam lounges that were so in vogue at the time. We worked hard, we played hard, we had a great sex life and we were upwardly mobile: two perfect stars in our very own orbit. Nick was regularly salesman of the month, and he'd just bought a better, brand-new Mercedes. A year after moving in, I was feeling like there was absolutely nothing that could stop us.

I did say nothing, not no one. So, here we go again. Her name was Sally.

I came home from work early one day, as I had a shocking headache (code for hangover). Jack had sent me home to try to sleep it off after I'd convinced him that it was a migraine. I was surprised to see Nick's car in the driveway and wondered what the hell he would be doing at home. He was always at the office, working long hours, or at the pub with his mates, having what he liked to refer to as a 'business meeting', as opposed to drinking too much in the daytime.

As I walked in the front door, I heard them before I actually saw them. There was loud moaning coming from our bedroom, which must have disguised the sound of me coming inside. Sally was supposedly a friend of ours, or so I had thought, and yet here she was, completely naked, underneath my boyfriend, and in our bed.

"What the bloody hell are you doing?" I yelled, shaking and deeply shocked as I tried to steady myself while feeling like I was going to throw up. I was smart enough to know exactly what they were doing, of course, so I have no idea why that was the question that came out of my mouth. Nick turned around with a look of total panic: busted, big-time.

"Jacq, babe, it's not what it looks like."

"Hi, Jacq. Sorry," from an insincere Sally.

Really? Am I blind? What does he think it looks like? While Nick jumped up, grabbing for his pants that had been thrown onto the floor, Sally just lay there, making no attempt to cover herself up, unfazed and smiling like a bloody Cheshire cat. Charming!

Without waiting for any further illumination on what it did or did not look like, I grabbed my car keys (not a Benz – I drove a sensible little Honda), ran out the door and drove erratically down the road to the beach that we both loved so much. It had been one of the main deciding factors in us ultimately making a higher offer on the place than we had initially intended.

As we didn't have mobile phones yet, I was looking for a pay phone to call Karen, who hopefully would be at home. She worked a lot of night shifts as a hostess at a ritzy club in the Eastern Suburbs and was usually home sleeping in the day. As much as I loved Di and Meg, Karen had so much more in common with my current lifestyle.

I didn't want to just drive to her place without calling first in case she was at her boyfriend's house or not home for some reason. She was the only one of my current friends to whom I could talk about any of my dramas, the rest of my friends being more drinking buddies who I could have a good laugh with but not a serious heart-to-heart.

Phil, her boyfriend, was a really nice guy, especially after the last one, Rex – an overprotective and rather abusive guy who hadn't been able to handle her working at the club. Rex had reckoned that she was paying too much attention to the male customers and he would often push her around at home to make his point loud and clear. *It's her job, you idiot* was what I wanted to say to him. More than once, I'd noticed bruises on her neck and arms. She had put up with it until one day he kicked her dog instead of her. Although she didn't stand up for herself, as far as I could see, there was no way he was going near her precious baby. She had called me and I went over and picked her and Bibi, the Maltese terrier, up and brought them to stay at our place until she had managed to find a place of her own.

Phil was absolutely fine with her work and treated her so much better, without any judgement or distrust. She was such a sweet and loving person; she definitely deserved someone who wasn't such a total psycho.

I found a phone booth near the fish café that Nick (the prick!)

and I loved going to. Karen's number was ringing. *Pick up, pick up,* I was saying to the phone willing it to obey me. It rang out. *Damn!* Frustrated, and determined, I tried again, and again for a third time.

"Hello, who is it?" said a tired and husky voice.

"It's Jacq. Thank God you're home. I'm coming over; stay where you are. You won't believe what he's done!"

Not waiting for her to answer, I jumped in the car and after a bit more erratic driving, made it safely to Karen's place, which was about a fifteen-minute journey. I think it took me five! Poor Karen. She looked stuffed, but she opened her arms and held me like I'd held her after her dramatic break-up with Rex. I cried, much like I'd cried for Harry, but this was grown-up crying: a future ruined, a trust that was now broken forever. I may have had my share of promiscuity, but I didn't abide with cheating. If you were with someone, you didn't fool around with someone else, especially Julie or Sally, whose boobs were as fake as her blonde (natural brown) hair.

Not long after I'd saturated Karen's shoulder, there was a knock at the door and Nick's voice called out.

"Jacq, I know you're there. Your car's out the front."

Clever boy, Nick. Points for observation, but no points for keeping it in your pants. It's amazing how devastating sadness can turn to white-hot anger in a split second.

"Piss off, Nick. I want nothing more to do with you. You can pack your bags and go live with Sally, happily ever after."

I didn't say that the anger made me smarter with the words that came out of my mouth. At this point, I felt like a gutted, helpless little girl. The power of the great job, the perfect house and the perfect boyfriend all felt completely worthless now. His infidelity had snapped something inside me, and I knew that I would never be the same again.

Realising that he wasn't going to go away, I decided to leave Karen to have some sleep and took the argument with Nick outside. I'm pleased to say that he was looking dreadful, and he had the good grace to have some tears in his eyes.

"Please, Jacq, can't we talk about it and try work things out? It won't happen again. I promise. Think of everything we have together. It was just once, and it was a huge mistake. Please."

As much as I was enjoying the grovelling, I knew that I was done and that I wouldn't back down. One strike and you're out – a bit like my dear old mum.

"Did you think I wouldn't find out, you bloody idiot? Don't you reckon I would have smelled her on my sheets? Seriously, fuck off. We're done," I screamed, climbing into my car.

"Come on, Jacq, calm down please. I wasn't thinking. We had some drinks at the pub at lunch and she came on to me. It was one stupid mistake. Forgive me, babe," he begged.

Reluctantly, as there was no way that I was going to forgive what I had just witnessed, Nick agreed to stay at a friend's house overnight to give me some time to calm down. I drove, less erratically, back to the house that I had loved, where we had entertained our friends and families – the house that I had wanted to share with the man whom I thought I'd be with forever. We had talked about marriage and kids after another year or two. That wasn't going to be my future now.

I stripped the bed and changed the sheets, unable to get the vision of fake-boobs Sally out of my head. I couldn't sleep, I couldn't eat; I just cried. Having paced the house for most of the night, I called Jack the next morning and told him that there was a family emergency and I wouldn't be able to come to work for a few days. He was not happy, as I was his main revenue generator, but I just couldn't think about work right now. It was going to be necessary for me to piece together my next steps, and there was no doubt that meant talking to Nick. I was feeling too gutted to even contemplate how it would be possible to move on with my life from this point.

Nick called me on the house phone (how did we survive without mobiles?) early in the morning and ended up coming around with coffee and croissants at about nine a.m. *What is that supposed to fix, you prick?* We both cried a lot, but it was no use. I may not have been raised to be a good, church-going Christian, and I may have had more than my fair share of sex, drugs and rock-and-roll, but there was still my strong moral compass when it came to relationships. He packed a few things and said that we'd have to discuss what to do with the house.

"We're selling it!" I virtually spat in his face. "And I'm burning the bed."

"Don't be so dramatic," he replied. "We need to behave rationally."

I have always loved it when people who are in the wrong are able to behave so condescendingly. I guess he thought that I would be able to forgive and forget.

So, seeing that I was supposedly being so 'dramatic', I took off the ring that he'd given me for my birthday and threw it in his face. He bent down, picked it up and put it in his pocket, walking away without looking back. That's one decision that I partially regretted for quite a while. It was stunning – white gold with a row of tiny diamonds, from one of the best jewellers in the City. But it would always have been a reminder of Nick and what he had done to destroy my trust.

After speaking a little more calmly and logically, Nick and I came to the difficult agreement that we would have to sell the house. I just couldn't stay after a week of sleepless, miserable nights, and neither of us could afford the mortgage on our own, no matter how much we were earning. We briefly discussed renting it out, but I insisted that it needed to be final and we both needed to move on. Perhaps I was being dramatic and could have given him another chance, but it wasn't what I felt capable of doing; the pain of his betrayal was unbearable. It left me wondering just how long he'd been unfaithful, and I simply didn't trust him to tell me the truth.

I moved into Karen's spare room to try to sort myself out. I had to gradually disentangle my social life from Nick's after he realised that no amount of pleading was going to win me back. Mind you, the pleading didn't go on for as long as I thought it might. Maybe he came to the conclusion that he would be able to have more than just fake-boobs Sally now that he was going to be single again. The hardest part for me was going to be that we went to the same places and had a large number of friends in common. It wasn't going to be a problem for a while yet, though, as I couldn't imagine ever being happy again or going out and having any fun. He was also going to be staying with a friend – not Sally – until the house was sold and he figured out his next move, apparently.

I did have a few spies, who told me that he was going out a lot over the next few weeks while I wallowed in my pain and grief. It seemed that he was moving on with his life a lot faster than I was. I didn't ask anyone about Sally or other women. It was hard enough knowing that he was able to go out at all when all I could manage to do was watch TV and eat chocolate. Why do so many of us women do that? It's not just in the bad movies that it happens. Many of us, from my experience, do exactly just that. I guess that's what they must base the bad movies on. As much as Karen tried, I wasn't interested in going anywhere, barely even able to get myself organised to get out of the house to go to work. I would turn up, do very little compared to my usual working day, and come straight home as soon as it was time to leave, for more TV and more chocolate. I was drinking a lot too to dampen my ever-present sorrow and disappointment.

It was becoming increasingly difficult to concentrate at work. I was making silly mistakes and had a sense that some of my clients were starting to lose their patience with me. Jack and my staff were all trying to be kind, but I felt that they were getting more than a bit tired of my constant long face.

"Why not go away for a week, Jacquie, and come back all refreshed and ready to put everything into the job again?" Jack suggested.

As soon as he had said it, just the thought of not having to go to the office every day and pretend that I was okay made me feel a whole lot lighter instantly.

"Thanks so much, Jack, for being so understanding. That sounds like a great idea. I promise I'll be my old self again when I get back," I replied, grateful to have such an understanding and caring boss. Derek would have told me to piss off, I'm sure.

In my lunch break that same day, I decided to go to the Travel Agent two floors below our office to book a holiday, somewhere relaxing and free from the possibility of running into Nick on a daily basis. After exploring the options, I booked a one-week holiday in Fiji, leaving in two days' time, and went back to tell Jack and my staff, who at least had the decency not to breathe a sigh of relief that they wouldn't have to see me looking so sad every day. I knew that Karen could do with a break from constant whining as well. Decision made; I went home to pack, feeling a sense of excitement for the first time since I had broken up with Nick.

Chapter Seven
Backgammon Queen

When I first arrived on the pretty little island, I was stunned by the beauty of the ocean surrounding me, so light blue that you could see right to the bottom in the shallower waters close to the shore. I remember still being in my usual fast-paced, go-getter Sydney frame of mind. One of the staff asked me with a huge grin and the brightest white teeth if I'd like a drink while I was waiting to go to my room.

"Black coffee – no sugar, please," I said, perhaps a little more curtly and efficiently than I had intended. This was my usual workday drink, times about ten. No artificial sweetener for me either, just straight black, being very discerning with my poisons after all. He smiled politely and wandered off, I presumed to sort it out for me.

After I had waited for what seemed like an eternity, he finally returned with a small wooden tray, my coffee and some local fruit laid out in a pattern like a star. As much as I was impressed by the presentation, I must have looked a bit annoyed by the timeframe. He just gave me the broadest grin and said with a sweet, gentle voice, "Fiji time, Miss," as he slowly moved away – swaying, it seemed, in time with the sway of the palm trees around us.

Over the next week, I managed to get very used to 'Fiji time', and was relaxed and happy for the first time since Nick and I had split. The other guests were a bit younger than I was, as nobody had bothered to tell me that it was the singles' party island that I'd booked for my holiday. They were mostly students, ranging in age from eighteen to around twenty-two, and as I'd recently turned twenty-five and was a career girl, there was quite a gap in many ways initially. Wanting to make the most of my current situation, of course I partied, I swam, I sun-baked and I played backgammon with my young friends, as well as having a bit of a fling with a very cute twenty-year-old Canadian guy called Ross.

Someone had brought the backgammon board from the games room outside to the long trestle tables near the beach. It was all such silly and simple, uncomplicated fun. All week, I kept winning most games and was eventually crowned Backgammon Queen of the island, a title bestowed upon me by my new friends. I didn't ever want to go back home to normality and reality. I was feeling better with each passing day, and this had turned out to be just the escape that I had needed.

I tried hard not to think of Nick, but as much as I was having fun, he would creep into my thoughts every so often, visions and memories of his betrayal still too fresh in my mind to erase as yet.

When my idyllic week in paradise was up, there were hugs all round with all the people I'd met, with a flurry of exchanges of phone numbers and addresses and promises that we would all keep in touch. Sadly, it was back to facing reality for me.

On the flight home, I felt such a conflict of emotions. Of course I wanted to see my friends and family, but I didn't want to go back to the pressure of my high-flying career just yet, if ever. Feeling doubtful that I would be able to give the job my all again, I wondered if there could possibly be something lower key and less demanding that I could do while I sorted myself out completely.

When I saw Karen upon returning home, she said that she was relieved to see me so relaxed and tanned. She always used to say that 'Brown fat was so much more attractive than white fat'! Not that either of us ever carried more than an extra kilo or two at any given time.

"I had such a fantastic time; I don't want to go back to work ever. My brain doesn't want to work that hard anymore!" I whined. "It would be great to do something more mindless for a while."

"Well, I don't think you'd like it, but we're looking for a waitress in the restaurant above the club. It would be a come-down from the corporate life for you, though," she suggested.

"I'll take it. Is it hard?" I asked, just a little too over-eager.

"I guess I could put in a good word for you if you're serious; and you've had all that waitressing experience when you were in Canberra. But just a word of advice – please don't tell my manager that you think it's 'mindless'," she laughed.

The next day, she spoke to the Club Manager at her work and organised for me to go for an interview with him two days later. Before I went any further with this new potential career direction, I had to make the rather difficult call to Jack to tell him that at this stage I really still wasn't able to come back and give the job what it required and what he deserved. He took it reasonably well, and suggested that we could perhaps 'keep the door open'. A good man was Jack, patient and kind – worlds apart from Derek.

I had, before my crippling breakup from Nick, trained my staff very well, especially Kellie, who was effectively my 2IC. It was better that Jack had people who were committed and ready to give the job their all than someone whose mind had vacillated between how to murder one's boyfriend and then thinking *I wonder if I should take him back!*

I dressed more casually than my regular corporate wardrobe for the interview with Karen's manager, Mark. We hit it off straight away, luckily, Karen's kind recommendation possibly giving me a bit of an advantage, and I was offered the job on the spot. He was, however, a little bit concerned about the level of my experience.

"How long do you think you'll stay with us? You're obviously a career girl," he pointed out at the beginning of the interview.

"Honestly, Mark, I'm excited by the opportunity to work in hospitality and I'm happy to start off in waitressing and maybe progress later on if there are any more senior opportunities," I replied confidently, always able to turn on the charm and act the part as and when I needed to. As long as I didn't have the mental pressure and demands of the career that I had been used to, as well as a decent steady income, I was happy.

Fortunately, I really was quite accomplished at the interviewing process. Often, as part of my role, there had been a need to coach applicants on how to best behave in an interview situation. I was also used to convincing clients that they should hire the applicant that had been referred to them. It wasn't difficult for me to walk into any interview situation without any level of anxiety and be who they wanted me to be.

Perhaps I was a famous actress in a former life. Not that I was a believer in all that back then, remember? Spirituality was still firmly on the back-burner at this point in my life. If only I was as good at picking decent guys who didn't want to cheat on me as I was at being offered every job that I went for. Now, that would be a useful skill.

I started my new job a few days later on the lunch shift. It was completely crazy – so hectic and fast-paced. Maybe my brain might be able to get a bit of a break, but my body was absolutely wrecked after my first shift. Who needed an overpriced gym anymore? The other staff members were a bit slow to warm to me, which I hadn't had in any of my other jobs. Perhaps it was the 'high-powered career girl' stamped on my forehead. It was clear that I would have to work damn hard to earn their respect. Funny how easy that had been for me up till this point. There were only attractive younger women working there as wait staff. It was a predominantly male clientele, and the manager encouraged us to flirt a little with them, to encourage them to stay longer and buy extra drinks. It was all a bit sleazy, really, but I was still very good at flirting, as I soon discovered, and the tips were amazing.

Karen worked all sorts of different shifts to me in the club below the restaurant, so our paths rarely, if ever, crossed at work. We used to catch up on everything at home whenever we were both there, or we'd head off to our favourite pub on the lower North Shore whenever we could.

"It's good to see you a lot happier at last, Jacq," she said not long after I started. "Well, at least not as stressed and miserable," she added. "Waitressing must agree with you, and I hear that Mark's really happy with you."

"Thanks, Kaz. The girls don't love me yet, but I'm trying to wear them down, and the work is great."

Fiji had helped me get back into the idea of wanting a social life again, but I was still a bit uncomfortable in my local haunts. Karen and I used to go out together, meet up with various friends and check out all the good-looking guys – that is if Phil wasn't around and I wasn't pining over Nick. Alcohol and cigarettes seemed to help, particularly on those occasions when Nick would appear, and I'd have to pretend that I hadn't seen him. We didn't speak to each other and tried to avoid any eye contact. In my gut, I knew that it would still take a very long time to heal my wounds.

The ice melted with my new workmates on our first night out for drinks together. Sandy, one of the senior girls, had asked me if I'd like to join them and of course I quickly accepted, wanting so much for them to get to know me and to like me. We weren't allowed to drink in the club with the clientele, so instead went to a small bar just down the road from the restaurant. Another bonus for me was that it wasn't an area that Nick frequented, so there was virtually no risk of me running into him. I quickly slipped into trying on my most entertaining funny-girl routine, dragging out my best jokes, and thankfully I had them all in stitches after a few drinks – hard work, but worth the effort. The family wit had come in very handy. It was one of the many things that I had been grateful for, growing up. We could mostly, not always, have a good laugh, even though it was often at someone else's expense.

"Well, it appears that we have a clown among us," giggled Sandy. I was so grateful for her approval that I went home feeling a lot more positive about my new choice of job, however long it might last.

One of my favourite things about my new job was the Friday routine after the lunch shift. It was the only day that we were allowed to hang around and mix with the customers at the restaurant, as long as we didn't go to the club. Chris, the piano player, would start playing around five and get us all singing along with him to a wide variety of well-known songs spanning a couple of decades. As you know, I thought I was an amazing singer, so I'd be belting out tune after tune as loud as I could. Everyone was too drunk to make a judgement on my talent or lack thereof, thankfully.

I was also enjoying my new wardrobe change, apart from our slightly-too-sexy uniform. The high heels and expensive suits and dresses were swapped for stretchy lycra leggings, lurex tops, enormous, fake gold earrings, and big teased hair with a whole can of hairspray to keep it in place. I swear mine would have stood up to a gale force wind. Ahh, the eighties: the decade of big, glitzy fashion and disco music. Fortunately, Chris played better music than disco, which has never been my favourite.

I was laughing again, genuinely enjoying myself, with no boyfriend – lots of male attention, but nothing at all serious. My heart felt a lot lighter and as much as I knew deep down that this job was temporary, it really was a lot of fun for the time being, however long that turned out to be.

It was at one of the Friday night after-work drinks that I met Chad. He was American, with the coolest accent I'd ever heard (I still prefer that east-coast accent over any others I've heard. Maybe it's an Aussie thing). He came into the restaurant with a local soap opera star, Michael Moore, whom we all recognised. I found out later that they had been to school together in Boston before Michael's family had moved to Australia ten years ago.

"Oh my God, look who it is!" Sandy gushed, star-struck.

All the girls were staring longingly at Michael, while I only had eyes for Chad. I fell for him immediately: enormous, soulful brown eyes;

dark brown hair just that bit too long, giving him a slightly bohemian, carefree look. I couldn't stop staring at him, and he was staring right back. While all the other girls were fawning over Michael, I was in the midst of another of my love-at-first-sight moments, although the intensity of this one was mind-blowing. This was the first time that I'd felt anything like this since Nick. I certainly wasn't looking to meet anyone. He was just there, right in front of me, eyes connecting with mine and sexy as hell!

We all went out dancing and drinking champagne, of course, to a nearby club; Chad and I couldn't keep our hands off each other. We jumped into a waiting taxi outside when it was fast becoming clear that we might just have sex on the dance floor if we didn't leave soon. Once back at his apartment in Manly, we spent a wildly mind-blowing night of passion together – one of those nights where you just feel that this is the real thing. And I was very good at knowing what that felt like ,with my experiences of romance so far in my life.

Leaving the next morning was hard; neither of us could bear the thought of being apart now that we were instantly in love. And so we spent every spare minute that we could together from that moment on. He had already told me that he was going back home to Boston in just two weeks, having come to Sydney for a few months on business. We certainly made the little time that we would have together count, and we hardly left each other's sides except for going to work. I already knew that it was going to be devastating having to say goodbye to him as the time for him to leave crept closer and closer.

Chad was very different to Nick: just as sophisticated, but more real somehow, with a depth and sort of soulfulness that I hadn't experienced before. We used to have deep and meaningful conversations about all sorts of stuff, and he was fascinated by absolutely everything about me and everything that I had to say. I hadn't been overly interested in any sort of philosophical discussion since uni, and that was fast becoming a distant memory.

While he was just as into what money could buy as Nick was, there was also a healthier balance in terms of the topics we would discuss. He would just stare at me all the time whenever we were together, seemingly transfixed by me, with the slow sensual smile that I was fast becoming accustomed to. I would feel a rather pathetic fluttering in the pit of my stomach every time he looked at me that way.

I had just turned twenty-seven and was finally, once again, ready to give love another chance. I didn't laugh as much as I had with Nick and we preferred to be on our own for the most part, talking intensely and doing a lot of gazing. He wasn't into cocaine, thankfully; we just preferred to have a few drinks, talk, go to bed, make love, and talk more in bed. We did go out occasionally with my friends and Michael, to bars and clubs, but we didn't surround ourselves with constant noise and shallow small talk.

Chapter Eight
The Whirlwind

Two weeks came around way too quickly. After a teary airport farewell, promising to call each other and write (oh, for a mobile phone!), I went back to Karen's feeling empty and confused.

What I felt for Chad in such a short time seemed to be deeper than the feelings that I'd had for Nick, in some strange way. With Nick, it had always been all about the party, the drugs and the booze – a life of hectic pace and money. With Chad, at this early stage it was more about soul-searching discussions and pure passion.

Poor Karen. Here I was yet again; another drama and another reason to mope around the house in tears. She hadn't had me back to my old bubbly self for very long, and I knew that this must have been frustrating for her. Sometimes I felt like I was the star of my own personal soap opera, and I'm sure she must have felt the same.

"Come on, Jacq. Let's go out," she pleaded with me. "I know you really liked him, but he's gone. You need to stop moping around and have some fun."

"Sorry, Kaz, I just want to stay in my room for a while," I said. I heard the huge sigh as she left me alone to wallow in self-pity once again.

At least the job wasn't too demanding emotionally or intellectually, and the physical demands were good for me. I was always busy, with little time to think about any personal stuff, even though I missed Chad terribly. Also, once I'd managed to survive the first two weeks, the after-work drinks with the girls kept me busy, entertained and distracted from my brooding. They really were accepting me more and more each day, and I was happy not to be in an office all day for a change. It also helped that I was still making quite reasonable money when I included all the generous tips that I ended up with each day.

Karen had refused to take much rent from me right from when I had left Nick, and I was actually managing to save some money – a hitherto foreign concept to me. I was used to spending it all on the wildly extravagant lifestyle that Nick and I had both enjoyed. In my bank account there was now a good lump sum from the property sale, and I felt quite secure about everything, financially at least. The restaurant was never going to make me the big bucks like my last job, but with the decreased expenses I was doing more than just fine.

Chad and I used to call each other nearly every day. It was super expensive, and we often used to get the time difference wrong. I would have to speak quietly so that I didn't wake Karen if he called when she was asleep.

"I miss you so much," I'd whisper.

"I miss you too, honey. You're too far away from me." That voice!

He was doing really well with his business in Boston, and asked if I'd come to see him for a holiday. He offered to pay for my ticket, and was hoping that I'd say yes and come as soon as I could manage it. He suggested that I consider staying for two months, so that we could really get to know each other and decide if we had a long-term future together. I could hear in his voice that he really was genuine, and I wanted to say yes immediately.

It was a big step for me, as I'd only ever been on holidays in Australia and my short trip to Fiji. Of course, I'd been to a great many of the best hotels and resorts with Nick, but I'd never been far away from home before. I always found enough excitement and fun locally and just hadn't had the urge to travel. I would have to get time off work and pack enough for a long stay.

What will I take to a place so far away, where it is currently snowing? I pondered my dilemma. I only had high-heeled boots and had never really needed a heavy jacket. The wardrobe crisis seemed to be my biggest issue. As much as I was a tiny bit more of a thinker these days, a tad less shallow, the way I looked still was a very high priority.

The next thing that I had to do was say yes to Chad and tell my family and friends about my impulsive decision. He had bought me a ticket and sent it by mail (no internet or email yet either!), and I received it a week later. We actually survived all this, as we didn't know the joys of having everything instantly. It was such a different and interesting time to be alive. People spoke at dinner, their heads not looking down, buried in their phones; you didn't have the need to see daily posts of someone's breakfast, and you had to make plans and trust that people would show up. Some of us had answering machines, but a lot didn't, and you could sometimes go for days trying to track someone down.

My friends were excited for me and my family were supportive, whereas poor Mum was struggling to understand why I would do something so seemingly crazy.

"Will you ever come back?" she asked.

"Of course, silly. It's just a holiday," I reassured her. Was it, though? A big part of me hoped that it would be more, but another part of me just loved Sydney too much to ever consider a relocation to the other side of the world.

I promised her that I would write and call when I could and that I wasn't going forever. At least that reassured her temporarily.

Next, I spoke to Mark about having some time off, hoping that he'd still have a job for me when I came back to Sydney. At this stage, I'd only been working there for five months and I was having a great time. I just had to see if this thing with Chad was what it appeared to be on the surface.

"I'd really love to keep working here when I get back. I'm so sorry to stuff you around so soon after starting," I said.

"Of course, honey. I didn't expect you to stay this long anyway. People come and go all the time in this line of work. Be in touch when you get back," he replied. There are definitely some nice guys in this world; fortunately, they're not all like Derek.

Before I left, I called in to see Meg. I missed her and wanted to reconnect and tell her my news. When I arrived, she opened the door and immediately proceeded to go into a coughing fit. She sounded really ill.

"Have you seen the doctor?" I asked her.

'I'm fine. Stop worrying." She tried to smile. I didn't believe her. "Now tell me everything about this trip."

That was so like Meg – put everyone else before herself. Before I left, I said to her in my bossiest voice, "Megs, you have to see a doctor ASAP. You sound dreadful. Promise me that you will."

"Okay, Jacq, I will, I promise," she replied unconvincingly. "Now, for God's sake, just go and have fun!"

I was more than a bit concerned, but she had Sean to look after her, and I was off on my big adventure. Surely she would be fine, wouldn't she?

Last, but not least, came the mega diet. Nothing but cigarettes and black coffee till lunchtime, then some crackers and tuna and a tiny dinner of steamed vegetables – with some wine, of course. Although my weight was fine before I started, I was determined to look even more perfect for Chad.

Before I knew it, the time had come. I was packed (well, over-packed!) and as ready as I ever would be for my big adventure to the United States.

The outfit to make my grand entrance when I hopped off the plane was red and gold from head to toe: red pants, a gold top, red and gold shoes and a matching scarf. No one was going to miss seeing me. I wore comfy clothes until we were about an hour away, then went into the bathroom and changed, did my scary, over-the-top makeup and put on a gallon of perfume. I liked what I could see of myself in the small mirror. I tried standing on the loo for a better view, but nearly fell in when the plane lurched. I had to trust that what I could see was as spectacular as I thought it was.

When I walked out of the arrivals door, I scanned the waiting area for Chad. I almost didn't recognise him, until I saw that unmistakable smile of his. He had put on quite a lot of weight in the three months since I'd seen him. He was wearing one of those puffy jackets (I have always absolutely hated them, practical but ugly), a lot more sensible for the climate than my choices, but yuk! Part of the problem was that I was ever conscious of my appearance and thought they made me look fatter. My heart didn't stop, as I'd expected it to and hoped it would; he looked so different. For the short time that I'd known him, he had always dressed so well and had the most perfect physique. There were no Facebook posts or Instagram feeds to warn me of the changes in him. However, I was here now, after an eighteen-hour flight. I had to be positive and make the most of it. He was still the same person, after all.

Why did I bother to lose all that weight? I was wondering. *Stop being so shallow,* was my answer.

"Hey, babe, looking good," he said. Very smooth – the same sexy voice, the same self-assuredness. I felt sure that, with all the sex we would be having, he would be back in shape pretty quickly. Plastering on the very best and most sincere smile that I could muster, I replied, "Well, hey yourself," and hugged him.

We held on to each other for a long time and kissed briefly before heading to the car park to make our way in the freezing cold to his apartment, which would be my new home for the next two months. My stomach was doing flips as I tried resolutely to remove the creeping sense of disappointment that I was feeling.

It was a bit strained between us at first, and it felt like I was making love to a different person. But then we really started talking like we had done for the whole time that he had been in Sydney, way into the night. His worldliness and his self-confidence above everything else made me feel so young and naïve around him, even though he was only five years older. He had travelled the world and was used to mixing with well-known celebrities.

Pretty soon we were laughing, and he told me about his mom's (not 'mum' – different language) home cooking, which apparently included huge amounts of butter and pastry. I, of course, said that I would now cook healthy meals for him – steamed veggies and wine, I was thinking. Well, it had worked brilliantly for me!

"Don't worry, babe, we'll be eating out mostly. I want you to meet all my friends and really get to know the place," he assured me.

The next morning, Chad had to go to work and left me alone in the apartment with a spare key in case I wanted to go exploring. With no idea of what time zone my body was in, all I knew was that I was starving. Upon discovering some peanut butter cup ice-cream in the freezer, I thought that that would be a good idea for breakfast. After my extreme pre-flight diet and way too much of this sweet sickly stuff, it wasn't too long before my head was hovering over the toilet bowl for what felt like an eternity.

Finally feeling a tiny bit better, I ventured outside wearing a very thin jacket, the only one that I owned, and the lowest of my many high-heeled shoes. I lasted for about two minutes before having to race back inside and sit in the central heating, watching American TV (so many channels!) until Chad eventually came home at around eight o'clock at night. I'd managed to have a short nap, but had been so lonely in a strange place without the confidence, knowledge or the appropriate clothes to go anywhere.

"Sorry, babe – big day. What did you get up to? Hope you had fun." *You're kidding, right??* "Let's head out for, dinner and I'll take you to the local club to meet a few people," he said.

Judging by the admiring looks (from the guys) and glares (from the girls), my new fashion choices were very popular in Boston when we went out to his favourite places. I tended to take this eighties look to a whole new level – shades of Sandy from the movie Grease.

Apparently, even for the much more, I thought, sophisticated and trendy Americans, I was a big hit. The glitzy look that I had been cultivating so well in Sydney wasn't quite as glitzy in Boston, which surprised me, and it pleased me that I could be seen as a trendsetter. I was, however, freezing, and spent quite a bit of time on my behind after slipping over in my extremely impractical boots. Just as well I had my penchant for self-deprecation, which usually sustained me and had others around me having a laugh at me if not with me.

"Watch out for the crazy Aussie girl," I'd say, or "Just as well I don't drink!"

The days and nights continued in much the same vein. As exciting as it was going to the best clubs, eating primarily lobster and drinking expensive champagne in the best restaurants, it didn't take me long to know without a doubt that I just wasn't happy. I had very little to do in the daytime when Chad was at work and had been used to living such an independent lifestyle at home.

Sometimes his 'mom' would pick me up and take me shopping for old lady clothes for herself, trying to take me to shops that might interest me as well. We'd go to these tacky cafes where she'd order doughnuts and cakes, and it was clear that she expected me to do the same. Whenever I'd try "I ate a big breakfast. I'm not hungry", she'd reply with exasperation and disappointment in me, "Nonsense, you're way too skinny. Come on, I insist!" She was trying her best, but it just wasn't like home.

Of course, I'd tell Chad that I'd had a great time to make him happy while I was trying to figure out how my feelings had changed so drastically since the grand love affair in Sydney.

He did offer to hire me my own car for the time that I was there, but after a few lessons in his car, a Cadillac which I swear was bigger than my bedroom at Karen's, I didn't have the confidence to drive on the other side of the road. I did catch buses into the city and wander around the shops, but I was just plain lonely and terribly homesick. I didn't particularly like any of his male friends; they were way too flirtatious, even right in front of Chad, and the girls that I'd met didn't seem to like me. Maybe the Sandy look was a bit too much competition for them – I don't know.

They all drank even more than my Aussie friends, and there was a never-ending supply of a variety of drugs. The depth that we had experienced when I had first met Chad in Sydney was not as I remembered it to be or wanted it to be, except on the rare occasions when we weren't too out of it at night and we would stay up talking. I wondered if it was just because he was working so hard or if this was simply the real Chad, the one that I had met being a delightful illusion.

I missed my friends and family much more than I had thought I would. Mum had been writing letters, trying to sound upbeat, but I could sense her sadness between the lines and concern that I was so far away in a strange country. She had never even been on a plane and had never dreamed of going further than Canberra to visit Tom. Our farewell before I left had been rather teary, with me trying to reassure her that I'd be safe and that I'd be back before she knew it. I just wanted to hug her, and she was too far away.

I knew for sure that I wanted to leave this place that didn't feel like home, go back to Sydney, and maybe even pursue a role in recruitment again. My brain had been a bit rested with the waitressing, and totally rested now with the trip to see Chad. I was hoping that I could potentially kick-start my career, and had found myself thinking about Di and Meg a lot lately too. Having been way too neglectful for quite too long now, I wanted to see them badly and to start to become a better friend to both of them.

At this stage I'd been here for six weeks and was due to go back home in another two. Chad told me that he wanted me to stay longer and had talked about making it permanent – even marriage. My feelings for him were waning, and I was still thinking about Nick. Here was a great guy compared to Nick the Prick, but I couldn't help how I felt. For me, the spark between us had fizzled and faded. I don't want you to think that it was because he'd gained weight; I'm not quite that shallow, having also managed to stack a bit of weight on again myself with the lifestyle that we were leading. Between Mom's doughnuts and the peanut butter cup ice-cream, which I was now firmly addicted to and which no longer made me throw up, my skinny clothes were now a whole lot tighter.

The time had come to talk to Chad and to tell him that I wanted to go home permanently as soon as possible.

"I'm so sorry. I'm just so homesick," I told him, which wasn't a lie. I didn't want to hurt him by telling him the truth – that I just didn't have the same feelings for him anymore.

"But, babe, I want us to be together and I can't go back to Sydney. Please stay," he pleaded.

"Just let me go home and see my family and friends, and we can see how things are after a while," I reassured him, trying to protect the feelings of a decent man who deserved better than I was able to give him.

He said that he understood, and after another very sad farewell at the airport, I walked away knowing that I'd never return. I had to improve my ability to choose the right guy – or perhaps it was time for me to just stay single for a while.

When I took my seat on the plane, there was an enormous relief and sense of purpose that came over me. I felt overwhelmingly excited to see my family, Di and Meg. Of course, I wanted to see my new friends as well, especially Karen, but really needed to be with people who had played such major parts in my history.

Throughout the flight, I found myself wondering if I'd really given it my best with Chad and whether I'd regret my decision in the future. I simply had to go with my gut, doing what felt right for me and also doing the right thing by Chad. Picturing his sad face at the airport as I was leaving, I couldn't help the tears that started running down my face: tears for Harry and Nick and now Chad. *Perhaps I just suck at relationships,* I concluded. *No more whirlwinds!*

Chapter Nine
A Homecoming and a Friend in Need

I'd only been gone for two months, and yet it felt like much, much longer. It was early summer in Sydney, bloody hot, and I decided to go shopping for some new clothes to take my mind off the decisions that I now had to make about my career and where I was going to live. It wasn't fair or reasonable for me stay in Karen's spare room forever, after all. Before I headed out to the local mall, I called Mum and Dad, then Annie and Tom just to say hi and to sort out some time to catch up.

Annie also lived in Sydney, and worked as a teacher in an inner west high school. We were only about a twenty-minute drive from each other, but I rarely made enough of an effort to see her. That was definitely going to change. Tom was in Canberra, where he had been working in the Public Service and sharing a house with some uni friends. He said that he'd come up for the weekend, as he really wanted to see me. What was that all about? They both seemed so happy to hear from me and so excited to catch up. I felt like I didn't deserve their enthusiasm after my slackness at keeping in touch. Annie said that she was free on the Saturday to see us both if that suited. I felt like a little kid again. It was only Tuesday, and I couldn't wait for the weekend and for us to be together again.

Having made the much-needed connection with my family, now I could go shopping. When I had gone away, the shops had been full of the Grease look. I'd come back to window display after window display of pastels and linen. I had always hated linen! It crushes as soon as you put it on, and I look absolutely awful in pastels. Yuk. As if that wasn't bad enough, the layered look was in – a sensible way of hiding your body under different lengths of fabric, mostly linen, and calling them clothes. I was not comfortable with wearing sensible, apart from which it was summer, and who wants layers in summer?

Despondent, I went home to have a serious chat with Karen about this horrible new fashion mistake. She agreed with me wholeheartedly, being a lover of the glitzy look herself, and we prayed that it would soon be over.

Saturday came at last, and I drove to the beach for the meet-up with Annie and Tom. Annie was going to be the first to arrive while we were waited for Tom to arrive from Canberra. She'd told me that she was bringing a friend with her, if that was okay with me. I wasn't too happy initially, wanting my siblings to myself, but when she arrived grinning from ear to ear with a woman whom she introduced to me as Jo, I don't think I'd ever seen her so happy and so animated. Little did I know then that she was the woman who would become the love of Annie's life.

"So good to meet you," said Jo. "Annie talks about you all the time," she added.

Good start, I thought – *impressive.*

I knew that Annie had never been into boys like I was, but this was the first time that there was an actual confirmation of her sexuality. To see her so happy made me want to cry, but instead I just grinned happily back at the two of them, their pure joy at being together and obvious feelings for each other infectious.

When Tom arrived, he wouldn't stop hugging me, which was so unlike him. The days of fake knives, teasing and nasty comments were now gone for good.

"Thank God you're back. We all thought that you'd be staying over there forever. Poor old Mum has been on the phone bawling ever since you've been gone," he said.

"She sure has," agreed Annie, rolling her eyes. "It has been tragic to say the least."

What had I done to my family? I looked at my siblings and felt a love that was different to anything I'd ever felt for them before. We were all grown up, we were living our lives, and we were family. We made a plan to go and see Mum and Dad the next day. I couldn't wait to see them and to tell them that I was in Sydney to stay and wasn't going back ever.

When we arrived at my parents' house, they were standing out in front of the house waiting for us to arrive. They were exactly the same as always, and both of them were unable to hide their excitement.

"You look so thin, bubs," said Mum. "Have you been looking after yourself?"

"I'm fine, Mum, just happy to be home." This started us off babbling on about our latest diets, just like old times. She showed us some new dresses that she had made for herself, and Dad kept going outside for a smoke, whistling happily, taking Tom with him to show off the latest additions to his veggie and herb garden. After neglecting my family for so long except for Christmas and the occasional birthday, I loved being home. All the sophisticated, million-miles-an-hour lifestyle was nothing compared to this feeling of safety, security and familiarity. We laughed so much that day, comfortable and totally at ease in each other's company. I felt a peace settling over me and a knowledge that it was time to make some changes to the way that I was living my life, starting with a break from men and drugs. I'd just stay with some alcohol and my beloved ciggies!

I spent the night in my old bed, and Tom stayed in his. Annie and Jo went back to Sydney, but not before I made another plan to meet up with them the following weekend. Mum came into see me before I fell asleep, her voice shaky and tearful.

"We thought you were never coming home again. We thought that you'd stay over there forever. It's so good to have you home."

"I love you, Mum." I grabbed her hand. "Don't worry, I'm back for good."

I hugged her and saw her properly for the first time: a woman who had struggled to raise three kids, with constant moving and resettling; a woman who just loved us all so much. As I was falling asleep, content, I started to think seriously about the need for something to feed my soul.

Even though it hadn't worked out with Chad and me, he had brought out a new depth in me on those occasions when we weren't out at clubs and actually sat and talked. My life had been so shallow and focused on the material for too long now, the never-ending party being more important than anything else. It was time to start properly growing up. I had always told myself that I was having such a good time, but now it just left me with a feeling of emptiness after another failed relationship.

So God didn't fix everything, boys didn't fix everything, and money didn't fix everything. *What next?* was the big question.

This constant busy, busy, busy mentality that had been running my million-miles-an-hour lifestyle had to stop. And I needed to continue the reconnection with the most important people in my life. After my family, I now wanted to see Di and Meg. I made a commitment to myself that I would contact them as soon as I arrived back at Karen's place. And that was another thing – to talk to her ASAP about getting a place of my own and letting her have her own space again. After a short time thinking about a possible new future, I fell into a deep sleep in my old bed in the red brick house.

When I woke up and said my goodbyes, it was time for me to return to Sydney, knowing that I was going to have to go back to the restaurant for a while, as I hadn't been earning any money for two months now. I hadn't had to spend much while away in Boston, as Chad had been incredibly generous, and I still had the majority of my savings left. I'd already decided that I wanted to return to recruitment as a career, but just wanted some security and familiarity while I got back on my feet. I'd start looking as soon as I felt more settled back in Sydney. It felt good to be contemplating new beginnings and a better way to live my life.

I'd made a great start with my family and smiled to myself as I thought about our usual craziness when we'd all been together. Jo had seemed okay with it all and hadn't run for the hills. I really liked her, and the fact that she was able to make Annie smile gave me a good feeling about the two of them already. Tom had been great company as well as we talked about his job, which he didn't love, and more about his real love – the band that he was playing in on the weekends. They played old bush music in country areas close to Canberra in converted woolsheds, and people would come from all around to dance wildly to the jigs and reels that they played.

When I called Di after arriving back at Karen's place, she told me that she'd already moved to Sydney and was working in Legal Aid at the other end of the city to where I had been working before the restaurant. We both became quite emotional and cried a bit – happy tears, though, as we also laughed about some of the old times that we had shared. It had been too long since we had seen each other, and we agreed that we couldn't wait to meet and catch up properly.

Having made an arrangement for the following week to meet during her lunch break, I said goodbye and hung up the phone, smiling happily to myself. She had sounded so genuinely pleased to hear from me and just like my old friend. I was looking forward to reminiscing about our time at school, with our witches' britches and our séances, among other memorable moments.

When I called Meg not long afterwards, she sounded so quiet, breathless and frail. She was happy enough to hear from me, and I could tell that she was making an effort to sound positive. When I suggested going out for a coffee or a drink, she told me that she didn't feel up to going out, so I made a plan for the next day to go over to the old apartment where she still lived.

I rang the doorbell and Sean answered. His face was drawn, and he looked really stressed.

"Welcome home, Jacq," he said, attempting to smile and failing. "She's not well," he mouthed.

"What's wrong?" I whispered back.

He didn't answer; he just led me inside so that I was able to see for myself. My jaw dropped when I saw her. She was so pale and thin.

"Hey, Jacq," Meg said in a hoarse, strained voice, and then started coughing uncontrollably. Sean raced to the kitchen to get her some water. When the coughing stopped, she smiled and tried to look happy, but I knew her too well. She was struggling to try and sit up.

"I've been begging for her to see a doctor, but she reckons that she's just tired and needs to rest. She won't let me take her," Sean said desperately, unable to hold back his concern and worry.

"Well, guess what, Megs? We are going to see the doctor today. Your bossy friend is not taking no for an answer. Come on, Sean. Let's get her down to the medical centre before it closes," I said, more than a bit forcefully.

The relief on Sean's face was obvious as we refused to listen to her pleas to stay home, somehow managing to bundle her into my car and drive up the hill to wait for the first available doctor to see her.

"We're going to run some tests. Your throat looks extremely inflamed, your chest doesn't sound too good, and your blood pressure is rather low," said Dr. Parker after an initial look at her condition, not knowing who to look at as the three of us all stared at him intently.

"Will she be okay, Doctor?" asked Sean nervously.

"We will have some results within a few days, and then we should know more. We'll just take her to pathology to get some blood taken. Are you all coming? It's pretty cramped," he hinted rather pointedly as we all stood up, Sean and I set to follow.

Chapter Ten
A Battle to Survive

Four days later, the test results were back. The news was not good. Then there were more tests, and even more.

After two weeks of waiting, the diagnosis was official. Meg had stage four lung cancer, and needed to start chemotherapy immediately. Sean and I were devastated, while Meg just nodded and accepted the news calmly. I guess she was relieved that she finally knew, after all the tests and doctor's appointments, poking, prodding and endless waiting. She looked worn out and defeated, while Sean and I remained determined that we could make her better through sheer will and the love that we felt for her.

Meg's parents came to Sydney to be with her, looking broken and exhausted. We were all going to take turns being with her while she was undergoing treatment. I had to take a few shifts at the restaurant, and Sean was also able to work part-time temporarily. Between the four of us, there was always someone by her side. We had a plan, and we were united in our efforts to achieve what we didn't know at the time was the impossible.

After the chemo and the tests to check her progress, the news was even worse. She wasn't getting better. The cancer was still in her lungs and had now spread to her liver. The doctor said that all we could do now was make her comfortable and suggested a hospice. He said that there were no further treatment options. I was desperately suggesting alternative medicine and more doctors. Meg just looked at me, tired and accepting.

"Jacq, it's over. I don't want to fight anymore. Please just be my friend till the end."

Her parents wanted her to go home and be with them, but she wanted to stay with Sean in the little apartment by the harbour until it was time to go. Sean and I, as well as Meg's parents, did everything we could for her to make her comfortable, but she was gone in just over a month, passing away quietly in her sleep without any fuss or drama in the early hours of the morning with Sean devotedly by her side.

Not long before she died, she asked me to come and sit by her bed.

"Can you please promise not to be too sad? Don't let everyone sit around sobbing at my funeral. If anyone can make them smile, you can."

"I'll do my darnedest," I promised her, trying not to break down in front of her and not knowing if it would be possible to keep that promise.

The world lost a beautiful soul that night, and I lost a beautiful friend who could never be replaced.

For my eulogy, I chose a beautiful T.S. Eliot poem to read, initially breaking my word to her that I would make people laugh. I didn't know how I was going to get through it, but for her sake I sure as hell was going to try my level best.

Sorry, Meg, I said to myself. *Just one sad moment, I promise.* I knew that she would have forgiven me considering what was to follow. So I began.

"Everyone that knew Meg well knew how much she loved T.S. Eliot, so I have a beautiful poem to read which I would like to dedicate to her," I said, barely holding it together. Breathing in and out to calm myself and to steady my shaky voice, I continued, "The poem is called *Eyes That Last I Saw In Tears.* I hope you all like it."

This is my affliction
Eyes I shall not see again
Eyes of decision
Eyes I shall not see unless
At the door of death's other kingdom
Where, as in this,
The eyes outlast a little while
A little while outlast the tears
And hold us in derision.

I broke down at the end, but had to pull myself together for the next part and to now keep my promise to my beautiful friend. And so, I continued.

"I made a promise to Meg that we all had to have a laugh. Well, you know how much Meg and I loved our makeup. This was one of our favourite songs at uni: *Makeup* by Lou Reed. I'm going to try to sing it and you are all allowed to join in, laugh, dance or whatever you feel expresses how you feel about our beautiful Meg. So, here goes." Sean handed out the words for the song so that anyone who wanted to could join in.

As I sang, I thought about the words and the fact that we had both been called slick little girls at uni. Our love of dramatic excessive makeup had led one of our closest friends, on one of our many very-out-of-it nights, to officially dedicate the song to us. It seemed only fitting that this was the song I chose to sing for her as a memory of the many happy times that we had shared.

When I finished singing, I noticed that people were smiling and crying at the same time. Some had sung along with me and a few people were on their feet, swaying along to my somewhat shaky yet passionate rendition.

Sorry, Lou, but it was for Meg. I didn't think that he'd mind too much. *Bye, Megs,* I whispered softly to myself. I couldn't imagine my life without her.

Chapter Eleven
Growing Up

After the funeral, we all had to find our own ways of moving on with our lives. Meg's parents went home, never to be the same again, having buried their wonderful daughter. Sean couldn't bear to stay in the apartment and decided to move in with his parents temporarily while he grieved the loss of the woman he had loved so much. I knew this was going to be a long road for him and for us all.

I finally managed to catch up with Di for lunch in the city. We hadn't been able to have our lunch, as I was busy helping to look after Meg. She had been at the funeral and we had spoken briefly, but not nearly as much as we needed or wanted to. We both craved some one-on-one time together.

"I didn't know her that well, Jacq, but you know I really liked her and I know what she meant to you. If there's anything I can do..." she said when we sat down.

"Just having you back in my life is the only thing I want right now," I replied, grabbing her hand and not wanting to let it go.

After a while of talking about Meg and reflecting on the distance that had been between us for too long now, we did manage to have another laugh about old times.

"I've missed you while I've been living the high life. The drugs are gone forever. It's time to grow up," I said to her, meaning it.

"I'm so happy to hear it, Jacq. I want you around for a very long time."

We hugged and promised to see each other on the weekend. I was going to go around for a drink on Saturday to meet her flatmate, Gary.

I had been recently feeling the need to reconnect with and apologise to Chad. We'd spoken a couple of times briefly when I returned to Sydney, and I'd told him about Meg. While he had been sympathetic when I had spoken to him, I could also sense an underlying coolness to his tone – completely understandable, given the circumstances under which I had left him. He'd invested a great deal into making a relationship work with me, and it felt like I owed him some sort of an explanation.

We hadn't been in touch at this stage for about two months. He may not have been what I wanted long-term, but he was a good person who had genuinely cared about me.

When I called his number, there was no answer. I decided to be brave and call his mom to see how he was doing. When she answered the call and realised that it was me, she said rather abruptly, even smugly (could I really blame her?), that he'd moved out of the apartment we had been living in and that he was getting married the next month! I was in total shock. There had been no mention or indication of this new love when I'd last spoken to him. Another whirlwind, I supposed.

"Please tell him hi and give him my best," I told her after I'd recovered, trying to sound sincere and in control. She had hung up before I had even finished speaking. I felt understandably confused, but also happy for him. He had been so sad when I had left, and my weak attempts at trying to convince him that I might come back had not been fair to him; I had had no intention of ever going back. Another door closed, another chapter that hadn't ended well, another reason to start living my life on my own and to grow up.

I told Karen that I was going to look around for a new place and try living by myself for a while. She understood and offered me the chance to come back any time that I wanted. We planned that we would get together at our pub at least once a week when it worked out with both our shifts. I started looking, again in the newspaper, but this time in the real estate section with no male/female categories; just for rent or for sale. That got me thinking that maybe one day I could even buy my own place again, especially if I could make it back into the recruitment world and potentially earn some decent commission. At least I had a plan while I was doing my own grieving for my dear friend, whom I would miss so much.

It didn't take me too long to find a very small apartment to rent, really close to the place that Meg and I had lived in when we first came to Sydney and where she had stayed until the day that she died. It was pretty basic – not a place that I would become attached to, but conveniently close to everything, clean, and adequately furnished for my short-term needs.

When I moved in, I would often walk past our old place and just stop and stare, remembering the two of us, so excited to be starting this amazing new life, buying cheap stuff to make it look posher.

I miss you, Megs, I said to myself, wiping away one of the many tears that I had shed for her since she had left my life.

I stayed in the new apartment for about six months, not dating anyone, and continued working at the restaurant while looking for a new job that would take me back into my career, though hopefully this time without the chaotic mindset and lifestyle that had gone with it before. I bought the newspaper and began my search. Mark was such an understanding manager that I wanted to be honest with him about my intentions.

"I always knew that you'd leave for good one day. I understand completely, but if you could just give me two weeks' notice so that I can cover you, that would be great. There are always heaps of girls looking for more shifts, but you'll definitely be missed," he reassured me. It felt better knowing that it wouldn't come as a shock to him or put him out when I did leave. He'd been so good to me with my trip overseas and my time off looking after Meg.

A few of the old uni crowd had moved to Sydney by this stage. I didn't see them too much, apart from at Meg's funeral, as they were still into being hippies and smoking pot. Being a corporate success and now working in the restaurant were both very alcohol-based and more sophisticated than my old life in Canberra – definitely not like the hippy I used to be. There was one girl whom I had always liked called Becca and I did see a bit of her, but she was still smoking pot and that was a bygone era for me. I wasn't interested in drugs anymore, just alcohol and my ciggies (which of course weren't drugs!), but definitely not pot or even cocaine.

Whenever I did see the old group, they were so out of it that it brought back too many mixed memories – the silly laughter and then the tears for Peter. Becca was really good fun, though; we would often walk across the Harbour Bridge just for fun, as neither of us ever tired of the magic of Sydney's harbour. When we spent time together, we would mostly end up giggling and talking about the best part of our old times together. We would often end up at her apartment close to the north end of the bridge and drink a bottle of champers. Funny how discriminating I was with my drugs; champers, wine, scotch and ciggies – these were all fine in my book.

I called Jack one day to say that I wouldn't mind coming back now if he had an opening. He told me that he didn't have any need for me at the moment, as things were going well with the staff that I had trained. I felt happy and sad in equal proportions when I spoke to him. I was pleased that my old staff members were doing so well, but it would have been great to go back to something comfortable and familiar.

"Sorry, Jacquie. I wish we could have you back, but everything is flowing nicely at the moment. Please keep in touch, though. You never know," he said warmly. "You may want to give John Smart a call. Apparently, his company is looking for someone to do internal corporate recruitment and some other HR duties."

John had been one of my best clients, and had known me really well before the Nick and fake-boobs Sally incident, when I was still focused one hundred percent on my job.

"Thanks, Jack. I'm not really sure if that would be my forte, but I'll definitely give him a call if nothing else in the recruitment consulting side comes up," I said, deflated and not at all confident that it would suit me.

I continued to look in the paper every time it came out, but there weren't any jobs that suited my skills, so I finally decided to take a chance and to give John a call to see if the job was still available and whether he would consider someone with my background.

"Come on in and we can have a chat over lunch. If you could just bring an up-to-date resume with you, that would be great,' he said when I called him, sounding happy to hear from me.

I couldn't help but be grateful yet again that I really was one of the most fortunate people alive when it came to getting jobs. I always seemed to get a referral and a lucky break just when I most needed it. As much as I did know that I was good at all my jobs and worked bloody hard, I had to admit that I was damn lucky as well. "You do have the gift of the gab!" my dad used to say to me on many occasions – I was indeed always, and still am most of the time, the biggest chatterbox on the planet.

"Hi, Jacquie." John smiled at me. "Great to see you. Please take a seat."

Returning his smile, I sat in his office, feeling a bit more nervous than I usually did in these situations. I guess this time it felt like I was reinventing myself and finally starting to properly grow up.

John and I talked for hours, and he sounded confident that he'd be able to train me fairly easily to pick up the additional skills that I would need. As the job was primarily writing advertisements and screening and interviewing applicants, I would at least feel quite comfortable with that part of the job. The woman who was leaving the job on maternity leave would train me as well before she left at the end of the month. We agreed on a reasonable starting salary and date.

"I'm sure that you'll be an enormous asset," he said as we stood up.

"I'll certainly try my absolute best." I shook his hand, feeling a bit more at ease.

I now just had to give notice at the restaurant. Feeling excited at the thought of pursuing a career once again, I went to the pub with Karen to celebrate.

It still upset me every time that I saw Nick, and there he was at the pub, staring at me as Karen and I walked in. Even after having had the relationship with Chad, there was something about seeing Nick – a hurt deep down in my gut that made me feel like I was going to throw up. Whenever I'd smell someone using the cologne he used to wear, I'd have to stop and breathe deeply to calm myself down. Love had come as easily to me as the jobs I landed, but it also seemed to be taken away just as easily.

"Hey, Jacq. Welcome home," he said. I hadn't run into him until now, thankfully.

"Hey, yourself. Nice to see you," I replied, with my best acting skills on display, trying to stop myself from running away immediately. It was time to be civil at last, even though I still felt like I'd like to punch him in the face. We lived in the same area, went to same pub and still had some of the same friends.

Ice firmly broken, I walked with Karen on shaky legs to the nearest table. I probably had a bit too much to drink, but I had survived the Nick encounter as best I could. Maybe I was finally growing up.

A few days before I was due to start my new job, I noticed that there was a two-bedroom apartment for sale in the building next door to mine. On a whim, I went to see it when it was open for inspection on the weekend. It would need quite a bit of tarting up, perhaps from the cheap import shop that Meg and I had gone to all that time ago, but I just loved it instantly. If I did actually buy it – *am I actually even thinking of that as a possibility?* – I would be on a strict budget, for a change, and cheap would have to do.

I went to the bank on the following Monday before I made any sort of offer, and they agreed to lend me the required money for the mortgage, as I had a good deposit that I hadn't managed to fritter away. I decided to take a chance, impulsiveness being a part of my nature, after all. New job, new home, new start. This was exactly what I needed. That, and no men for a while longer. Little did I know at the time that this purchase was to be the beginning of my love affair with real estate – a tad healthier than many of my previous ones.

I started the new job, feeling completely like a fish out of water for the first week. Every day my head ached from concentrating so hard to pick everything up and from the effort of using my brain again. It was going to be a huge challenge, and I was going to have to put everything possible into making it a success. After all, there was the fact that I was soon going to be a home-owner. The deposit had been paid, contracts had been exchanged, and settlement was due to happen in six weeks' time. The excitement that I felt was mixed equally with thoughts of *What the hell have I just done?* and a feeling of total panic.

Sometime in the second week of the job, just after my predecessor had left, everything really started to click. It helped that John was so helpful and patient. I also had two staff members, Geoff and Leonie, who were welcoming, knowledgeable and impressed by my expertise at the recruitment side of the job at least. As I was used to an extremely fast pace working with Pat, Derek and Jack and at the restaurant with Mark, hard work didn't faze me at all. In fact, it was a welcome relief to be totally immersed in something so exciting and stimulating to the brain again.

I quickly discovered that Geoff was absolutely hilarious, with my sort of humour. We loved the same music and movies and used to sing quite loudly when there was no one around. He used to enjoy quoting the funniest lines from movies that we'd both seen and making up different words to songs to make them sound ridiculous. We'd be doubled up at our desks until I would have to switch back into being a serious corporate woman. Leonie was a bit more sensible and would just roll her eyes and keep on working.

I didn't have any time to dwell on Meg or my failed relationships in the daytime. Night-time, when I finally made it home after a long day, was when I really missed her, and when on occasions a sense of loneliness would creep in. Fortunately, I usually fell asleep pretty early, totally knackered from my day. I wanted to do this by myself: grow up, be responsible and make my own decisions; scary, but a real independent life.

When the time finally came to move into my new apartment, I was beside myself with excitement and couldn't wait to paint things the colour I wanted and to make it my own. Sean, Karen, Di, Annie and Jo all came to help me with the move. There wasn't a lot to move, so we were pretty quickly into the champagne that Annie had brought to celebrate my purchase. She was moving into Jo's house in the inner west in a few weeks and they were both beaming, in love and blissfully happy. They were simply the cutest couple, Annie being, as my dad called us both, a real 'short-arse' and Jo being very tall and statuesque. Sean was quiet, still visibly distraught, dark circles under his eyes and lines on his forehead that hadn't been there before. He was also a lot thinner and paler these days. I think the distraction of being surrounded by busyness and laughter was good for him. Those of us who had known and loved Meg would take a very long time to heal.

The space that I now had in the new apartment was exactly what was needed after being in a tiny room at Karen's for quite some time now. There was a spare room where I kept my guitar, a sewing machine and a typewriter, among other things that I'd stored in Karen's garage before moving in. She came around for a visit one day after I was almost set up and asked me with a mischievous grin, "What is this, pet, the room of failures?"

We laughed our heads off at the time, but this feeling and practice of never completing anything and always being too busy and distracted for a meaningful hobby would continue to plague me for many years to come. As I joined in with the laughter, I felt an ever-so-slight twinge of disappointment, wondering whether there was more to life than the way I was currently living it and why none of my supposed hobbies had ever been successful. The door to exploring my spirituality opened and closed on a regular basis, with questions like *Who is God?* followed closely by *Who cares?*

Karen knew that I'd done some weekend typing lessons years ago and had quickly become well and truly bored — apart from which the teacher had been extremely condescending towards all of the students in the class, and I was more often than not too hungover to pay the attention required to be successful. The lessons had been meant to go for four weekends and I had lasted one, never to touch the typewriter again after that.

The two of us had bought sewing machines together and, determined to save ourselves some money and learn how to sew, had booked ourselves into sewing lessons close to where we lived. After a few lessons and making some pretty ordinary-looking clothes, we had both decided that we preferred to do our usual thing and go shopping for clothes readymade by professional designers. The patience involved in getting things to look and fit exactly right seemed to elude us both. The teacher was always so patient and encouraging.

"Looking good, girls," she'd say, or "That's going to suit you so well. You're bound to get a lot of wear out of that outfit," or my favourite, "Your husbands will be so proud of you."

My God. My husband, if I ever found the one (or the fourth), was not going to be someone who admired my amateur homemade clothes; surely they would be able to buy me whatever I wanted. At least, that had been my rather shallow thinking at the time. Now that I was such an independent woman and a property owner, there was not going to be any relying on a husband or any man for the foreseeable future.

I was used to making a very good income and had been surrounded by other people who also did, for the most part, since starting work in Sydney. Although I had grown up in a family with very little money, it was now something that I had learned to take for granted. I didn't think that would ever change at that point in my life. So, that was the next hobby ditched. After about five lessons, Karen and I left and went to the pub, knowing that we would never go back. The clothes that we made were never worn again; they looked amateurish and homemade, and nothing at all like my very talented mum would have been able to create.

I still feel a bit sad today about not keeping the guitar lessons going, but I just didn't have the instant talent that I had thought that I would have, nor the time to learn and practice properly. My musical tastes centred around the music that was played at the clubs I frequented, and the radio I listened to in the car or in the kitchen. The guitar playing would have to be left to Tom; instead, going out dancing and singing with great passion and enthusiasm to all the modern music was my preference. The guitar was packed away in the spare room with the other failed attempts at having a hobby that didn't involve never-ending partying.

Maybe one day I'll play again, I thought wistfully, *far too busy now.*

Chapter Twelve
Mr Sensible?

My new home was fabulous; it was close to everything that I knew, and it felt comfortable and secure. There was nothing I'd kept from the house that Nick and I had owned. Most of it had been his from his previous apartment, and I'd left everything that Meg and I had bought with her, not needing anything for the glamorous new lifestyle that I would be living with the supposed man of my dreams. There was just my personal stuff and my 'room of failures', as my rental apartment had been furnished. This was a good excuse for a trip to the import shop and the local second-hand furniture store. I was hoping to be able to buy better things once I was more established at work and able to manage my mortgage repayments. For now, there was no need to be too fussy as long as I was comfortable and independent.

Catching the ferry to the city every day never ceased to move me, and I was eternally grateful for the shimmering harbour and this magical city that was now my home. The trip to work was my time to reflect on my losses and the blessings that had come my way. These moments of introspection were a much-needed meditation before the workday would begin its unrelenting pace. It wasn't the same pace and pressure of my recruitment consulting roles, fortunately; people were less frenetic in this environment, thank goodness. There was, however, a lot expected from me in my position. I had to travel interstate for senior level recruiting assignments and attend never-ending staff meetings. The hours were long; the rewards were huge.

After only six months in the job, John called me into his office one day for a meeting to discuss my progress.

"I'm so happy with your performance, Jacquie," he said. "As part of your six-month review, I've decided to give you a ten-percent pay rise and a company car as part of your salary package." He shook my hand, congratulating me on the work that I was doing, and I was so happy that I was almost – only almost – speechless.

"Thanks so much, John. I'm so grateful to you for your patience and support. I love my job." My words rang true; I really meant it.

The new car meant that I would be parting with my now rather ageing Honda, symbolising the end of an era for me in many ways. I remembered the erratic drive to the beach after the Nick and Sally incident and the countless kilometres that I had clocked up tearing around like a mad woman, always in a rush. It did mean that I'd now drive into work, rather than my ferry ride, which was a bit sad, but I could now sing along to the radio the whole way – a decent enough compromise.

I enjoyed every moment of this new chapter in my life, knowing that I had given the job everything that I possibly could. Walking through the front door of my own home every day, even with my occasional loneliness, it felt so good to be able put my working day behind me and simply relax. I wasn't drinking too much – just a glass or two of wine most nights with dinner; my only addiction was to ciggies, which I loved with a passion. I was pretty close to pure, in my head, certainly compared to my slightly shady past, and therefore entitled to this one vice. As much as quitting was on my list of things to do, I just wasn't ready yet. Most of my friends smoked; people smoked in the pubs and clubs and even in their offices. Imagine a non-smoker coming into my office for an interview to see an overflowing ashtray and be hit with the stench of stale tobacco smoke – how revolting, but that's what was acceptable back then.

When I said I didn't drink much, I wasn't a teetotalling Methodist either, nor an Anglican, of course. There were the regular Friday after-work drinks still, this time with my new workmates. Geoff and I often went to the hotel across the road (way too fancy to be called a pub!) with a few of the people who worked in our HR department and some other staff members from the same floor of our building. Geoff's girlfriend, Jen, would sometimes join us as well. She was such a sweet girl, not as funny as Geoff – more level-headed, conservative and 'self-contained'. I think they made such a good couple because they were close to opposites. I didn't ever get very drunk, happy just having a good laugh and a lot of fun. It was a much-needed release after a long and productive week. The band at the hotel were fantastic, playing songs that I loved, giving Geoff and me an excuse to sing even louder than usual, while Jen would just look at us both and smile. We danced ridiculously in a group on the dance floor, others around us possibly thinking that we weren't as funny as we thought we were.

Occasionally Carole and Wendy would join us, as they were both still working in the city. Carole had moved to a competitor, and Wendy was still with Pat the sleaze. We weren't as close these days, but it was still good to keep in touch with people from my first job in 'the big smoke'. Di would also sometimes meet up with us, as her legal-aid friends were a lot less bawdy than we were, preferring to discuss politics and world affairs. For me, once I left the office, there was zero interest in any heavy discussions about anything at all.

There were a lot of good-looking men at work, and I enjoyed a bit of flirting but just didn't want any sort of a relationship at this point in my life. If it's 'once bitten, twice shy', this was three times bitten, six times shy. One Friday night, Geoff looked over at me and said, a bit too loudly after a great many drinks, "Don't look now – heavy alert!"

The heavies were the senior executives in the company and the heavy that he was referring to was Simon, who headed up our marketing division. We had spoken quite a few times, and he seemed nice enough – just too bloody serious for my liking and rather self-important, I thought. He was looking at me and smiling, a strange expression on a usually expressionless face. He spoke in a very posh voice, wore very expensive-looking clothes and drove a Jaguar, which I'd seen in the company car park. Even though both Nick and Chad had been doing well financially while I was with them, they had been less intense, a lot less serious. Simon certainly wasn't my type in terms of a relationship, and I had clearly been so good at picking the right type so far!

So, thinking *Why not?* I gave him one of my warmest smiles. We didn't actually make it to the speaking stage.

Not long after the smiling incident, Di popped into the hotel for a quick drink and to say hi. She looked exhausted, with huge, dark circles under her eyes.

"Hey, babe. Good to see you. You look totally whacked," I said, hugging her.

"Bloody work and bloody Gary," she blurted out. "I'm so overloaded at work, and when he gets home, he starts having these raging parties with all the guys from his club. I can't sleep with all the thumping around in the lounge room. You'd think that they did enough prancing around at work.'

Gary worked at a gay nightclub in Kings Cross as a dancer with a whole lot of other guys who liked to dress up as Barbara Streisand,

Liza Minnelli or some other famous female singer. I'd met him a few times now and just couldn't take to him. He was barely civil to me, and rather rude and bossy to Di.

The house that they'd been renting together had come up for sale a few months ago, and they had decided to take the opportunity to buy it so that they could stop paying rent and have an investment. The deal was supposed to be that either one could buy the other one out as long as they had a proper valuation, and they had both agreed. I didn't know a lot about the law when it came to real estate at this point, but I thought it all sounded a bit dodgy. Di had been confident when they had decided to do it, as they had been getting on really well, and she said that she trusted him. She had been becoming less sure of her decision the last few times that I'd seen her, and had expressed the desire to sell and disentangle her life from his. Apparently, he wasn't having a bar of it.

"You can always come and stay in the room of failures for a break and a decent night's sleep. I'd love to have you. Have you tried having it out with him?"

"Thanks, Jacq, and yes, several times. He reckons I'm being a total drama queen. Me! And he's refusing to discuss one of us buying the other out or selling the house."

She only stayed for under an hour, before kissing me on the cheek and going home to try to get some sleep. I was worried by how exhausted and defeated she looked.

Simon was still there, on his own, staring at me. Geoff and Jen were dancing, so I thought I might as well go over and talk to him. He offered to buy me a drink, and I noticed that he was slurring his words a bit. He said that he was drinking straight scotch, and I said I'd have the same. Weird, as I only ever drank wine or champagne these days.

"That's a serious drink," I said. (*For a serious guy,* I thought!)

"It's been one hell of a week. I need to let off a bit of steam and get away from the execs for a change," he replied, barely intelligible. *How many has he had,* I wondered? The execs, or heavies, usually drank in the boardroom, all men, and no one else was ever invited.

I took another look at him: a bit too Country Road for my tastes, but kind of handsome, with large, intelligent-looking green eyes and brown hair that flopped over his eyes, making him look a bit more boyish and vulnerable than I had previously thought. Rose or scotch-coloured glasses perhaps, but I was beginning to find him quite attractive.

We had a couple more scotches, and then he said he would wait with me till a taxi came along. Well, all I can think is that it must have been the scotch. Next thing I knew, we were in a wild embrace, barely able to stand up, and then stumbling into a taxi on the way to my place. As he lived a lot further up the North Shore in the old money area, we thought that my place would be closer, and we wanted to get each other's clothes off pretty quickly, apparently. We just made it through the front door before we did exactly that in the hallway of my apartment. God knows how we managed it – we were both so drunk.

The next morning, I woke up feeling like someone was hammering on my head repeatedly and as though I'd swallowed a bottle of sand. Simon was snoring away beside me. I rushed to the kitchen and drank several glasses of water, which was followed by what seemed like an eternity of throwing up. Not being accustomed to drinking scotch, I felt absolutely wretched. After I finally made it to an upright position, I went back to the kitchen to grab some paracetamol and some more water. I steadied myself and made it back to bed without any further trips to the bathroom and eventually managed to get back to sleep.

Before Simon left to go home, he kissed me passionately – the last thing that was on my mind – and said that he would like to take me out for dinner that night. Wondering why he wasn't a complete wreck as well, I declined, still feeling pretty ordinary. I guessed that he must be a lot more used to heavy drinking than I was.

Even though I didn't feel that mad about him, he was different to the other men that I usually found attractive, and I thought that maybe I should give him a chance. He wrote down my number and I agreed to go out with him on Saturday week, as he was away on business next weekend and I wasn't too keen on midweek dates. It was usually way after seven each night before I'd end up finishing and then all I wanted to do was to get home, eat something light with my glass of wine. and watch a bit of mindless TV, often crashing out on the couch.

We saw each other at work a few times through the week and nodded or smiled politely, and he called me twice at home for a chat. He was nice – very gentlemanly – but not very funny. Oh well; that was my domain, anyway. The sex had been okay, at least from what I remembered of it, if not mind-blowing. The time went by quickly, and it was soon time for our date.

He picked me up right on time, handed me a huge bouquet of roses, which I put in water, and then we left to go out in the Jag. We went to a beautiful restaurant overlooking the harbour and had the most amazing service and the most gorgeous food I'd ever eaten. The manager knew him and kept coming to check that everything was okay. Nick and I had never eaten here, as it was rather too quiet and classy for us. We had always preferred trendy and loud. We chatted easily about Simon's family from the upper North Shore, his expensive private-school education and his ambition. He had come from extreme wealth and was heading the same way.

He told me that he was buying a house not far from his parents' home and was fast establishing himself as an upper-North-Shore, highly successful, upwardly mobile corporate executive. I let him talk, not saying too much about the red dirt house or the red brick house; I just made a few jokes to lighten the seriousness of our conversation, wondering just how I could ever fit into his picture-perfect life and if in fact I would even want to.

As we were driving home, to have a nightcap from the bottle of scotch - *Yuk, not again* - that Simon said he had left in his car, I realised that he would be expecting to stay with me again. Not feeling really sure that I wanted him to, I did think that I probably should give it another go and see how I felt about him. He did appear to be very taken with me. After the first scotch, I felt queasy and thought that I was going to throw up again. *Is this becoming a pattern? See Simon, drink too much, throw up?* I tried to forget about it and just kept on drinking slowly, steadily, but the sick feeling wouldn't go away. I found some antacid to settle my stomach and suggested that we go to bed. He was more than keen about my proposal, and my stomach eventually settled. The sex was okay, pleasant, which to me was a lot like sensible. Perhaps it was time for sensible.

The next morning, the queasiness was back and the paracetamol and antacid weren't working. I acted like there was nothing wrong and Simon eventually left to go to a family lunch. This guy must have a cast-iron constitution! I went straight to the bathroom, where I spent a large part of the day. He wanted to catch up again that night, and I made up an excuse of having to see an old friend. I promised to have dinner with him, though, the following weekend.

After another few days the queasy feeling was still with me, and I decided that I should go to see the doctor. I was rarely sick enough to bother, and didn't know any of the doctors at the medical centre that well. The doctor that I saw, fortunately not Dr. Parker this time, took my blood pressure and my temperature, which he said were both normal.

"You couldn't be pregnant, could you?" he enquired.

What the hell? I'd been taking the pill, and often kept taking it instead of taking the sugar pills if I didn't want to have my period for some reason. Had I done that this time? I couldn't remember. Surely I couldn't be. I was always so careful.

After quite a long silence, he asked when I had last had sex and when my last period had been. It had been two and a half weeks since the first time I'd had sex with Simon. He suggested that we do a blood test, as this would be a more reliable indicator than a urine sample at such an early stage. I told him about the throwing up after the first night we'd spent together, and he wondered if perhaps this could the reason.

"You do know that vomiting may have caused the pill to be ineffective? When do you usually take it?" he asked.

"Usually first thing in the morning..."

Oh my God! I must have taken it before I started throwing up, after the head-hammering had started on the morning after our first night together.

He said to call the next day for the results.

So, the next day, I found out that I was indeed pregnant. After the initial shock, I realised that I was going to have to tell Simon to discuss what we would do about it. I called him straight away and suggested that he could come over to my place for dinner. He was surprised by my invitation, as I had told him that I didn't like to socialise during the week.

"I'd love to see you. I didn't want to wait til; the weekend. I've missed you," he said, sweet and flirtatious. *What??* That was quick.

I was unbelievably nervous throughout dinner, spilling my water, feeling shaky and finding it difficult to pluck up the courage to tell him. We finished eating, he complimented me on my culinary skills (lamb chops and salad!), and it was time to bite the bullet. I honestly thought he'd get up and run out the door when I broke the news to him. Instead he smiled broadly, sincerely, and reached for my hand.

"That is great news! I'm so happy. I'm mad about you," he said, looking straight into my eyes with what I could only describe as adoration. It was lovely and scary having him look at me like that.

"But we've only just started seeing each other. It's way too soon," I replied shakily. "I think it's better if I have an abortion. I just didn't think that it was fair to make a decision without talking to you first."

"Look, Jacquie, I'm financially secure, I adore you already, and we can make this work. I'd like to marry you. Please don't consider getting rid of our baby. Think about it. I will look after you, I promise," he said earnestly, pleading with me.

I couldn't believe what I was hearing. What a great guy – but I didn't love him, or feel anything even close to what he was clearly feeling. On the other hand, I was now thirty. Maybe it was time to be with a sensible guy and let my head rule for a change, even though he was not very funny and drank a lot. I said that I'd think about it over the next couple of weeks and we'd discuss it further. *Do I want this baby? And if I do, can I contemplate a life with Sensible Simon?*

"Please, Jacquie. I can give you and our baby a wonderful life." He wasn't being fake, I could tell.

After promising him that I'd think about it, we went to bed. I figured that I needed to see if the sex was good enough, apart from everything else. Average, sensible and pleasant – my favourite words.

Chapter Thirteen
Marital Bliss?

Something in me felt that maybe this just wasn't right, and yet I ended up saying yes to Simon. I really didn't want to have an abortion, knowing too many friends who had been through it and having witnessed their internal conflict and sometimes regrets. As much as I needed to consider it as an option, such was my level of uncertainty, I made my decision, and I did want to keep this baby.

Simon was there, offering me security, and he was determined to do the right thing. I was sick of the heart-stopping, gut-wrenching love at first sight that I'd felt for Harry, Nick and Chad. Simon was successful, sensible, and absolutely adored me; just maybe we could make each other happy. He wouldn't cheat on me – I just knew it. I was increasingly concerned about how heavily he drank, but then I was no angel myself, so I told myself that it was just work stress and it wouldn't be an ongoing problem. I wanted to have this baby, and he was the father; there was no denying that.

After breaking the news to our families and hurriedly making the necessary preparations, it was time to move ahead with my marriage. I walked down the aisle with my dad, feeling nervous, the whole time wondering if I was perhaps making a huge mistake, but it was too late now. Di was waiting for me at the end of the aisle as my only bridesmaid, and my family and friends were all smiling. I was four months pregnant, and I was going to make this work.

"Love you, bubs," said my gorgeous dad, kissing me on the cheek.

"Love you too, Dad," I replied shakily, holding on to him, unwilling to let go of his arm just yet.

Simon beamed at me as we made the commitment to be together for the rest of our lives. He loved me, and I knew that he would take care of me and our baby.

It was a beautiful ceremony, with the reception held at the home of Simon's parents, Ida and Frank, on the upper North Shore. Their house was the biggest and poshest place I'd ever seen. Tom and his wife Jen played the music and sang at the reception on my insistence; Simon's family would have preferred a string quartet. I had said that you couldn't sing along to that sort of music, and I think I noticed an eye roll and definitely heard an exasperated sigh from Ida.

Tom and Jen still lived in Canberra and had been married for two years now, with their sweet little daughter, my niece Ella, and Jen was pregnant with their second baby. They had formed a small band with two friends and were extremely talented. I really liked Jen; we were very close whenever we managed to find the time to see each other at family gatherings and the occasional weekend visits.

Of course, at the reception, I joined them on stage for a few songs, grabbing the microphone and singing a bit too loudly as I was prone to do. There was quite a bit of tut-tutting from Simon's parents, while he just gazed indulgently, adoringly, at me, as if I could do no wrong.

"This is who I am," I said under my breath. "You'd better get used to it." Anyway, I thought that I was a fantastic singer – no one had had the courage to tell me otherwise – so they were lucky to have me entertain the guests.

After a couple of hours, I noticed that Simon was once again very drunk, staggering a lot and slurring his words. When he made his speech, it was hard to make out what he was saying for most of it. Everyone clapped and cheered anyway, so I figured that it was just because I wasn't drinking that I was noticing it and being overly sensitive. He kissed me sloppily and placed his arm heavily, possessively, around my shoulder.

His parents clearly idolised him. His mother came up to me at one point just to tell me how lucky I was and what a wonderful son Simon was. There was a sight chill to her smile as she sailed off to mix with her wealthy friends and relatives. They weren't too interested in spending much time talking to my family, as I don't think we quite came up to their social status. I did notice them looking rather judgementally at Annie and Jo once too often, and was about to give them a piece of my mind. *Settle down, Jacq,* I muttered to myself, not wanting to cause a scene.

My friends and family all did what we did best: laughed too loudly, sang too loudly and stuck to each other like glue, to me representing a unified front of normality and simplicity among the opulence and extravagance surrounding us.

Throughout the whole day and evening, I missed Meg so much as I thought of her beautiful smile and happy nature. I also missed Karen, who had moved to Carolina recently. She had broken up with Phil, as he had told her that he wanted to start seeing other people for some inexplicable reason. She had initially been sad, but very soon agreed; things had become somewhat stale between them. Not too long after their split, she had met a gorgeous, somewhat older, American man, Bob, whom she declared to be 'the love of her life'. She had called to wish me all the best. Sadly, I didn't think that we would be able to keep in touch as much as we would have liked to, with me now being a wife and about to be a mum. We were still confined to letter writing and the occasional very brief phone call when the time difference worked out for both of us.

After the ceremony, Simon and I went off to a beautiful hotel in the city near the harbour. The room was huge and absolutely gorgeous, overlooking the twinkling city lights and the sparkling, inky water rippling gently as the boats and ferries glided past the window. Simon lurched forward, fumbling rather roughly with the zip on the back of my dress, and tied to kiss me, but ended up tripping over and falling onto the bed. Within seconds, after some unintelligible mumbling, he was completely out of it, snoring heavily. I changed out of my dress into the ridiculously expensive lingerie that I had bought for the wedding night, thinking that I would be able to wake him up. He didn't stir from his prone position when I tried to rouse him. Thinking *What's the point?,* I changed into a sensible t-shirt and leggings, packing away what had been meant to be a special treat for Simon on our wedding night.

I stood at the window for hours, taking in the glimmering harbour, the lights and the night noises, holding my expanding belly, wondering for what felt like the hundredth time whether I'd done the right thing. Surely it was just the excitement of the wedding, I thought. It had to be okay, for the sake of the baby. I refused to be sad; the night had been fun and Simon and I would be just fine, I convinced myself. I went to bed and slept fitfully, feeling anxious and alone. I kept thinking that my choices so far hadn't been great, and I did know with absolute certainty that Simon loved me. We would be happy; he would stop drinking and he would always be true to the love that he declared for me.

When I woke up the next morning, Simon was raised up on one elbow, staring lovingly at me, as usual appearing to be unaffected by the excesses of the evening before.

"What a fabulous night. I love you so much," he declared, and started kissing me gently, stopping for a while to kiss my belly and look up at me, smiling. I felt like I could breathe out and relax, and that everything was fine as I had hoped it would be. I responded to his kiss, and we made love for the first time as husband and wife. We ordered a huge breakfast and made love again, falling back to sleep in each other's arms.

Once we had finally surfaced, showered and packed, we set off to explore the markets close by, and enjoy our first day as a married couple. We were heading off for our honeymoon in Fiji the next day and had to go home and pack. We would be staying at a beautiful resort on the mainland – not on the island for singles that I had enjoyed so much last time. The world was bright; we were going to be just fine and stay together forever. I was determined that this would finally be my happily ever after. Simon was starting to really get my humour and managing to crack a few jokes himself, lightening his often overly-serious nature. He could be quite funny, I noticed, when I gave him a chance.

When we arrived in Fiji, I was once again captivated by the sweet, gentle nature of the locals, with their genuine smiles as they said 'Bulla' to us whenever they saw us. The honeymoon, for the most part, was wonderful. I spoke to him honestly about his excessive drinking rather than letting it build up inside me, and he agreed that he would not drink too much. He didn't argue about it, happiest when he could find a way to please me – or so I thought. He kept to his word except for one of the nights that we were there. I noticed once again that he was drinking a lot, and extremely quickly.

"Don't you think you've had enough to drink?" I said, feeling that he would be cooperative and realise for himself how he was behaving. I didn't yet know much about the inner workings of the mind of an alcoholic.

He immediately reacted, becoming quite abusive towards me. Grabbing my arm roughly, he held it a bit too tight and glared at me threateningly, a look that I hadn't seen before.

"For God's sake, stop being such a damn prude. Lighten up and give me a break. I'm paying for this, so I'll drink as much as I like!" he said with a nasty sneer.

Not being used to this sort of behaviour from anyone in my life before, I was frightened; I stormed off to our bungalow, leaving him alone in the restaurant. He followed me back a relatively short time afterwards and apologised profusely, pleading with me and assuring me that he was sorry for his actions. My hands were shaking, my doubts moving further forward from the back of my mind where I had firmly placed them.

"Please, Jacq, I love you. I promise it won't happen again," he begged. I so wanted to trust him, having made this difficult choice to be with him – and, true to his word, he kept his drinking under control and we had a fabulous time for the rest of our holiday. We enjoyed the beautiful beach and magnificent sunsets and relaxed, happy in each other's company. While I could see that he wanted to drink more, I tried to reassure myself, *surely he can also control it – can't he?*

The slight knot in my stomach that had started ever since I had discovered I was pregnant to Simon was ever-present, and yet equally mixed with the joy of watching my usually flat belly expanding. I was becoming quite adept at squashing negative feelings, putting on a smile and masking any insecurities with humour and a positive attitude. Whenever I thought about the new life that was growing inside me, I could push away the doubts even more. I wanted this baby with a love that was bigger than anything I had ever felt or known.

Chapter Fourteen
Max

When we returned home from Fiji, it was time for us to settle into married life. We had moved all of my stuff into Simon's house. My apartment was being sold so that I could put the proceeds into Simon's mortgage, which was surprisingly large for someone on such a high income. I guessed that it must be his extravagant lifestyle. Anyway, we were married, we were committed, and we were about to be a family. I had felt sad packing up my little home that I had loved so much, especially the 'room of failures', which was now the garage of failures, or at least one corner of the garage that Simon had told me I could use for storage. I had left all of my furniture in the apartment, as it looked better from a sales point of view, and would either sell it to the new owner or get rid of it, as Simon had beautiful, expensive furniture throughout his home. Everything was rather beige and perfect.

"If you want to do any redecorating, that's fine, darling," he assured me. "Mum has a wonderful decorator if you need any tips."

Yeah right, I thought. *I think I can make any improvements myself. And it might just have to start with the (lack of) colour scheme.* But out loud I said, sweetly, "Thanks, darling, I'll think about it."

As my pregnancy advanced, it was becoming increasingly difficult to keep up the usual hectic pace at work. It was time to concentrate on getting ready for the birth of my baby. I left my job feeling an equal mix of sadness and excitement. John was supportive, understanding and disappointed to see me leave.

"All the very best, Jacquie, from all of us. You have been a pleasure to work with," he said at my farewell drinks. "I hope you will be able to return at some point, as we'll miss you terribly. It just won't be the same without your smiling face."

"Thanks, John. I'll miss you all too," I replied, and I meant it. "Geoff is going to have to work overtime to make you guys laugh. Big job, buddy!" I grinned at Geoff. Of all the jobs that I'd had, this was definitely my favourite. I was going to find it a challenge to be without the mental stimulation and my own income, as well as the fabulous people I worked with. It was time for my next chapter, and it was time to say goodbye.

The next few months flew by as I bought bright cushions to liven up the beige, found a red kettle to scare the hell out of the pure white kitchen, and decorated the baby's room in bright colours with a beautiful, antique rose gold cot. As much as Ida and I were getting on really well these days, there was no way that her decorator would be coming anywhere near my home. Simon was happy as long as I was happy. He had a temper that I had only seen once before, on our honeymoon, and it would surface occasionally when he had had a tough day at work, and particularly when he was hungover. He was under a lot of stress constantly at work, so I tried to do nothing to provoke any anger towards me. After all, I did know just how tough the corporate world could be.

Perhaps it is me provoking him? I wondered. After all, I definitely could be feisty at times. *I'll try to keep my mouth shut.*

We entertained a bit – mostly Simon's work friends. Simon was a fantastic cook, often spending hours on a reduction sauce or something equally as fancy. I could never be bothered with that much fuss. There was a whole aisle of sauces at the supermarket and a deli close by with readymade ones that were more than good enough in my eyes. Still, it made him happy and I rather enjoyed my kitchen-hand role. At these times, I felt a real closeness with him and more confidence that perhaps our marriage would be just fine.

I had Di and Becca over a few times. It was a bit of a hike for them both, as Di lived the other side of the bridge and Becca didn't drive, so had to come by train. My family also visited a few times before the baby was born, usually when they knew that Frank and Ida were out of town on one of their many overseas holidays. Everyone seemed to be smiling a lot, looking positive – and yet not totally genuine, I thought. I could usually tell what people were feeling when I looked into their eyes. The expression 'the smile that doesn't quite reach the eyes' was the dead giveaway for me. I guess they might have been picking up on my stomach knot. Things felt more forced; my laughter didn't sound as sincere. Was I waiting, ever-vigilant, for the nasty person I'd experienced on our honeymoon to resurface?

We attended quite a few corporate functions where there was loads of drinking by everyone except me. Where had my usual laughter gone, I wondered? Was it just that I was used to being drunk as well? I smiled at everyone and everything, trying to be amused by the stupid drunken jokes. *Fake it till you make it,* I thought. Once the baby was born, I'd be able to drink again and maybe I wouldn't have to feel like I was being so fake.

After five months of marriage, we were settled into our routine, and we were – if not blissful, then at least pretty happy. One night, about five days before my due date, I was woken up by an agonising contraction heralding the start of my labour. We rushed to the hospital, Simon in a state of pure panic and me in shock that it could hurt as much as people said it did. I had thought that they were just being wimps. And then I experienced the greatest joy that I could have ever imagined – if you deduct the eight hours of pain and screaming at nurses, doctors and Simon. Max was born and I was completely and utterly in love. His pale hair and beautiful blue eyes, his tiny hands – everything about him was to me perfection. He was a lot more like me to look at than Simon, but blonder and angelic – I don't think I've ever been called that, even as a baby.

Simon was clearly very happy, and yet more intent on fussing over me than his son. He was a bit awkward when he held him and handed him back to me the moment that he cried. He did, however, hug me incessantly, telling me that he was proud of me. On my second night in hospital, he came in with a beautifully wrapped gift for me; nothing for Max. It was an absolutely stunning diamond necklace. Odd that there wasn't anything for Max.

Ida was absolutely wonderful when she and Frank came to visit, leading me to wonder, not for the first time, whether I had perhaps been a bit too harsh in my initial judgement of her. I hadn't come from posh and I simply didn't understand it. She fussed over Max, making it abundantly clear that he was loved and welcomed into the family. The following day, Simon took Max and me home. He carried the capsule, eyes only for me and not the baby. He guided me in through the front door gently, lovingly, as if I were an invalid. He placed the capsule on the floor without looking at Max and took me in his arms.

"How long before we can make love?" he asked. "I've missed you in bed with me so much."

"The doctor said about six weeks would be best," I told him, rather shocked that he would ask such a question and thinking that there could be nothing further from my mind. All I wanted was to hold and feed my beautiful baby boy.

"Surely that's a bit long, don't you think?" he said rather testily, almost petulant.

I didn't reply, as Max was stirring. I bent to pick him up, glad of the distraction.

The days literally flew by as Max developed quickly from helpless newborn to his first real smile at five weeks of age. Each day my love for him grew more and more. Simon tended to leave us alone a lot; sometimes he smiled and occasionally played with Max, but there just wasn't as strong a bond developing between them. Any doubts that I had ever had about having Max were completely gone, and I felt pure joy and laughter return to my life, as I laughed at everything he did, he would giggle back at me, lovingly, happy to be just with me. I loved him unconditionally, feeling like my heart was connected to his.

Simon started to get frustrated at the amount of time and energy that I spent on Max, and particularly if I didn't want sex when he did, which was all the time! Often a cloud would appear over his face, heralding the displeasure that he felt towards my rejection of him. He occasionally pushed or shoved me, especially when he had been drinking, and I learned to move quickly, to get out of his way. If ever I was too busy with Max and didn't pay him enough attention, he tended to get even more upset, saying something like "What a mummy's boy", or an equally sarcastic comment. *What a spoiled brat,* I often thought, *and just who's the mummy's boy?* I was not totally surprised by his behaviour, having seen the way Ida, particularly, doted on him.

We would often have to get babysitters to attend a corporate dinner or function. I hated leaving Max, but Simon insisted that I had to always be by his side and available to entertain and be entertaining. He was very successful, totally career-obsessed, and incredibly generous as long as I continued to be the dutiful wife — still quite an uncomfortable and unusual role for me. I could have anything that I wanted from a material perspective; we appeared to be the perfect glossy couple to anyone who ever saw us together. Having been used to my independence and success in the workplace, it was a weirdly alien feeling to be so dependent on another person, and a person that I didn't always trust. I watched myself morph into something that I had thought I would never become.

As Simon continued to drink way too heavily, I tried to ignore it and think of how much we had and how spoiled and lucky I was. On the occasions when he would become aggressive, I mostly learned to keep quiet, not to provoke him any further. I was also drinking again: not heavily but steadily, most days especially just before Simon came home. I found it easier to have sex with him if I'd had a few drinks to alleviate the edginess I felt around him a lot of the time. I wondered for the first time when Max was almost one if I should leave him. I had tried to talk to him about how I felt many times and he would always convince me that he loved me, that it was work or he was tired, and that he would never ever do anything to hurt me. *Well, you'd better not,* I thought. My love for him had not grown as I had hoped it would, and leaving was definitely always an option in my mind. It was just different with this relationship, and of course more complicated by the fact that I had no income of my own and Max to consider. I loved being impulsive, but had to keep a more level head as a mother and give this marriage more time.

I started seeing a bit more of Becca, as she had twins not long after Max was born and wasn't smoking pot anymore. I used to drive to her house, near where I had lived with Meg, and we would talk for hours. As Dan, Becca's husband, was also a bit controlling, we supported each other over a few glasses of champagne on many occasions. No pot, but she did love a drink. I didn't tell her about Simon's occasional aggressive nature; we just made light of our husbands' behaviours and enjoyed our time without them. The kids played really well together, leaving us to have a drink and a laugh. Before driving home I would trade the champagne for a lot of coffee and water, hoping that I wasn't over the limit and could get Max home safely. Above anything else, including myself, he was my priority at all times.

I also saw Di occasionally – not as often as I would like to, as we were living in very different worlds. We still had a very deep and strong love for each other, having shared so much at school and at uni. I would never forget that. She wasn't married, and kept flitting from boyfriend to boyfriend with nothing lasting very long. Each time I saw her she was looking increasingly stressed, chain-smoking and agitated. She still wanted to sell the house she was in with Gary, and he still refused. He couldn't afford to buy her share. She didn't know what to do.

"I'm so confused, Jacq," she said. "I can't see my way out of it. I'm popping pills to sleep, drinking too much and can't focus at work. He's such a jerk."

I didn't know what to suggest, so I just hugged her and promised to be there for her no matter what. I didn't tell her about my life. I'd made my decision, and as of this moment in time I was sticking by it.

Simon would go out for drinks after work quite regularly. He would come home expecting me to jump into bed with him. Even if I had a few drinks, I was finding him less and less attractive, with his controlling nature and the ugly red wine stains (his drink of choice along with the scotch) crusting unattractively around the corners of his mouth. If I turned him down, there would be the usual push and shove that I had become accustomed to – nothing too violent. I usually just gave in and went to bed with him. I kept asking myself why I was still there when I clearly doubted my love for him. I couldn't answer that. Maybe it was the lifestyle, the security for Max; I just didn't know. My customary confidence had faded, that was for sure, and still I had this unwavering determination that we could make this work.

Time marched on; our lives were incredibly busy, and superficially we had it all. There were the fabulous holidays overseas, and locally, our lovely home with everything that I could want and great friends. Simon was mostly good to me, and I had the good sense to try not to provoke him. Max was growing up so fast, from baby to toddler to the sweetest little boy, always preferring to be with me than his father.

When Max was around two and a half, Simon came home one night after another of his huge drinking sessions. He was staggering and slurring and kept trying to kiss me. It was disgusting. I was getting fed up and, perhaps stupidly, decided to have it out with him.

Not thinking at all logically, I lost my temper, pushing him away from me as he tried to make advances, not realising that it was pointless trying to reason with a drunken man.

"I'm sick to death of your drinking. You're so unattractive and sloppy. Get away from me," I said, shoving him again. Huge mistake.

Crack! It felt and sounded like a whip slapping across my face. There were no words as he then put his hands around my neck, squeezing tightly. He kept squeezing until I must have blacked out briefly. When I came to and opened my eyes, I saw him sprawled across the bed, fully clothed, snoring. Feeling repulsed, confused and angry, I got up slowly, shaking, took a very long shower and went to the spare bedroom, where sleep eluded me until the early hours of the morning.

When Simon found me asleep the next morning, he tried to hug me, seemingly oblivious to what he'd done. "Why are you sleeping in here, babe?" he asked, blurry-eyed and still reeking of alcohol.

When I pulled away from him and told him what he had done, he was mortified; he had no memory of it at all. The bruises on my neck had already started to show. He fell to his hands and knees, apologising, begging for forgiveness, hugging me and assuring me that it would never happen again. I so wanted to believe him, but couldn't bring myself to hug him back. Not long afterwards, Max woke up, giving me an excuse to disentangle myself from Simon's arms. *Where is that happy, strong person you have always been, damn it? This is not you, Jacquie!* I silently admonished myself.

The knot, the disquiet, mixed with the determination, spun round and round in my head and in my gut. In the mirror I saw the ugly purple of the bruises and the red marks on my cheek. After settling Max with some toys to play with, I quickly applied some makeup and found a scarf that would hopefully hide the marks Simon had left on my neck. I felt ashamed, confused and trapped. *He says he loves me so much, but how can he do this?* was my constant worry.

I kept quiet, I kept smiling, I told no one, and I couldn't fathom why. Simon became the perfect husband in every way, treating me with the respect, care and concern that he used to display before Max was born. And so we entertained family and friends; we had some moments of laughter and closeness. Socially, together we were well matched, with both of us being able to talk endlessly on any topic: it was glossy and glamorous. Our guests all thought that we were the perfect hosts. We both enjoyed planning our menus and cooking together, chatting about the different wines and cheeses that we would serve. There were no more violent outbursts, I could breathe again, it was going to be okay. I was blindly operating in an ever-increasing fog and willing everything to work out. My shoulders were always that little bit raised, my neck just that little bit too stiff to allow me to sleep well at night. I didn't trust this nice Simon, not when I'd seen just how ugly he could be.

I became even more vigilant around his drinking, trying my best to make sure that I ignored his behaviour when he drank too much. It was hard; I would roll my eyes and say to anyone who would comment, "Oh well, you know Simon," as my shoulders lifted and my neck tensed and tightened further. His friends and family accepted him this way; there would be no allies there. *I guess it must be me then,* I often thought, as I kept wondering just how much of this was actually my fault. I was tired all of the time, he was so sorry, and I knew that I had really provoked him. I felt like I was a character in a movie, detached from reality, afraid of leaving and afraid of staying. I kept rushing, always busy; there was no time to look too deeply inside. My brain hurt with the effort to figure out what was right and what was wrong.

Sometimes I'd take Max over to Di's house, and she'd play the piano and we'd sing songs for ages while Max played with her black Labrador, which she had named Bubba. Both of us were overly bright and happy on those occasions, laughing and singing too loudly, a determination in both of us that we were okay. I saw the sadness and exhaustion in her eyes and noticed how quickly her full glass would be emptied and refilled. If only we had spoken openly to each other then.

I found an excellent local Kindy for Max and decided that I wanted to go back to work part-time, feeling concern that my brain might just be atrophying! The faster I moved, the more I did, the less time for thinking.

John was delighted when I called him to say that I wanted to come back, and suggested that I could work two or three shorter days a week to fit in with Max's Kindy hours; I could start straight away. *You're a lucky girl, Jacq, I said to the mirror in the hallway,* smiling when I hung up. The work wouldn't be quite as challenging, but it would keep my brain busy and give me a purpose when I wasn't with Max.

As well as the knot in my stomach, which now felt more like an empty space, the stiffness in my shoulders and neck was getting worse, with the pain sometimes heading towards a migraine. I ignored it as best I could. I wasn't going to allow anything to stop me. There were drugs for the pain. Work, take care of Max, shop, clean, see friends, and go out with Simon: that was my new plan. On and on went the rollercoaster.

"Why do you need to go back to work?" complained Simon. "Surely you have everything you need." I knew that he wanted me at home and available when it suited him.

"I just want to use my brain a bit," I explained. I begged and promised that nothing would change.

The excitement about returning to work also helped me want to persevere with my marriage, for some odd reason. I was often afraid of Simon, but I also knew that he loved me, and he was always so remorseful whenever he was at all aggressive with me. Wanting to believe him and to convince him and myself that it would all be okay, I made love with him more regularly. I hadn't been on the pill for a while now, as it didn't agree with me, but we had always used condoms or withdrawal to avoid another pregnancy. So far so good.

Being back in the working world was the most liberating feeling. This was where I excelled, and I was happy. Max settled into Kindy after we had worked through the separation anxiety (mine, not his) and I dragged out my corporate gear for my triumphant return. It was strange on the first day, having Geoff and Leonie tell me what to do. They were both still working there and had been promoted – Geoff into my role and Leonie as his 2IC. I think they secretly liked this role reversal, as I'd always loved bossing them around, even though I was always a fair boss. The gratitude that I felt being back and the sense of achievement that I experienced translated almost in equal measure to me being happier in my marriage. Simon saw the positive change in me and we even had more sex, sometimes at my instigation. My headaches weren't as bad, and my future was looking brighter.

One morning when I didn't have to get up for work, I had forgotten to set the alarm. Simon had left for work early and hadn't woken me. Max came into the room and asked me for some breakfast. When I saw the time, I jumped out of bed, rushing around like a madwoman, getting Max organised for his day.

"Oh shit, oh shit!" I yelled.

Max looked up at me in my state of panic. "Naughty Mumma."

I'd told him how bad swearing was, and he loved, even at such a young age, to pick me up on it whenever I'd slip up. I flew out the door wearing grotty old sweatpants and slippers.

Arriving at the Kindy centre, I screeched to a halt, angle parking in a parallel park, and ran Max inside, avoiding the looks of the other mums and staff members. When I came back outside, I saw Clara, the mother of one of Max's little friends, in her car, gazing intently into her lap. I really liked her; we'd had a quick coffee a few times – she was so quick-witted and funny. When I came up to her window to say hi, she looked up, startled to see me, and burst out laughing.

She wound the window down and I could see that she had a tray of lamingtons on her lap.

"What the bloody hell are you doing?" I asked.

"Well, the note said that we had to bring homemade food in for the stall. I'm trying to squash them so that they don't look so even. I don't bake!" She grinned.

"Well, my friend, I have no plate of food and no ability to dress myself either, apparently. I didn't even see the note," I replied, grinning back at her.

As much as I'd liked her before, there was now a certainty that I had found a lifelong friend. I adored her sense of the ridiculous, and she always told me how annoying her husband Patrick was, which made me feel better about Simon. We planned to go out for lunch on one of my days off when both of our kids were at Kindy.

We started to meet up quite regularly, talking endlessly about everything, including the tarot readers, psychics and coffee readers that she frequently went to see. I was fascinated and asked for some numbers so that I could maybe go and see someone myself. I wasn't planning on going straight away, but really wanted to at some point. For the time being, I was content to buy a book on star signs, one on numerology and another on fortune-telling. I was instantly hooked. A throwback to my witch days, but a more grown-up version, I thought. With all of this new knowledge, I came to realise without a doubt that everything I did must be because I was a Gemini and a number three. It helped to have this new obsession as an ongoing interest to add to the welcome distraction that work was providing.

When I was with Clara, my laughter returned; when I was at work I felt smart and of value; when I was with Max, I felt pure happiness. When I was with Simon, I felt emotionally conflicted and still doggedly determined.

One morning, about a month after the sweatpants, angle-parking and lamingtons morning, I woke up feeling really ill, the same feeling that I had felt when I was pregnant with Max. After another trip to the doctor, it was confirmed, as I suspected, that I was indeed pregnant. "Bloody condoms!" I muttered to myself.

Simon, smiling broadly, was clearly thrilled, and I was numb. I wondered why he was so thrilled when he didn't seem at all connected to Max. Something was still definitely not right in my marriage, but perhaps with another baby I would feel more settled, wouldn't I? Simon and I did manage to have some fun times – and not every marriage was perfect, after all, I convinced myself once again.

Simon treated me like a precious gem right through the pregnancy, and Max was so excited to think that he would have a baby brother or sister. I continued to work until I couldn't manage to lug my enormous belly around anymore. John was understanding and happy to consider me coming back after the baby was born if there was enough work at that time, and we agreed to keep in touch. I loved my job and needed the ongoing mental stimulation. I was definitely hoping that I would be able to go back. For now, I had a new baby and Max to think of.

Chapter Fifteen
Charlie

When Charlie was born, I didn't think that it would be possible for me to love someone as much as I loved Max, but I sure did. It was incredible how much she looked just like a mini Simon: the same huge green eyes, more like his than my hazel ones, and the longer, thin nose and hands. We both adored her from first sight, but for Simon it was like she was perfect and Max didn't exist.

From the time that we brought her home from the hospital, the more I paid attention to Max, the meaner Simon was and the more he gazed lovingly at Charlie. I couldn't work it out; it was like Max couldn't do anything right. *Did Simon feel that he was in a competition with the poor kid?* Whenever I confronted him, he said that I was exaggerating and being overly dramatic. *Was I?* I just wasn't sure of anything anymore. Simon had such a confident and strong character that I found I doubted myself much of the time when I was with him.

The months rolled by, my joy in being a mother outweighing my doubts, being far too busy to think about what Simon did or did not feel. I loved both of my kids and that was enough. Max loved his little sister and she looked at him like he was the most important thing in her life. She gurgled especially for him and smiled most brightly whenever he was around. This often made Simon try too hard with her, again seemingly competing for attention.

We continued to have an active social life with old friends of his and Becca, Dan, Clara and Patrick, as well as some new friends we'd made in our local area. It was all jolly and bright, lots of drinking and laughter. This was family life and surely, I kept telling myself, Simon's drinking was normal for a man with his level of responsibility. Considering all that I had, his slight aggression and sarcasm weren't too hard to deal when once again I would remind myself that our home was beautiful; we had friends who wanted to spend time with us and two amazing kids.

Max was popular with the teachers and kids at his Kindy, and Charlie was adorable, her big eyes taking in everything around her, as if she knew exactly what was going on at all times. A friend said to me, when she first saw Charlie, "She is an old soul, that little girl," and I tended to agree. I used to call her my little koala, as she loved clinging to me when Simon wasn't around, and she wasn't absorbed by something that Max was doing to entertain her.

One night, after I'd stopped breastfeeding Charlie, Simon suggested that we should spice up our sex life. He had bought a porn movie and wanted to watch it with me. I tried to protest, laughing it off as a lame idea, hoping that he wasn't serious. He grabbed my wrist, and said rather forcefully, "Come on, Jacquie. I work hard. You're always tired. We need a little bit of fun. You'll enjoy it, I bet."

This left no room for discussion as he led me to our bedroom and placed the movie into the video player (still no mobiles, and no DVDs either). The way he looked at me made me realise that it wasn't worth creating a scene. As much as I knew that I should have stood up for what I wanted, I was too tired to argue and felt empty and powerless.

Just looking at the video cover made me feel sick. It was all big hair, big boobs, big bulges and lips that brought a whole new meaning to the word pouty. The movie was awful, the sex was awful, and I felt like a whore.

Come on, Jacquie, I said to myself once the sex was over and the credits started rolling (credits for what? Certainly not for a clever plot or character development!) *Wake up. This is not who you are!*

The next day, I started to think even more seriously about leaving him. He hadn't hit me again, but he frightened me. His tone of voice, his sarcasm and controlling, unpredictable manner all contributed to him being a man that I simply didn't want to stay with. I was frightened about starting off on my own, but I was equally afraid of the effect that he would have on my children if I stayed. Particularly there was the impact that it was already having on Max as Simon's favouritism towards Charlie continued on a daily basis.

The main issues facing me with this difficult decision were financial, as I had very limited funds in my own bank account, and the physical energy it would require to forge a life on my own. I was emotionally and physically exhausted. I wondered if I had the strength to do it. The days rolled by, the inertia took hold of me yet again, and I stayed. *One day,* I thought, *I'll have the courage to do this.*

I hadn't returned to my usual weight after Charlie was born, and Simon had recently started teasing me about it on a regular basis.

"Look at you," he would say. "You're looking a bit chubby, babe," grinning as if he'd said nothing wrong. The cruel, nasty comments became a constant most days, no matter what I wore or how hard I tried to lose the weight. Even knowing that he was just being a complete arsehole, I took it to heart and decided it was time to take action. So I joined Jenny Craig. As Simon kept telling me that nobody else but him would want me if I was overweight, I was determined to prove him wrong.

I took to this diet with a vengeance. Upon reaching my goal weight, a whole four kilos lighter, I couldn't stop. There was no need to go back to speak to the diet coach; I had it sorted and could do this myself – men were even flirting with me, I noticed, on occasion. Down and down went my weight, until one day I collapsed in the kitchen, faint from hunger. Hopping on the scales to weigh myself the next day, I was shocked to see that I'd dropped to forty-nine kilos.

Stop it, I said to myself. *Pull yourself together, and fuck you, Simon!* Or preferably, not fuck Simon, if this was how I was going to continue to be treated. My weight didn't drop any further and I went back to eating normally, sensibly. I was wondering what Simon could choose to pick on next.

There were many times when I just knew that Simon wanted to hit me and I sure as hell wanted to hit him when he was drunk and so nasty towards me and particularly Max. Often, when we became angry at each other, usually about his drinking, he would push me up against the wall, holding my throat, his face close to mine, sneering and mocking me. He didn't hit, though; he just threatened to, wanting to exert his physical power over me, I guessed – it worked. I moved faster to get out of his way and into another room when the dark cloud passed over his face, but I didn't learn to shut up, as he wanted me to. Always having been one to speak my mind, I poked the bear on occasions, almost willing him to do something, perhaps so that I would have to make my move at last and stop living with this ongoing tension.

It was time to stop this bloody whingeing and to talk to someone who could perhaps help me to go through with this and to create a new life. I thought about a counsellor or maybe Di, Becca or Clara, but just wasn't sure who would be the right person able to help me unjumble my foggy brain and bring me some clarity.

When I did actually make an appointment for the following week to see a counsellor who was recommended by Clara, I found that I actually relaxed a bit, breathing out and feeling my shoulders drop ever so slightly again; I had taken my first positive step and it felt good. As well as arranging to see the counsellor, I wanted to talk to Di. She was my oldest friend, or as she liked to say, 'Not oldest, Jacq, longest standing!'

It was becoming harder, though, with all that was involved in raising two kids, to keep in touch with her. Our lives were very different in so many ways. When I did manage to speak to her she sounded so down. We both were, and laughter didn't come as easily as it always had in the past when we were young without responsibilities.

I made an arrangement on a Friday to bring Max and Charlie over to visit on the following Sunday morning. I was going to tell her exactly how I was feeling about Simon. I needed to reach out to someone who really knew me, and I felt that she needed to talk to me too.

"Can't wait to see you, babe," I said, and meant it.

"Yep, me too." She was making an effort to be bubbly, but instead sounding so tired and defeated; I was worried, and happy that I would be seeing her.

Between that decision and the counsellor, I was starting to feel more powerful. Having battled on alone for way too long, believing that Simon could change, it was now abundantly clear that I couldn't make this work through sheer will alone.

Charlie, who was six months old at this point, was sick the night before I was due to visit Di and so, exhausted from being up half the night, I called and cancelled, leaving a message on Di's answer machine. When I didn't hear back, I wasn't overly worried. We were a bit slack in more recent times, in terms of the regularity of our contact. I thought that I'd call her on Monday and make another definite plan. We needed each other, and hopefully we could support each other through these tough times and get back to being as close as we once used to be.

On Monday afternoon, I still hadn't heard from Di and was about to call her and tell her how slack she was. Before I could do that, her sister Mary called me, sounding just awful, and told me to sit down.

"I don't quite know how to tell you this, Jacq." She started sobbing. I heard her give a huge sigh, as if she was trying to pull herself together. "Di has committed suicide," she continued, before breaking down completely. I was speechless, numb and disconnected from my body. I don't remember the rest of what was said. I just remember hanging up the phone and not moving from my chair in the lounge room for a very long time. How hard must it have been for her to call and tell me this; and yet all that I could think of at the very moment in time was my own feelings and how devastated I was.

Di had left a note written to her friends and family, saying that she felt that we all had something to sustain us: partners, children or something that brought us joy. She felt that she didn't have anything to bring her the level of happiness that we experienced on a daily basis.

What about us? I said to myself. *Why didn't you talk to me or anyone in your life who cared about you?* Feeling a mixture of irrational anger at her actions and deep sadness that she had really felt so helpless and alone, I spent time beating myself up, wondering why I hadn't told her that my life was not the glossy, shiny picture that appeared on my surface. I couldn't budge the feeling that perhaps I could have saved her. My guilt was savagely gnawing away in my belly, relentless and ever-present.

Compared to the absolute raw, debilitating grief that I had felt when Meg had died, at least I had time with her to speak to her, to hold her until the end. With Di, the shock was unbearable. If only I hadn't cancelled, just maybe we could have helped each other – but I also knew that if I kept thinking like this, I would go completely insane. When the anger that had been my predominant emotion after the shock subsided, next the sorrow set in, dark and heavy. I cancelled the appointment with my counsellor, not wanting to share my feelings about my marriage anymore, not having the energy that I felt was needed to talk to a stranger. Simon was gentle, supportive and considerate during this time, as I was facing such an awful tragedy in my life. Damn, I was going to miss her.

Thank God, Di's sisters and her dear friend Robbie spoke at her funeral. I couldn't do that again. Mum said to me one day when we were talking on the phone about it, "It's like your whole past has been ripped away from you. Your two closest and dearest friends. I'm so sad for you."

'Thanks, Mum. I'll be okay. It's just really hard right now."

The two people who had been such integral parts of my life for so many years and through so many crazy experiences were now both gone from my life forever. I stopped myself from telling her about my troubled marriage. It didn't seem to be the right time.

For the sake of my beautiful children, I would go on, jaded, sad and lost, but I would not let them down. They had known Di and Max was old enough to share some of my sadness, hugging me protectively. Charlie just snuggled into me, sensing that that was what I needed.

Di, how could you do this? Why didn't I take more time to talk to you? Could I have saved you? These and several other pointless questions ran round and round in my head day after day as I backed down on my decision to tell Simon that I wanted to leave him. The fog in my head became increasingly thicker; my legs felt like they were being dragged into quicksand. Too tired and too sad to do anything, I chose to stay, to try to survive this, hopeful that a miracle would happen and my feelings towards him would change.

Simon seemed totally oblivious to my conflicted feelings about him and our marriage, acting as if nothing at all was wrong. He was concerned for my sadness about Di, but didn't see a problem with the marriage, or didn't want to. He had what he wanted: a wife, two children and a fabulous career. I wasn't ready to have the conversation that I needed to have, not yet. And I kept thinking that so many women were worse off than me. Why couldn't I just shut up and learn to live with it?

Chapter Sixteen
I Hate Linen

As normality slowly returned, the loss of Di never too far from my mind, the kids needed me to be strong again. It was soon going to be time for Max to start school, and as Simon had had a huge pay rise, we thought about moving to a bigger house, closer to the best school in the area on the North Shore. None of the kids from Max's Kindy would be going there, as it was out of area for them. I felt concerned that it might be difficult for him, as he was such a sensitive kid, but when I raised my concern with Simon, he was adamant.

"For God's sake, Jacquie, stop smothering him. Don't you want your son to go to the best primary school in the whole area?" he said.

My son? I thought. *Surely he's our son.* I kept quiet.

We ended up buying a massive house on the top of a beautiful street with equally enormous houses all the way down it. Our house on the hill was Simon's pride and joy. We had really made it now, surrounded by beautiful homes and beautiful marriages – or so it seemed to me, as my marriage was definitely showing some very significant cracks. I wondered over and over again if there was a way to make this work and if I could quell the negative feelings for the sake of the beautiful existence that Simon provided for us.

He kept up the heavy drinking and I continued to keep quiet, to be the best wife and mother that I could be, and to be grateful for all that was good in my life. And there were things to be grateful for; there had been no real violence for a long time now and Max knew that I was in his corner at all times, even if his father wasn't.

The house was like a palace, with chandeliers and gold fittings in the bathrooms, heavy brocade tie-back curtains and overly-patterned, expensive-looking wallpaper throughout. It was a tad on the tacky side but great if you were into glitz, a lot like eighties fashion.

"Maybe I should get out the lycra leggings and big earrings again," I said to Simon, chuckling at my own joke, particularly when I saw the ensuite with gold fish-heads for taps. He at least agreed with me and saw the humour – the taps would definitely have to go!

When Mum, Dad, Tom, Jen, Annie and Jo came to visit for the first time, their jaws dropped collectively as they entered through the opulent foyer and made their way down a very long and wide hallway. The ceilings were super high and every room was oversized. Along with my family, I felt overawed by such an extravagant demonstration of wealth. Simon was beaming.

"I never thought that I'd ever know someone who lived in a house like this," said Mum, wide-eyed, "let alone be related to them!"

During their visit, Tom and Jen's now three gorgeous little girls played happily with Max and Charlie, while Simon made sure that everyone, especially himself, had their glasses constantly filled. I loved having my family there, even if they were totally overwhelmed. Once everyone had finally relaxed, we all joked around as we always did when we were able to be together in one room. As I felt myself becoming more and more at ease, especially with my family around, it was great to see genuine laughter returning after the loss of Di and the continual ups and downs of the should I stay/should I go saga. Honestly, I was beginning to get bored with myself and the constant drama surrounding my marriage. *Make a bloody decision, Jacq, and stop bloody whingeing* was one of my favourite admonishments these days.

When I wasn't with family or friends, I had my spiritual books to read to help me make sense of my otherwise mixed-up world. I loved becoming lost in the insights that they provided as my soul searched for answers, something to make me feel less confused and lonely within this life that I had chosen to stay and live. I still had Becca and Clara to talk to about living in a less-than-perfect marriage, and wondered if now was the right time to speak to one of them. Having lost Meg and then Di, it was becoming more important to keep connecting with my friends. The only problem with that was that they didn't appear to be as unhappy as I was. *Maybe soon,* I thought.

One night, Simon found me crying over the two friends that were now gone from my life and he sat with me, trying to be of comfort. He was so loving and sweet that for a very brief moment in time my guard was let down completely; I temporarily put aside the aggression, the sarcasm and the drinking. I needed a shoulder and his was the only one available right now. In this state of vulnerability, we made love and once again I found myself considering that surely for the sake of everything that we shared, I could try to talk to him again and explain more clearly how I was feeling. Perhaps we could see a counsellor together. *Good idea, Jacquie – it's been long enough coming up with that bright idea.* More often than not there was a feeling of being resigned to my fate now, the good in my marriage just enough to give me hope to believe that happiness with Simon could be still possible. I was too tired and nowhere near brave enough to forge a life on my own anyway, so a counsellor it was that was going to be able to sort us out. With that thought, and my new mindset of 'give it another shot', condoms went by the wayside and I fell pregnant with Eddie.

Charlie had already started at the Kindy that Max had been attending, and we didn't want to move her. I was going to have to drop Max at his new school and then rush Charlie back to Kindy, about a twenty-minute drive away. There were some great friends that I'd made at the Kindy, especially Clara, who was no longer there; her son had also started school, but a different one to Max. I felt that I would need to make friends with the mums in the local area to build some sort of extra network for my kids moving forward.

At the orientation day for new students at Max's new school, I managed to superficially befriend a few women, chatting away, with my 'gift of the gab' coming in very handy. They certainly weren't my cup of tea, but Ida would have loved them. They all appeared to be so well-spoken and dressed beautifully; linen, linen and more linen, subtle, neutral-toned makeup, plus very heavy gold, antique-looking chains around perfect necks. I had chosen my best denim jeans and a black non-iron blouse, minimal jewellery and my favourite bright red lipstick. Not the right choice for the majority, apparently.

There were two women who appeared to be a bit more approachable, talking together at the back of the room and not wearing bloody linen. I went up to them and instantly felt a stronger connection, I guess because apart from anything else because they were dressed a lot more like me. They were funny, down to earth, not at all snobby. In fact, they were busily making fun of all the other women around them. Silly giggling not being appreciated in such a posh environment, we were met with many disapproving glares. Apparently giggling wasn't allowed at this school. Maybe I'd have to behave myself if I wanted to fit in more.

The next week, when it was time for Max's first day, I tried to find Alison and Lola, the two women I had met the week before, but couldn't spot them at first. Eventually, just as the bell was ringing for the kids to line up and go into their classrooms, I spied them together and made my way over, somewhat relieved to not be totally alone.

"Hi, Jacq!" They appeared to be genuinely happy to see me.

"I hope our kids are in the same class, so that I have some allies," I said, smiling at them both. Unfortunately, when the names were read out, their kids were in the same class – a different class to Max.

I had to leave him to adjust and settle in, the separation, as it is for most of us first-time parents, gut-wrenching. It felt like forever until I could go and pick him up after collecting Charlie from Kindy. I was so exhausted looking after a home and two children, now pregnant with my third, and just hoped that he had had a good first day. He came out smiling and chatting happily to another boy, while there appeared to be a whole gang of boys all together behind him. I didn't notice the girls, as they were not my immediate concern. *Oh well, he only needs one friend,* I told myself.

Over the next week, he told me stories of boys being rather mean and deciding who could and couldn't play with them, clearly leaving Max and his one new little friend out. Well, maybe it was pregnancy hormones or maybe it was just me being an overprotective mother, but at the end of the next school day, I marched into the classroom as soon as the bell had gone and asked Max to wait outside for me. There was another mother waiting (a linen lady) to see the teacher as well, but that didn't stop me.

"Max tells me that there has been some nastiness among the boys," I said to a rather surprised teacher. And before she could form the words to reply, I added with flair, "You do know that ostracism is tantamount to bullying, don't you?"

I wondered where that little gem had come from, but God it felt good, and I sounded so smart. Feeling impressed with myself, I spun around and marched right out of the classroom door, leaving the linen lady and the teacher with their mouths wide open, staring after me.

Anyway, it must have done the trick because Max told me that the teacher had spoken to them all about bullying the very next day and told them that they must include each other in their games. *Well, look at you,* I patted myself on the back. *You go, girl!*

Chapter Seventeen
Buddhas on the North Shore

So it turns out that maybe Buddhas aren't just really cool ornaments. Around this time everyone decided that they wanted to buy a whole bunch of Buddhas for their homes. A very posh, overpriced Bali shop had opened up that sold all this must-have trendy stuff to the North Shore housewives. Very interesting that nobody seemed to have crosses and pictures of Jesus around. Maybe that wasn't cool enough, or maybe they shared my mum's viewpoint about the pointlessness of Christianity.

They came in so many shapes and sizes that I could see the North Shore mums trying to frown with the effort of making such a tough decision (difficult with the recent introduction of Botox to curb those nasty lines). I mean, what colour, how many, what sizes, indoor or outdoor, the fat ones or the skinny ones, and what about matching the décor? I was in the shop having a look myself when I overhead two of the linen ladies that I vaguely knew from the school talking about their latest dilemma.

"My decorator has just completed an off-white furnishing theme that really works with the antique white walls. Will the gold and blue Buddha clash, do you think?" said one woman called Trixie (yes, really).

"Well, Trixie, I'm sure that blue and gold will work perfectly, as long as everything else is in the white tones," said the other one, Poppy. "My decorator told me that it's good to have a couple of items that pop." They nodded sagely, flicked their immaculate hair, paid for their purchases and scurried off to a brand-new four-wheel drive parked in a no-standing zone right out the front. Were they serious? I think the point was acting like you knew and speaking with the confidence that a truckload of money can buy.

They considered me to be below their social level on the local hierarchy. They, like their other friends, had a somewhat impenetrable bond and I definitely wasn't included by many of the socially elite. I didn't even rate a nod as they sailed past me, over-perfumed, with flawless makeup and perfect teeth. I guess the doctor or lawyer or banker hubby would sort out any parking tickets, as long as his guests were entertained and his wife continued to look young, thin and gorgeous.

Even though Simon and I also had the big house and a great income, I wasn't from the North Shore and had the distinct feeling that I would never be in their league. I hadn't been born there, nor had I gone to school there. Many of the women that I had met at Max's school had attended the very same school when they were kids.

I did, however, buy a few Buddhas for myself after they left – not at all worried about my colour scheme, though. Beige or off-white were never going to be favourites of mine.

I also loved going to a place in our local shopping centre which I called my 'crystals and dolphins' shop, selling, among other things, crystals and dolphins (the ornamental kind, of course!). I saw a book on the shelf called *Buddhism for Busy People* which I thought sounded hysterical. It sounded just right for me; I was definitely (in my eyes) the busiest person on the planet, and now that I owned a few Buddhas I could find out a bit more about this religion to see if it might provide the answers I had been looking for since my family's desertion of Christianity.

I started reading it, instantly thinking that I could perhaps become an expert at this. The principles that I did manage to absorb among my own busyness were around the concepts of Karma, Attraction and Aversion. It made sense to me that 'you reap what you sow', as I had at one point been a good little Anglican girl. I also got the concept that we all feel like we would like some more of this and a lot less of that to enable us to be truly happy, that we are never just happy as we are in this very moment in time. That certainly resonated with me.

I didn't, however, have time to get much further than that as, ironically, I was far too busy. Maybe I needed a book called Buddhism for Busier-Than-Average Busy People. And so it ended up on the bookshelf of failures, rather than the room of failures, along with some other self-help books that I'd bought to try to help me deal the dramas and shortcomings of my marriage and my life in general. *Maybe one day I'll read more, but for now, simply not enough time,* I told myself.

My next craze, a few months before Eddie was born, was deciding to take up folk-art, thinking I would have a go at something creative. I painstakingly traced and painted brightly-coloured flowers and leaves onto placemats, coasters and little boxes for jewellery, expecting that they would be lovingly displayed on people's tables and dressing tables. For a while it became a great escape for me, consuming endless hours of my time. Everyone I knew during that period ended up with some tacky little masterpiece that I had created, for birthdays or Christmas or any other event that I felt might warrant such a prized possession.

My new-found creativity was helping me creatively avoid any sadness and confusion I felt around Simon. And now there was to be another baby, I would have to work harder to make this marriage work. The folk-art was a way of escaping into my own little world, where worrying about my life could be placed firmly on the back burner. Quite often, I'd become so absorbed in my fabulous artworks that I'd lose track of time. I remember, one night, Max and Charlie coming out onto our enormous deck overlooking our equally enormous pool, where I had chosen to set up my creative corner.

"Are we having anything for dinner tonight, Mummy?" asked Charlie.

"Yeah, Mum, we're hungry!" Max joined in.

"Sorry, kids – coming!" I quickly packed up my precious supplies and rushed in to create the quickest meal I could think of. Two-minute noodles again. It was seven o'clock and Simon still wasn't home, which was quite normal for him.

Not long afterwards, possibly much to the relief of the many recipients of my handiwork, I gave up the folk-art craze and all of my art supplies sadly joined the 'room of failures'.

Chapter Eighteen
Eddie

Eddie was born, and I was once again completely besotted. Whereas Max looked more like me and Charlie looked more like Simon, Eddie was a complete mix. He had the cheekiest face, enormous hazel eyes, my slightly thicker, shorter nose and Simon's chin.

We took him home, and as much as I loved him and my other two children, I knew without a doubt not too long after he was born that any happiness in my marriage was gone. The pretence and effort of trying hard to make it work were now making me feel like I was in a constant state of depression. Eddie was still too little, but Max and Charlie were starting to notice and kept hugging me, asking if I was okay. The feeling that it was over had been building for far too long now; it simply had to end – if I could figure out the best way, with three kids and not a lot of my own money that I could access without Simon finding out.

I had just enough self-esteem left that he hadn't managed to knock out of me either physically or emotionally to start to plan. His drinking seemed to be increasing (to 'cope with the pressure at work', he said), his treatment of Max was getting worse, and my laughter was rare, except when I was playing with my kids. While he still hadn't hit me again, he continued the pushing and shoving me whenever I annoyed him, and he would grab my arms so hard that I would end up with bruises that were hard to cover.

Even knowing that it had been a huge mistake staying before I fell pregnant with Eddie, I was never going to let any of my children know or feel that. He was so precious, and I would never ever regret having any of them. They were, and still are, my world. I had made a commitment to love this child and my other two – to protect them to the best of my ability every day of my life.

Bravely, as a last-ditch effort in the midst of my on-again/off-again planning, I suggested counselling to Simon, and he laughed at me.

"There's nothing wrong. Why the hell do we need to talk to a stranger about our lives?" he said, clearly not impressed.

"Yep, everything's just fine, arsehole," I said under my breath, not looking at him.

"How about we plan a holiday? I'm sure that's all we need. You're just tired from being with the kids and I've been working too hard. How about you book us a trip to a resort up north?" And that was my idea totally dismissed. Problem solved, Simon-style!

The thing about Simon was that, along with his controlling, aggressive behaviour, his regular sarcasm and nastiness, he was one of the most generous people on the planet. He held firmly to the belief that you could throw money at any problem and it would simply disappear. Anything the kids or I wanted, within reason, we could have. Anything, that is, except for my peace of mind. I considered my kids and what was best for them. It made it harder when I thought about what they would lose and how lucky they were to have so much. *Do I have the right to take that away? Will it be a struggle for us on our own?* I worried. We were all used to not having to question money. The turmoil was never-ending, with my dilemma over what was best for my children paramount in my mind.

I agreed to look at some options and talk to him about it the next day. At this point, until any plan was properly formulated, I had to act as if there was nothing wrong. I felt a bit lighter yet again, and wondered whether I would have the courage to do what I so badly needed to do. God – I felt tired, worn down and worn out, as well as feeling overwhelmed with the effort it would take to disentangle myself from this life we had together. I was feeling hollow and stuffed, just like my favourite T.S. Eliot poem, with my head filled with straw.

Whereas Max was a gentle, sweet soul and Charlie was a watcher, intense and alert to everything around her, Eddie from the word go was what could only be described as quirky. He always did everything differently to the other two. He was independent and a complete handful, always into mischief. Having three kids and being in an unhappy marriage was tough, but I adored them, for their differences and for just being the individuals that they were. When I was with them, we giggled at the most ridiculous things. At those times, I was relieved that just perhaps they weren't too badly affected by how I was feeling. They were all quick-witted, like my side of the family, while Simon preferred a more slapstick style of humour and shows like Funniest Home Videos, which I couldn't stand. I did worry more about Max, though. He was often tense and withdrawn when Simon was around, a lot more than the other two. He was the one that Simon would lash out at and pick on when he was in one of his moods.

Clara invited us around for dinner one night and was able to see first-hand exactly what Simon was like, coming to a greater understanding of my sadness. While we were eating, Max came up to me, politely excusing himself, to ask me a question. I interrupted our conversation to answer him.

"Stop bothering us!" Simon shouted at him, already slurring from the many glasses of red wine that he had consumed. "And don't you dare pander to him," he said to me. "This is adult time. Go away, Max, and leave us in peace!" he finished, as Max quietly, obediently walked away, head down.

I started to defend him, when Simon hit me with one of his death stares. Clara and Patrick didn't need to see any more of the ugly side of my marriage. It wasn't fair on them. So, after a slightly awkward silence, I tried to lighten things up. "Well, cheers, everyone. Thanks so much for having us around." And I promptly changed the subject to something lighter – having a stab at the school mums always had Clara in stitches.

I talked a lot to Clara after that evening about my wanting to leave, my fears and my overwhelming disappointment in my marriage. She had now seen Simon's behaviour and continued to offer me a beautiful friendship, listening and caring – a friendship which is just as strong today. Her husband had never been violent; she was staying in her marriage which, like many, was far from perfect. She wanted to support me as best she could, being a shoulder to cry on whenever I needed it.

"You know how much I care about you, Jacq. Don't ever feel that you can't come to me," she reassured me. "What a dickhead. And poor Max. He didn't deserve that. I wish we could have all said something right then."

I finally spoke to Becca as well and, although neither of them could totally empathise, they were committed to being loving and loyal friends. I didn't want to talk to my family just yet, as I didn't want to worry them until I'd worked out what I was going to do. I had always wanted this marriage to work, but any glimmer of hope was slowly but surely fading.

Time moved on at a crippling pace as I was always doing something with the kids or meeting up with women from the school, when I wasn't seeing Clara or Becca. I had realised from the start that it had been a mistake to move to the snobby area and the school where people were already entrenched with their friendships and social networks. They all seemed to have such perfect children. I did, however, manage to get invited to a lot of lunches, where I drank far too much champagne to give me the sparkle that I needed to sparkle. I had officially joined the North Shore treadmill, which was at times great fun, but mostly I just wanted to get off and stop trying so hard to fit in.

While I had managed to meet a few people – including Alison and Lola – who, like me, sat on the fringes of North Shore acceptability, it just wasn't my scene. I always felt that I had to try too hard; it was exhausting. I didn't want to be on the fringe, but I didn't want to be acceptable either. It would mean dressing differently, behaving more demurely (I've never been described as 'demure'). That was definitely not going to happen.

One day I had dropped Charlie off at preschool and arrived at the school gates, once again looking around for someone who might want to talk to me. I gazed into the sea of linen. *How does it not get crushed?* was my question. I'd only have to wear it for a minute – not that I ever did – and I'd look like I didn't know how to use an iron. I used to wear floral leggings and a rugby jumper – my uniform for school days, comfy with my extra kilos again that I hadn't shifted since Eddie was born, and no need of an iron.

I had Eddie in his stroller and had waved Max off to join a friend with a linen-clad mother. It's not to say that they were all horrible people; in fact, they were all rather 'pleasant' (one of my many favourite words!), and they had been noticeably better after my bullying comment. It was just that I stood out like a sore thumb and didn't look like one of them. As I turned to leave, I spied another woman with a son about the same age as Eddie. She was in a very similar outfit to mine, and was looking equally aghast at the perfection all around her. We looked at each other and smiled, connecting instantly. Her name was Nellie.

From that day we became inseparable for a large part of every week – kindred spirits. I was able to tell her everything. Alison and Lola sometimes joined us, as well as friend of hers called Tina, but we were happy with just the two of us in a world of our own, our little boys playing happily together. We found that we both laughed at the same and the most ridiculous things, and together became happy to sit on the fringes with a few others who also enjoyed our company and the difference from the norm that we represented. She had a similar sense of humour to Clara's, and although our kids were different ages and at different schools, occasionally the three of us would meet for coffee and laugh until the tears were streaming down our cheeks.

Nellie and I continued getting together week after week, and it was truly enough to keep me going along with my other friends. Nellie's son, Patrick, and Eddie started at the same Kindy two days a week. I had managed to stay on the treadmill now that I had Nellie to talk to, but the plan was always brewing among the fog that was forever continuing to engulf my life and cloud my thinking.

Once again, I thought about going back to work part-time, but I knew that I had to sort myself out first. It would be imperative for me to have my own income and a life of my own established for if and when I was on my own with the kids.

Even with Clara, Becca and now Nellie, plus a few others, I couldn't fix the increasingly large hole in my gut. I was boring myself with the same internal conversation, and didn't want to burden others with what was ultimately nobody else's decision but mine. In addition to my great friendships, I found that drinking and smoking helped me cope. I was waiting for the final blow to make me do what I knew that I absolutely had to do. My plan kept being shelved, but I knew the day would come; I became increasingly tired of trying to hide the bruises, which were not always so easy to cover – especially when the long, hot summers would roll around.

In amongst so much confusion and sadness, one of the things that I did love to do was have the few girlfriends that I had made from the school and local area around for drinks and one of my famous platters on our huge back deck, overlooking magnificently manicured gardens and the pool. I say famous, as I was known to many, and still am, as 'the platter queen'. Nellie used to tease me about the fact that there was never a gap on my platters, every space filled with a wide variety of delicious food. We laughed a lot on those days, helped along significantly by a truckload of champagne.

One day, Nellie came up to me with an unreadable expression on her face, struggling to make eye contact with me, which was unusual.

"What's wrong, Nel?" I asked her, concerned, as I picked up the rather strange vibe from her.

"I don't know quite how to tell you," she began. Then, taking a huge breath, she finally looked up, tears in her eyes, and told me that her husband had been posted overseas with his job. They were going to have to leave in four weeks' time.

I felt like I'd been ripped in two. She was my playground ally and a truly wonderful friend. Having lost Meg and then Di, I was more inclined to want to keep the friends that I did have as close as possible to me. Thank goodness, I still had Clara and the others with whom I shared the same sense of the ridiculous, but God it was going to be lonely without Nellie. I would so miss that support in the playground, being with someone who could laugh at my silly jokes and who truly got me and the way I thought. Lola, Alison and Tina had big shoes to fill now that Nellie wasn't going to be glued to my side. I so didn't want her to go, but she had no choice.

To take my mind off my devastation about Nellie leaving and to stop Simon's nagging, I planned our holiday. This was my last shot at trying to be happy and work out whether we could save this marriage. I would talk to him properly and he would have to listen – no work, no school, no friends over, just us. I already knew in my heart that it was pointless.

Nellie left; I cried for ages and then, realising that I had to get on with my life, started packing and getting everything ready for the five of us to go away to a small resort on the North Coast of NSW.

The resort was unbelievably beautiful, right behind a small hill that led straight onto a magnificent, sparkling beach with the purest white sand. The pool was enormous, with a slide at one end that became Max's favourite place while I paddled with the younger two at the shallow end. They were so happy, splashing around with each other and ordering endless amounts of French fries and lemonade to have by the pool. As they usually ate pretty healthy food at home, this small indulgence was just fine by me.

From the time we arrived Simon drank excessively, starting before lunch and continuing on until late into the evening, while I stupidly and pointlessly nagged him to stop. The days usually started out okay after he had consumed his hangover breakfast of bacon and eggs with a gallon of tomato juice. He would often play with the kids in the pool and even crack a few jokes with me.

Then the cravings for a drink became too much. He'd start with a bloody Mary or two before lunch, then a couple of beers while we were waiting for our lunch to arrive. He insisted on a bottle of wine with lunch and then back to beers until he crashed out, snoring, on a banana lounge beside the pool.

At night, he pressured me for sex all the time and when I said I was too tired, he would make nasty comments about my weight again. I was five foot three inches tall and I weighed sixty kilos – hardly what anyone would call grossly overweight. I was so paranoid about being fat that I believed him and ate virtually nothing for the whole time that we were away; fruit and black coffee for breakfast, a small salad for lunch and mostly just wine for dinner. That way, Simon didn't disgust me quite so much when I did give in to his demands.

We never did manage to talk properly; he would always avoid the topic – tell me that I was imagining things and that I was so lucky to have anything that I wanted. (Was I?) The ability to think or act rationally appeared to have left me. One of the biggest issues for me was just how totally unattractive he became as he slurred his words and slobbered all over me. *Yuk!* It was disgusting.

At times, I would think back to that funny little girl in the red dirt house, the teenager exploring her sexuality in the red brick house and the highly successful career woman that I had been. *Where the hell is she now?* I certainly wasn't prepared to live my life depressed and sad all of the time. I wanted that person back.

Chapter Nineteen
Marriage on the Rocks

When we came back, I went to see the counsellor Clara had recommended to help me make some sense of my life and what to do from here. During our appointment she wouldn't tell me what to do, even though I begged her to. Instead, she suggested that I read a book called *Marriage on the Rocks* which talked about being married to an alcoholic and about the fact that addicts tend to attract addicts. This was a book that I actually did manage to read, despite my constant busyness, from cover to cover. I had always been sort of addicted to something that I thought would fix me. It started with God, then boys, then diets, then sex, then cigarettes, pot, cocaine and drinking, followed by money and of, course, relationships. I continued smoking when I wasn't around the kids, and I was drinking more than my fair share of wine.

The counsellor also gave me some affirmations to say every day that she thought might help me. Initially they sounded lame, but I thought I'd give it a shot.

I am fine just the way I am.
I am strong and resilient.
I am loving and lovable.
I am calm and confident (on repeat!).

I also read some books about battered wives, as the book that I'd just read had piqued my interest in knowing more about the decisions we as women often make to stay in abusive relationships, against our best judgement. As I was reading the books, it felt like it just wasn't me, and I couldn't relate as much as I had thought that I might. The women depicted were more often than not from lower socioeconomic environments, and they were truly battered. Simon had pushed and shoved a lot but had only hit me really hard just once, even though he threatened to regularly. I felt like a fraud compared to those poor women and it made me feel worse in many ways. They stayed, they tried, and their lives were so much harder than mine. Maybe I should shut up and start to appreciate how lucky I was in comparison.

So, instead of helping me as I'm sure the counsellor had intended, it backfired; I couldn't relate to that sort of systematic abuse. At this point, nobody had ever told me that one hit is too many, and there were a large number of people who kept telling me how lucky I was to have such a gorgeous house and a successful, generous husband. Often I found myself saying, *Wake up, Jacquie, before it's too late!*

Of course, Simon and I managed to have some good times; it wasn't like I was miserable twenty-four hours a day. As crazy and dysfunctional as my life was, we still entertained friends and family and attended school functions; at times we could even laugh at each other's jokes. It was just that it often felt wrong, fake and forced, and I was always ever-watchful, vigilant, as I waited for the inevitable.

As I was constantly wondering what my life was all about, I started to go to loads of clairvoyants, tarot readers and coffee readers, most of whom had been recommended by Clara. They'd tell me whether to stay or leave, surely, I thought. One in particular asked me, "Are you happy in your marriage? I don't think it will last much longer."

Even though I knew that was what needed to happen, I almost resented her saying it. Of course, she was right, and yet the decision inevitably had to be mine. It was the effort and energy that it required, mixed with the fear of having no money, depriving my kids of a privileged life, that had kept holding me back over and over again. My life had well and truly started to feel and sound like a badly-broken record. In addition, wasn't it partly my fault?

"I know what I should be doing," I said to Clara one day after going to our favourite coffee reading lady. "It's hard to actually do it, though. Where am I going to live, and how will the kids feel about it?"

"I know it's tough," she replied. "Just remember, I'm not going anywhere." We hugged, and I knew that with people like her around I would never feel alone.

I enjoyed all the tarot readings that I had been to so much that I ended up buying myself a pack of Tarot cards from my 'crystals and dolphins' shop and thought that I might give it go. I did my own daily readings for a while and loved it, believing everything that the cards showed me. I wanted to learn more when I had time, but was still far too busy to find the time to progress this new-found hobby any further. Yet this one was one that really grabbed my attention and focus and gave me a sense of direction and purpose, if ever so temporary.

Still, while my readings were helpful, the gaping hole in my gut had increased so much by this time that it felt like I literally had no stomach. It told me clearly over and over again that this wasn't right, and yet here I still was. *Why can't I go ahead with my plan? Why am I still on this damn treadmill? Why am I so weak?* Blah, blah, on and on it went. I was simply too sad to stay and too tired to go. It didn't help that, deep down, I was convinced that I often provoked him. On some level, there was an unshakable belief that what was happening to me was perhaps somehow my fault. If only I could just shut up! No one that I had met was divorced or even separated among the parents of my kids' friends. I had nobody who could or who was prepared to tell me what was involved, and didn't know who to turn to for help.

Max had settled in really well at school. He was such a sweet, sensitive, gorgeous soul, even the snobby parents and their kids had come to adore him. I noticed, however, that he was becoming increasingly tense and frightened day by day around Simon. When they came back from sport, he would often go to his room, sullen, withdrawn, telling me that he didn't want to talk about it. I'd often yell at Simon, trying to find out what he had done to make Max so unhappy, which was dangerous territory with a man who had such a short fuse. He'd yell back even louder.

"Stop mollycoddling the kid, for God's sake. He needs to toughen up. Do you want him to be a loser?" he would say, or similar words, whenever I brought it up. He would grab a beer and a cigarette and go outside, slamming the door behind him. There was no point in arguing any further.

"Max, honey, are you okay?" I would say to his closed door, not wanting to invade his privacy.

"I'm fine, Mum." I could hear sniffling. "I just need to be by myself for a while."

"I'm right here if you need me." My heart was breaking as I reluctantly did as he asked and left him on his own. Wanting to challenge Simon and not wanting to create a scene played around in my head as I tried to figure out how to handle this. Max deserved better, that was for sure.

Charlie had started school by this time, and appeared to have some difficulties with settling in right from the start. She had been absolutely fine at Kindy and hadn't struggled at all. She wasn't reading or writing well, and stood out among all the perfect, bright little girls who were excelling at everything. I did manage to make some new friends, especially Alice, with the most infectious laugh and bubbly personality. Her daughter was in the same class as Charlie.

Simon was in total denial when I discussed her learning issues with him, refusing to see the need for any extra help, and thought that the school and I were overreacting. When we met with one of her teachers to discuss it, he became rather nasty towards her.

"Well, clearly, you're not doing your job properly, are you?" he told her in no uncertain terms. "Come on, Jacquie, we're leaving."

"Simon, we need to hear her out," I started to argue, but upon noticing the cold, hard glint in his eyes, I thought better of it.

The teacher looked at me sympathetically, trying to connect with me. I dropped my eyes in case Simon saw. We left and he refused to discuss it any further. I would continue to try to help her as much as I could at home and speak to her teacher by myself in future to see if we could come up with a strategy together, without involving Simon. I didn't have the energy or confidence to go back to work at this point and still had the knowledge that my marriage would end at some point in the future – the knowledge but not the courage. My plans would start, and then I would talk myself out of it.

One day when I was out having a coffee in one of my favourite cafes on the lower North Shore, I saw a sign on the building advertising counselling courses. It appealed to me, as I felt that I'd be such a fabulous counsellor and so, on a whim, I grabbed the leaflet from the small perspex box on the wall beside the sign. Having read through it and feeling like it could be an interesting diversion, I discussed it with Simon, who funnily enough was relatively supportive, perhaps because it meant that I wouldn't be going back to work. I could never figure out what was right or wrong with him. It was just so uplifting to think that I would be able to keep my brain active.

From the moment that I started the course, I absolutely loved it. It helped me cope with the loss of Meg and Di, as I was able to discuss my pain so openly. The wonderful teachers and other students supported and encouraged me as I kept planning my escape. There were single mothers whom I was able to talk to and a nurturing, caring environment without judgement of any kind. Simon tolerated me doing the course, "as long as it makes you happy", but he couldn't really see the point of it. While I was doing the course, I had assessments to complete as well as the kids and house to look after, and I was too busy to worry as much as I usually did. My brain was definitely working hard again, and it felt good.

I managed to finish my Certificate and was so proud of myself for actually completing something that I had the certificate framed and hung up in the study. It didn't go anywhere near my 'room of failures', the contents of which were still in our garage in my own little section, a testament to the fact that I was indeed a failure. But I simply couldn't throw any of the stuff out, just in case I might have the urge to type or play the guitar or sew or paint. Anyway, I had my Certificate, the first thing that had filled me with such pride since finishing uni – apart from my kids, of course.

One night, as I was now suitably qualified and an expert, once again I suggested counselling to Simon.

"Look, Simon, surely you must be able to see how unhappy I am? I think we need some professional help." If nothing else, I wanted us to be able to sort out our differences for the sake of the kids moving forward.

He started threatening me straight away, abusing me for having done 'that stupid, waste-of-time course' and then assuring me that I'd have no money if I ever dared to leave him; he'd make sure of that.

"And no one else would ever want to be with you." His tone was the same old cruel, mocking one that I had become accustomed to for too many years. "You must be able to see how much weight you've gained. You've really let yourself go."

I didn't even bother to reply. Again, I was still only between fifty-eight kilos at my lightest to sixty kilos at my heaviest – nothing had changed! Finally, after a lot of crying and begging, he reluctantly agreed that he'd come to a counsellor with me so that I could 'sort myself out', but said that it would be a waste of his time and money.

I made the appointment and he came with me, acting as if I'd literally dragged him there. When we were with the counsellor, he denied his drinking, his treatment of Max and his abusiveness towards me. He somehow managed to convince her that I was just tired and stressed, and it felt to me like she believed him. All the things that I had wanted to say when she encouraged me to talk became caught in my throat. He could be rather charismatic when he put his mind to it.

We left, me despondent, him vindicated.

"Why did you lie to her?" I yelled at him in the car park.

"You stupid bitch!" he yelled back at me, only inches from my face. He smelled of tobacco and stale red wine. "How dare you accuse me of such appalling behaviour in front of that woman? You made it sound like I'm always drunk and always hitting you. For God's sake, it's nowhere near as bad as you made it out to be. You're delusional. Clearly you have lost any intelligence that you ever had."

With that, he pushed me hard against the pillar next to our car where no one could see him. He was strong; I was scared of what he would do, and felt certain that if I didn't make a move, he would slam my head against it. It was there in his eyes. Where was the counsellor now? I pulled away from him just in time and ran as fast as my shaky legs would allow, out onto the street. I hailed a taxi and sat in the back seat, not making any eye contact or conversation with the driver for fear of breaking down in front of a complete stranger. Once safely at home, I had to try to calm down before it was time to pick up the kids from school and Kindy. Simon went back to work.

When he came home that night, he grabbed a glass and a bottle of scotch and disappeared into his study. It was a Friday night, my head hurt from an impending migraine, and I was done.

Chapter Twenty
Enough

The next day was Saturday. My head was still aching, I was angry, and I was not going to forget or get over his behaviour – not this time.

"Arsehole, fuckwit, bastard," I kept saying to myself, anger firmly taking over from my usual fear and fog. Max had a party to go to and I was taking Charlie and Eddie to the park. As usual, I was rushing around, trying to pretend that everything was normal for the sake of the kids. Simon came into the family room, where the kids were all sitting around the table having breakfast before I was going to take them all out. One look at him told me that this was not going to be a good morning. He was hungover; his eyes were bloodshot and he had a menacing look on his face. A sarcastic, nasty sneer appeared as he looked around the table and stopped, focusing his attention on Max. He started poking fun at him for the way he had just done his hair. Max had been trying to be a bit trendy of late and had gelled it back like the other boys at school were all starting to do.

"What are you? A bloody jellyfish?" said Simon, mockingly. He proceeded to laugh, thinking that he was hilarious, not seeing or caring about the wounded look in Max's eyes, but I could see the tears starting to form – the tears that Max wouldn't let his father see.

Charlie and Eddie looked nervous. They loved their big brother and hated seeing him upset. Simon never picked on them like he did on Max, Charlie being perfect in his eyes and Eddie always off in his own little world. They picked up on the tension. Fed up, tired and with my new-found fearlessness for once, I stepped in.

"That's enough! Stop picking on him, now!" I yelled. "Just back off and leave him alone." Max deserved better, and I was so over this ongoing bullying. I shoved a surprised Simon as hard as I could in the chest.

He turned to look at me, disdainful and bloody angry. The next second, he was pushing me up against the kitchen wall. Once again he put his hands around my neck, but this time it was in front of the kids. He kept squeezing. Shocked and confused, the kids started begging him to stop. My eyes connected briefly with Max; he knew the number to call. Simon dropped his hands, but it was too late now.

The police arrived and took him away for questioning. They had seen the marks on my neck and the state of the kids when I had opened the front door. The time had come; no more – I was done. An eerie calm started to take over from my usual state of vigilance and anxiety. I held all my kids close to me and cried quietly, softly. He was never, ever going to touch me again.

Max didn't want to go to the party, but I convinced him that I was okay and that everything was going to work out, feeling that the distraction would be good for him.

"I hate him, Mum. I never want to see him again," he said. These were the first words that he had said out loud to me against his father, and I could see the relief in his beautiful young face. Charlie and Eddie hugged him, and we all took a precious moment in time to be together, just the four of us as it was now going to be.

"Mummy," said Charlie, "is Daddy going to be okay? Why are they taking him away?" As much as she loved Max and hated seeing him so upset by her father, she still didn't believe that Simon was such a mean person much of the time. She had witnessed what he had done, but all that she had ever experienced from him was love and acceptance. The conflict was evident in her big, frightened green eyes. Eddie said nothing, just watched, detached and happy that we were hugging his brother to comfort him. This was not going to be easy; I had no idea exactly what would come next, but my life with Simon was over. The kids and I were leaving, and it had to work out – it just had to. They would adjust. We all would.

The police called me. Simon had been served with an AVO and would only be allowed to come home as long as I felt that I would be safe. Unafraid for the first time in so long, I agreed. When he came in, I could see the anger and disbelief building in him. Bullying me and begging and pleading weren't going to work with me anymore. After the policeman dropped him home, he glared at me, heat building dangerously in his eyes. I didn't care what he said or did to me.

"Look at what you've done now. How dare you embarrass me like that, letting the police drag me out of here in front of the neighbours?' he yelled. "This is my house. You'll pay for this!"

"Shall I ask them to come back? You do understand the meaning of an AVO, don't you?" My voice was stronger than usual; my sarcasm was outclassing his. "So hit me again, you fucking bastard. I am leaving you, and I no longer have any interest in anything you say. You're a disgusting human being," I finished, holding his stare. Sadly, the kids heard it all.

"I've told you before that you will have to fight me for every cent, and I mean it." His face was getting dangerously close to mine and yet I held eye contact with him, feeling the old, confident Jacquie making a triumphant return and refusing to enter any further into a war of words. He wouldn't dare to hit me again, now that he knew what would happen if he did. This was what taking back my power felt like. Adrenaline pumped through my veins. I could do this! I could do this!

I spent the next few days trying to keep the routine going for the sake of the kids, slowly packing our things, avoiding Simon and getting ready to find somewhere to live. They were quiet, well-behaved and stayed out of Simon's way. Charlie was the only one who went near him, their bond stronger than what he had with any of us. As much as I felt somehow a bit lighter, I wasn't a complete idiot and knew that there would be some significant struggles and challenges ahead. Taking Charlie away from her father was going to be a major one. I resigned myself to the fact that no matter what he had done, I would never deny him the right to see his children once we had left. We didn't speak to each other, except for the most basic of civilities. I cancelled any arrangements that we had made as a couple.

The time had come to sit down and tell the kids together of our next steps – that we were moving out. Simon was oppositional, as expected, and yet knew that I wasn't going to change my mind. At that stage, I think he honestly believed that I'd come crawling back once I had a chance to see how tough it was going to be without him. He had no idea of the strength that was now building in me, the strength that had been lacking for way too long. As expected, Charlie's reaction was the hardest to watch.

"No!" she said adamantly. "This is not how it's supposed to be. You're supposed to stay together." Such grown-up words for someone so young. *What am I doing to my daughter? Surely she'll be fine in time, won't she?* After all, she had the boys and she had me. *We all love her enough for her to be okay, don't we?* Max couldn't hide his relief, and Eddie sat quietly and smiled like it was all a big adventure – that was so like him.

The police had told me that I would need to see a counsellor at the court before going to the hearing about the AVO. Having made the appointment for as soon as I could possibly see her, I drove further up the North Shore to the courthouse where she had her office. She was so helpful and supportive when I saw her, and strongly recommended that I should go to a domestic violence group to help me recover from the trauma of my marriage.

"Domestic violence?" I questioned her, still confused by the books that I had read on the subject. For me, this was a label that I associated with women who had been severely beaten, not me. Somewhat reluctantly, I booked into the group that was running two days later, wanting to keep myself busy in between packing and looking at properties to rent.

The woman who was running it was a gentle, sweet person with the kindest eyes called Barb. All of the women in the group were asked to share with the rest of the group. When it came to my turn, after I had heard some truly horrific stories, I felt ashamed.

"But he only pushed and shoved me around a few times, and only two or three seriously. I'm not a battered wife. I feel like an imposter," I said to the group of women assembled in a room to the side of the main court building. "And I know that I provoked him." Regardless of my decision, I still held myself accountable for some of the blame.

Barb looked at me kindly.

"Once is one time too many, Jacquie. Domestic violence is never okay – not in any situation." This was the very first time that I had ever heard these words, and I chose to believe her.

As part of the AVO process, I had to attend court to testify as to whether I wanted to keep it in place or whether I would drop it. Simon was not going to attend, as it was up to me to decide, according to the police, but he had pleaded with me in a rare moment of playing nice to drop it, as it wasn't good for his professional life. Whether that was true or not, I agreed, but threatened him that it would be back in force if ever he came near me again.

Arriving at the steps to the courthouse in North Sydney, I met with my court-appointed solicitor. I had taken the trouble to dress professionally in a suit and heels, makeup, and hair neatly blow-dried. The solicitor came up to me, as I must have been looking lost, and asked for my name. After introducing himself, he looked me up and down.

"I hope you don't take this the wrong way," he said, "but you're not doing yourself any favours looking like you have it all together. If you want to keep the AVO in place, the magistrate will need to believe that it's in your best interests and that you're not coping." He was actually dead serious when he said this, not believing that he had said anything wrong.

"I do apologise that you won't have the opportunity to see my bruises, both external and internal," I replied with the appropriate and deserved sarcasm. *Fucking arsehole* was what I wanted to add. "I don't need you to do anything today except to say that I have agreed to drop the AVO. I am leaving my marriage. Not that it is any of your business. I'm going in." With that, I left him standing on the steps and went to find a seat inside.

After court, and a rather insincere apology from the solicitor, I went home and told Simon that the AVO had been dropped, as agreed, and that we would be leaving within the week. The time had come when it was finally enough.

I was too proud to ask my parents to help, as they were retired and had very little themselves. As Tom was struggling financially, raising three children on a rather low wage, I couldn't ask him either. Jen had returned to work part-time, but they were finding it difficult to make ends meet. Annie and Jo were buying their first home together and had a mortgage. They were happy, and I didn't want to bother them. I explained to them all that I was leaving, without elaborating too much on the why, assuring them that we were all going to be fine.

I continued to look after the kids, telling them over and over again that it would all be okay and that I loved them very much. I moved into the spare room and made sure that I did nothing to aggravate Simon any further. As much as it was clear that he was upset, nothing could change my mind now. There was too much damage done and too much fear of what might happen if I stayed.

Chapter Twenty-One
A New Home Will Fix Things

I finally left Simon and bought my first mobile phone – the kind we now refer to as a 'brick' and that could easily be used as a substitute hand weight. It was the fifteenth of August 1999. I had been saving as much as I could for some time and had just enough in my own bank account to rent a small house on a short-term lease, not far away from the big house on the hill.

When we moved in, I set about making the house as homely and welcoming as I could. It was the most liberating feeling doing this on my own, creating a new future for us all. I was breathing more slowly, and God, it felt so damn good. There would be no further need for long sleeves and scarves to cover the evidence of my marriage. Freedom at last!

As I did not want to move the kids out of area for their school and Kindy, the new house would work very well for all of our needs. Simon had agreed to me having some of the furniture – not the best stuff, of course, but enough for us to set up our new life. Leaving their father was going to be traumatic enough for them, I reckoned, so I was grateful that we were still close to everything that was familiar to the kids. We had left the big house amidst his protests that he would change and that he loved me, followed by his threats that he would not give me a cent and that I was disgusting, saying yet again, like a broken record, that I was fat and that nobody else would ever want me. He couldn't hurt me anymore, physically or emotionally, and yet I knew with absolute certainty that he would do his darndest to hurt me financially. That was the one power over me that he still held, and boy did he know it.

The house was small and neat and for the time being – while I could pay the rent – it was ours. The paintwork was chipped and awful colours, the carpet was an ugly dark brown, and the bathroom was green and pink – but no gold fish-heads, thankfully. We didn't have a pool or a big yard; we had a small, grassed front yard and a concrete courtyard out the back. As the kids all loved basketball, I went to our local sporting goods store and bought a cheap hoop. This turned out to be an excellent decision; they had a top-of-the-range one at the big house, but this would do for now and it was an activity that they could all do together.

I still knew very few people who were divorced at that point in my life and I knew nothing about child support, how to apply for it or who to talk to about it. So, imagining that I would have to wait until I saw a solicitor and the settlement was complete, there was no choice but to be under his thumb still from a financial viewpoint and to be more careful than I had had to be in many years. Simon didn't offer any assistance and, perhaps sensing my naivety, simply continued to pay me what we had called 'the housekeeping', which was the amount that he had been accustomed to giving me to buy groceries and with a little left over for play money. He had always taken care of the bills and now it was definitely time for me to learn the value of money. The main problem, though, was that I could see only too clearly that it was going to start running out – and fast. I hadn't been used to looking after my own finances since my apartment days, when I had had such a high income that money had never worried me.

Just for the moment, none of that mattered too much, as we had settled in and we were safe. The little house was comfortable, and we had all that we needed. My shoulders relaxed, my sleep improved, and I was no longer afraid of everything I did and said. The kids and I cooked together and played our music loud, dancing around the island bench in the middle of the kitchen. Charlie needed more reassuring and time than the others, but was coping, I thought, better each day. It helped that I had bought us a dog, the cutest little golden Labrador puppy, the first weekend after we had moved in. We named him Monty. We all adored him.

Of course, I knew that I would have to sort out when the kids would be seeing Simon and the money situation, but for now at least I didn't have to see him or talk to him, having quickly learned how to text! It was time for us all to have a bit of fun.

Eddie started school, and as much as he had always been an individual and quite different to his peers, he appeared to be okay. When I picked him up every afternoon, he was happy as usual, pottering along in his own world.

Max was relieved, and really started to go from strength to strength. His confidence grew; he started doing really well at sport and even improved in his schoolwork, whereas he had been struggling so much before we had left Simon.

Charlie, on the other hand, was devastated. She regressed at school further and further, never wanting to go and, according to her teachers, not trying very hard and being quite oppositional to doing her work when she was in class. She had always loved her father, and as much as she wanted to be with me and her brothers, she had been the closest to Simon and his clear favourite from the day she was born. She appeared to be at her happiest when she was with Monty and surrounded by her family. Every night, she would sneak him into her room, where he slept with her the whole night. Often I'd hear her whispering, thinking that I couldn't hear her.

"Monty, shhh. Come here," she'd say. "You can come on my bed, but be very quiet." With that she would close her door, and I knew that she would sleep better with him to keep her company. Neither myself nor the boys argued with her, sensing that her need for the comfort of our beautiful dog was greater than ours.

Not long after we had moved into our new home, I had contacted a solicitor who had been recommended to me by a friend to start the proceedings necessary for the final disentanglement from my marriage. She listed the separation day as the day that I left the home that we had shared with Simon and reassured me that no payment to her would be due to her until settlement took place. Simon, however, went to a supposedly better, more expensive solicitor. Next, I received a letter telling me that it was his legal right to see the kids every second weekend. I had never had any intention of stopping him seeing the kids, but I didn't want them to go.

As much as I encouraged them to still have a relationship with their father, Max flat-out refused to go, and Simon didn't fight it. Even though Charlie adored her father, she also didn't want to leave me, and I could tell just how conflicted she was. Reluctantly, she would be prized from my arms with the promises of some sort of a bribe from Simon. Eddie just went along, not wanting to cause any trouble, also happy enough to see his father, but happiest when we were all together, our solid little unit of four. Max stayed inside, as I refused to allow Simon any further than the front door. Why did I still feel scared of him, with that bloody knot making an unwelcome return to my stomach? We were safe, surely. When they came back on Sunday afternoons, we would do something special – either cook something together or go out for a cheap meal.

We were all used to living such a privileged lifestyle, but now Simon was making me pay with little or no concern for his children. Bravely, one day after we had been in the house for several months, I asked him, "Do you think that you could give me a bit extra while we're waiting for the settlement to come through?", already knowing what his answer would be. "Just to help out the kids," I added.

"You can't be serious! I'm not giving you another cent until I have to," was his angry reply. "You created this mess, and you can sort it out yourself." The phone slammed down.

By this stage, I could see that we were rapidly going to run out of money. There was a place called Cash Converters at our local shopping centre. So, packing up everything that I could from the 'room of failures' and all of my jewellery, I went to see how much I could get to help us out. The guy who served me was so lovely and quite generous, considering the age and state of a lot of my stuff. Second-hand folk-art stuff, a completely out-of-date typewriter, a very ageing guitar and thankfully some pretty expensive pieces of jewellery at least! We now had enough for another few weeks until I figured that I would finally have to ask my parents for help.

It was difficult on a daily basis to shake this feeling of financial worry, even though it was blissfully mixed with the relief of being away from Simon. It appeared to me that all around were the perfect couples who just didn't understand my position. They were all seemingly happily married and couldn't fathom why I had left the big house on the hill. In fact, a few people asked me outright why I would leave such an amazing house and lifestyle. Seriously, why would someone just up and do that if everything was fine? I didn't tell anyone the truth about the violence except for Becca and Clara. I also wrote to Nellie and told her what I had done. They were all supportive, as they had heard and seen the damage that had been done to me physically and emotionally.

On one of my many days of wondering how we were going to survive until the settlement came through, I had a most fortunate and unexpected godsend. We had been living in the house for well over six months now, and as I was leaving my front gate, I ran into one of my old neighbours from the same street as our house on the hill. She was out walking her dog. We weren't overly close, but had always enjoyed an easy, if ever-so-superficial, friendship. From the little I knew of her, she was a nice (a bit like pleasant, but better) person, petite in every way, always immaculately groomed with a magnificently-coiffured dark blond bob.

"Hi, Jacquie," she said, sounding genuinely pleased to see me and lightly touching my arm. "How are you? Are you managing okay?"

Well, that was enough. A kind word and I was barely holding back the tears.

"Sorry, Sandra—I'm okay really. It's been tough and we're struggling," I managed to say between sniffles. After a deep breath in and out, I finished. "But once the divorce is finalised and my settlement comes through, we'll be fine."

She paused for a moment, as if she was mulling something over. "Let me talk to Bill," she said, again gently touching my arm. "He may know of a way to help you and the kids out." Her husband worked in banking and was a nice guy from the few times that I had spoken to him. I thanked her, but didn't give it another thought, as I assumed it was just her way of being kind.

Later that day, just before the kids and I were going to have dinner, there was a knock on the door. It was Bill, and he said that he would like to talk to me for a few minutes. As always, he was dressed in the male North Shore uniform: chinos and boat shoes with a polo shirt. I was surprised to see him and even more surprised when he smiled, concern evident in his well-sculpted face, and proceeded to discuss his proposal with me.

"Look, Jacquie, Sandra told me that she'd spoken to you. She was very concerned for your welfare and I'd like to be able to help out," he told me as I listened incredulously. "I've spoken to one of the lenders at the bank, and it looks like we may be able to provide some financial assistance to you. As you will have what I would imagine to be a generous settlement, there will be no issues with repaying a loan, I would assume," he said, professional and business-like but with a real warmth and sense of caring.

I wondered why I hadn't thought of that. Too busily entrenched in my survival mode was my best guess. I was so grateful that I was speechless momentarily – not a common problem for me!

"How about you just come in to the bank tomorrow and we can sort out all the paperwork?" he said. "We should be able to process the loan fairly quickly."

"I can't thank you enough," I replied, reaching out to hug Bill briefly, sensing that he felt rather awkward, as we had never before shown any display of affection. He patted me on the back reassuringly and left me staring after him, struggling to believe that I could be so damn lucky.

Well, what do you know? I said under my breath. I went back inside smiling broadly and hugged the kids. We were going to be okay.

"I love you guys to bits," I told them, trying not to cry, even though they were tears of happiness and relief sliding down my cheeks as I spoke. "I always will, no matter what."

"Are you okay, Mum?" Max, perplexed by my sudden outburst of emotion, hugged me back, brow furrowed – ever the carer and nurturer, especially since he considered himself to now be the man of the house.

I went into the bank as soon as I had dropped the kids off at school the next day and signed the papers that would provide us with thirty thousand dollars, enough for us to live on while I waited for the settlement money to come through. It was now time to sort out all the terms for my divorce. I extended our lease to cover us for the remainder of the year, until we would be in a position to buy a property.

Hope having returned, it was time to shout myself a cappuccino and a manicure. My nails looked awful, and I was damn sick of instant coffee.

Yet another few months literally flew by; we were coping better and better with each passing day, particularly without the immediate concern of being broke. I regularly went to see teachers and the school counsellor at Charlie's school as we worked collaboratively on strategies to try to help her progress. The boys were absolutely fine, happy enough to go to school and hang out with their friends.

One day my solicitor phoned to tell me that she had spoken to Simon's solicitor and it looked very much like he was going to play dirty. She said that he would probably fight me for every cent and that she suspected there might be more money than he was declaring. I was entitled to a sixty/forty split apparently, but she recommended that I settle for the fifty/fifty that he was insisting on, as he had the funds to keep dragging it on. He was prepared to take it to court for as long as it took at a cost of over thirty thousand dollars a day.

Knowing that the bank loan wouldn't last forever, I just wanted it over and done with. I agreed to his terms and signed the papers, and we were due to settle in another month. I was over fighting and was moving ahead with my life. Even fifty percent was going to be enough for us to be well set up until I could hopefully find a part-time job that I could manage, while still spending as much time as I could with the kids. They needed me to be there for them, especially Charlie at that point, even though her difficulties at school were improving.

My settlement money came through exactly one month later. I was now completely independent, and was able to pay out the loan that Bill had arranged for me. Having dropped off an expensive bottle of champagne to them, I gave them both another big hug. Bill was still just as awkward, but I didn't care; I was so incredibly grateful for their kindness when I had been in such great need of someone to help.

Even though it was a great relief financially and I could stop worrying for a long time, I still often felt quite alone as a single mother, relieved to be away from Simon but often scared and confused about what my future was going to look like. I wanted to lighten up a bit and stop stressing so much. Even my own regular Tarot readings didn't help me as they used to. *How long will I be able to manage on the money? Will I always be on my own? Are the kids going to be okay? Did I really do the right thing?* These and many other questions swam around in my head on a loop most days. At least I did know the answer to the last one!

I was excited that we would be able to buy a place that would be ours rather than a rental, but I would still have to be extremely careful as to our ongoing living expenses. It wouldn't be the high life for us anymore, and we would all just have to get used to it. Simon was going to have to pay child support, but that wouldn't be enough for us to live on without me working. The thought of getting a job terrified and excited me in equal measure.

My confidence had taken a severe beating with the ongoing physical abuse and the continual putdowns. There was simply no way that I was going to let my fear cripple me and stop me from moving on with my life now. I had always managed to get a job before, so why not now? *I'm still clever enough, aren't I? So where's that newspaper?* I said to myself, a new determination and energy surging through me, and *where do I look this time?* I wondered.

Chapter Twenty-Two
Our First Home

With the settlement money, once our rental agreement was up I was able to buy us a rather small but very cute little Californian Bungalow in the next suburb from where we had lived with Simon. It was still driving-distance to the school, but in a slightly less posh area than the one we had left. From the moment I first saw the front courtyard, with filtered sun peeping through the large oak trees that lined the street and the verandah which opened onto it, I was hooked. I pictured myself sitting there with a cup of tea (probably more likely to be champagne!), watching the kids play on the trampoline that I was going to buy them, with Monty running round, checking on everyone as he loved to do.

There were three good-sized bedrooms, a combined lounge-diner, and a reasonably modern kitchen overlooking a small backyard currently overgrown with weeds. This would necessitate me getting in touch with my hitherto unused green thumb.

We all loved it, and I let the kids choose the colours that they wanted for their bedrooms – an interesting decision, in retrospect. As I handed them the colour charts collected from the local hardware store, I held my breath in anticipation and excitement, knowing their choices could be a challenge but that the house was ours and the decisions were ours to make.

"Mum, can I paint my room purple?" Charlie begged, bouncing up and down. "Please, can I?"

As the boys would be sharing a room, they huddled together over the chart before Eddie, after looking at Max for confirmation, confidently announced, "We want this one, Mum."

It was a very bright blue, hard on the eyes, but I couldn't care less. They were all happy.

For my room, I chose a deep, bright, washed gold. There was definitely going to be no beige anywhere to be seen, that was for sure.

Monty padded happily from room to room checking that we were all still there. Pets as therapy – there's nothing quite like the face of a big goofy Labrador to cheer up your day. God, we loved that dog.

It was such a relief to be settled; now to keep the bills from coming on such a regular basis. While the settlement was generous, our day-to-day living expenses were nothing short of scary, and left me constantly dipping into the cash that we had left over after the purchase of the house. I had already started looking and applying for jobs, and was hopeful that the right thing would turn up that would suit our needs. As I'd given up work when I fell pregnant with Eddie, there hadn't really been the time, the need or the confidence to return since then. Having made a brave decision, it was now time to get that old spark back, to dust off the business gear and get myself out there again.

Max started high school at the local Catholic school, where some of his friends were going. Simon and I had considered the snobby all boys' private school when we had still been together, but this was the school that Max wanted to go to; Simon wasn't interested in our choice, and I respected Max's wishes. I couldn't believe just how grown-up and handsome he looked in his uniform: he was a different boy away from the constant criticism that he had experienced with his father. It was wonderful to watch him blossom, free from the worry of trying to please someone who was always looking for faults. He settled quickly, made new friends and became obsessed with basketball and swimming. I knew without a doubt that I had done the right thing, at least for his sake.

"You are happy, honey, aren't you?" I asked him.

"I sure am, Mum," he replied, hugging me tight.

Charlie was still struggling academically, and I had her tested to discover that she was dyslexic. I organised some support for her after school one day a week, which she hated but went to reluctantly, probably just to please me.

"I hate it and I hate her," were the constant words out of her mouth each time she came out of her sessions. After a while, there was no significant improvement; her tutor confirmed that she simply refused to try. Charlie asked me after what was to be the last session that she attended, "Can't you just let me do my best? I don't care if I'm dumb. I just want to do dancing and play netball. Please, Mum, I'll try harder, I promise."

I agonised over the decision and even tried to talk to Simon about it, but he wouldn't listen and I couldn't force her to go. Honouring her wishes felt more important. She was still young, in primary school, and that there was plenty of time later on, surely – at least I hoped so. She had very few friends but seemed happy enough, especially when she was with her family and her beloved Monty, on a stage dancing, or on a netball court.

"Ok, I guess so, but I just need you to know that you're not dumb, and we can get help so that school's not so tough for you." I tried to reason with her, but she knew that she had won.

Eddie was buzzing along, enjoying school, and had made a few little friends in our local area. He was constantly asking to go down the road or have someone over and as long as he was happy, I let him do what he wanted. He also enjoyed soccer and t-ball with other little boys his own age, mostly from the same school. He was a busy kid with loads of energy, exhausting and equally engaging. I loved my kids, and watching them grow was a never-ending source of joy for me.

Not long after Max started at his new school, I was fortunate enough to meet two fabulous mothers whose kids were also in his grade, one called Julie who had separated from an alcoholic husband just before I had. She made the most amazing cupcakes and used to bring them over to my place for morning tea, which I'd exchange for one of my insightful amateur Tarot readings and a glass of champagne. The other woman, Linda, who used to pick her son up from the same train station as me, often joined us as well. She was happily married. Her son and Max became good friends, and we enjoyed each other's company whenever we were together. I had definitely started to gather some wonderful support around me now, and didn't care about the judgement from anyone else.

There were many more single mothers at the high school, which helped me feel much less of an alien, but my married friends were just as important to me. Clara, Becca, Alison, Lola and Tina were constants in my life, popping by for a drink and a chat and keeping me away from the 'smug marrieds', as I liked to call them, at the primary school – the ones who always said 'my husband' with such reverence. But even with so much choice for friendship, I still really missed Nellie.

Among the relief, the support and the positives in my life, I wondered why I sometimes still felt so down. My life was super busy, running around like a madwoman a lot of the time, trying to get the kids to all of their activities, friends, parties, et cetera. It was completely chaotic.

With the exhaustion ever building in me, I decided to see a doctor to see if what I was feeling was normal for someone in my situation.

"You're probably still having a major reaction to all of the trauma associated with your marriage and divorce," he told me. He suggested that it might be a good idea to consider taking anti-depressants. Even though it was something that I was hesitant to do, I agreed to give it a try. After all, surely it wouldn't be for very long – just a bit of help to bring back my perkiness while I looked for work.

The feeling when I took them was awful initially, but at least I was able to cope better each day. Eventually my body adjusted to the side effects, the worst of which was nausea similar to the morning sickness that I'd experienced with all of my pregnancies. Refusing to allow myself to feel any stigma around taking medication, I trudged on, looking at the smile in the mirror that I had thought would never completely return. No Simon, no abuse and no real money worries yet. My 'happy pills' proved to be an okay addition to my feelings of getting mentally well and getting the old Jacquie back.

I took out my Tarot cards a lot more frequently, reading my fortune, and played around with giving family and quite a few friends, as well as Julie, the occasional reading. I wondered if this could be my new talent. Around this time, I also grabbed the *Buddhism for Busy People* book again and managed to read a lot more of it this time, loving what I read. *That's what I'll be,* I thought, *a North Shore Buddhist – as long as it's okay to drink, smoke and read Tarot cards.*

One Saturday, at Max's regular baseball game I met a woman called Lucy who, it turned out, had had a horrible marriage and subsequent divorce too. She was working full-time but really struggling with the costs of after-school care, mortgage repayments and all of the usual bills that never ever go away. Her son was at an expensive private school where he had been going prior to the divorce.

"I don't want to move him. He loves it there, but my bastard of an ex-husband has just announced that he won't contribute to the fees anymore. I just don't know what to do."

We became great friends and enjoyed a lot of laughter in amongst the confusion we both often felt, raising kids by ourselves in an area where most of the parents were still together and loaded. We were both taking 'happy pills', always struggling, and lending each other money when we were waiting for child support or to be paid. I remember one time when she was really broke counting out all of my coins, copper and silver, and giving them to her so she could buy dinner.

"Thanks, Jacq. That should buy me some mince for a spag bol. You're a gem." We giggled away as we packed the coins into a plastic bag, drinking a bottle of cheap wine, relieved that there was common understanding and no judgement.

She had a reasonably good job in a recruitment firm and asked me one day if I would potentially be interested in coming on board part-time to do some marketing work for them.

"We've been thinking about advertising the job anyway. And I think you'd be a natural."

"I hope it's not the wine talking, but I'd love to! At least I do know a lot about recruitment."

"I'll set it up. My manager can be a bit of a cow, but it's good money," she said with a final hug, before heading off to buy her mince.

When I met Lucy's manager, she was tough but we hit it off rather well, and once again, I had a great job fall right into my lap. It wasn't ideally what I wanted, as it involved loads of cold calling to potential clients to see if they would like to use us as their recruitment consultants. However, the money was pretty good, it was part-time, and it was possible for me to start straight away.

My first day was the following Wednesday and I found it quite challenging at first, firstly because I hadn't worked in a while and secondly because I had to become used to a great many negative responses from potential clients. Handling the large number of them didn't bother me too much, though, as there was some extra money coming in.

My old suits from the corporate days came in handy, even if they were looking a bit out of date. One was bright blue and another was bright red; the third was hot pink and black. They all had extremely padded shoulders with quite short skirts.

There was a very popular show around at the time called Melrose Place where many of the stars wore clothes similar to mine. The staff started calling me 'Melrose Mum'. (Not very demure for a mother of three, that's for sure). It was fun being part of a team environment again, even though I knew that I wouldn't want to do this kind of job forever.

While another relationship was the last thing on my mind, I started to think that I would like some male company occasionally when the kids were with Simon or staying over with friends. My confidence was making a welcome and much-needed return. I started to go out to bars with Lucy or anyone that happened to be free whenever the kids were busy with friends or the younger two were with their father. For some very odd reason I found that I attracted a lot of younger men – a mother complex perhaps? I enjoyed flirting again, but never went any further as I simply wasn't ready, happy enough to just know that I was still attractive to someone – *See, Simon, men, and apparently boys, do still want me!*

Then, one night after a few drinks, I met the man who was to come to be known by all my friends as 'Bob the Bonk'. He was at my favourite lower North Shore pub where Nick and I used to go. Very tall, dirty blond hair, weathered face, broad cheeky smile – he could only be described as the quintessential Aussie larrikin.

"Hey, sexy, buy you a drink?" he said when he sauntered up to me – he did a lot of sauntering, I was to find out. Smooth? Not really, but it worked.

"Sure, why not?" I tried my best sexy voice back (the husky quality helped significantly by my many years of smoking).

He was to be the first guy I would sleep with since Simon, starting that very night. God, he was good in bed – not that I had had much to compare him to for a very long while.

Bob and I had a ball together whenever I could see him; nothing too serious, just blissfully uncomplicated and extraordinarily passionate sex. He was funny, easy-going, drank very little and thought that I was gorgeous – big ticks all round. We continued to see each other casually for about six months, until he moved out of Sydney for business reasons.

It wasn't sad, as I hadn't been looking for anything serious as yet. I was simply grateful to him for restoring my faith in my ability to enjoy a physical relationship that was neither abusive nor controlling. We kept in touch for a while after he left until he met someone else, which was fine by me. I had now completely proven to myself that someone actually did want me, despite what Simon had told me. And again I thought, *Fuck you, Simon!*

Simon had met a woman with three daughters less than three

months after our divorce was final, and Charlie wasn't happy about it. She had been his princess and now felt totally replaced. Her revenge was to flatly refuse to go to see him anymore, so now only Eddie went. He was quite happy to continue a relationship with his father, while the other two weren't. Max now hadn't been to stay with him since our separation and barely saw him except for the occasional sporting or school event. While he was a lot more relaxed and happier these days, I noticed that he would still tense up whenever he saw his father.

Initially Simon tried to insist that Charlie would have to see him every second weekend, but he finally came to realise that it wasn't worth the fight and the misery that it caused – apart from which he had a new family now, and only Eddie was happy to fit in with them whenever he had to. He was my Mr. Flexible in every situation; not a lot fazed him at all.

I had to leave my 'Melrose Mum' job, as there was no more money in the budget for the marketing role. It would now be necessary for me to find something else very quickly, preferably working in recruitment if it was at all possible. Confidence in my abilities well and truly restored, I kept on applying. Eventually I saw an advertisement (still the newspaper – no *Seek.com* yet) for a part-time recruitment teacher and thought that I'd apply. They weren't asking for recruitment qualifications, just a degree and recruitment experience, both of which I had. If I was accepted, this would mean having the school holidays off and still being there for the kids. I didn't feel like taking on anything full-time at this point in the kids' lives, as there was so much of my time and energy involved in looking after them and the home, as well as trying to have some sort of social life.

The interview went well and after a two-week wait, I received a phone call to offer me the job and it felt great – hopefully just what I wanted and needed.

Not long after starting my new role, I was walking down the corridor when I heard, "Oh my God, Jacqui, is that you?"

I turned around to see Sara, a gorgeous woman whose husband, coincidentally, had been an acquaintance of Simon's. She had three kids too and was, previously unbeknownst to me, struggling to cope with a bad marriage. We talked and talked as I tried to give her a balanced perspective on the pros and cons of being a single mother.

"Do you work here?" I was thrilled to think that I would have a friend in the new workplace. We immediately made a plan to catch up for coffee when we were both free.

To this day we are still able to compare notes and have a laugh and a cry together about the ongoing struggles that we have faced as single parents.

We considered ourselves fortunate to have jobs that paid quite well and allowed us all of the school holidays to be with our kids, but even more than that, we considered ourselves damn lucky to have found each other.

One of the things we talked about a lot was how the people in power within our workplace were capable of such condescension to those who were junior in position to them. There was quite a complex hierarchy to deal with. I had had my fair share of a range of different experiences in the workplace, from horrendous to amazingly supportive, but one thing I insisted on as a manager, was to be democratic and to treat my staff with respect. We discovered at our workplace that many people in high positions, especially the women, tended to walk along corridors very loudly and very quickly, with an air of incredible self-importance. We called them 'the foot stompers'. The men in power appeared to be more content and self-assured with their lot, with no need of stomping; instead they had a desperate need to call many unnecessary meetings.

As we were both part-time, we sat at the bottom of the teaching totem pole, content with just doing our jobs, staying clear of the 'foot stompers', and we were virtually never invited to the very important meetings. I was grateful and determined to do this job well while ignoring any power-plays around me. There was no driving need in me anymore to be the boss of anything or anyone. *Leave them to it* was my thinking.

I was learning to really, genuinely laugh again; wonderful friends, great kids and my freedom helped me enjoy my life more than I had done in a long time. Among the daily financial worries and the ongoing parental concerns as to whether my kids were okay, I needed to give myself a break and keep reminding myself of my courage and just what I'd managed to achieve. I'd always done the best that I could, like most parents do. We don't always get it right, but as long as we truly love our kids, then we must at least be partially on the right track.

My mobile rang (God, I loved that thing – not in the obsessive way that many Gen Ys love them today, though.) I loved the way we could contact each other without endlessly checking answer machines or picking up the home phone to check that it was, in fact, working!

"Hi, babe," said Nellie, a smile obvious in the tone of her voice. "Well, you'll never guess what?" A pause for dramatic effect. "I'm coming home for good."

"Oh my God, that is the best news ever!" I started to cry – joyful tears, though, not blubbery miserable ones. She had spoken to me on the phone, and written actual letters with a stamp to me, but she hadn't seen me go through what I'd been experiencing all these years. "When? Soon, I hope."

"In two weeks," she answered. "So you can stop crying and get ready to have a drink with me and a full day of talking – to start with, anyway. I want to hear absolutely everything."

We ended the call and it felt so exciting that we would be able to hang out all the time just like we used to. Much like Clara, we had an identical sense of humour, but I also knew that she would enjoy meeting the new friends that I had made. She hadn't ever known me as a divorcee, and I was sure that that wouldn't make a difference; I didn't want the married/single divide to be an issue for us as it was with many women. But not my friend Nellie: she was definitely not a 'smug married'.

Chapter Twenty-Three
Moving and Moving On

Nellie came home and we couldn't see enough of each other, meeting regularly at one of our favourite coffee shops when I wasn't working and talking endlessly on our mobile phones when we weren't together. We caught up with Alison, Lola, Tina and Alice for dinner and drinks to share our continual whinges about many of the North Shore mothers. We had coffee with Clara, laughing until we cried about anything and everything. Life was good at these times.

Nellie's son, Patrick, and Eddie reconnected, picking up their friendship just like they'd only seen each other yesterday. By this stage they were in their final year of primary school. I was now surrounded with caring friends, a good job and kids who were, for the most part, okay. The only major issue for me really was that my outgoings definitely exceeded my incomings, no matter how hard I tried to budget.

Sitting in the coffee shop close to my house, Nellie looked at me, searching my eyes for the truth. She knew me so well.

"So tell me, Jacq, honestly, how are things? Are you really okay?"

I gave a huge sigh. "Well, I made the right decision to leave him, but it's tough. I get lonely sometimes, and we're always trying to make ends meet. Money is a constant issue, and we're going to have to move again."

"Bugger!" Her hand reached for mine. "I'm sorry, and I wish that there was something that I could do to help." She had her own kids and her own life to worry about, but it meant so much that she cared.

Sadly, there was going to be simply no choice but to sell and move to something smaller and cheaper so that we would have some additional cash to live on. In many ways, that was fine by me; I loved going to open-home inspections and could spend hours going through the real-estate section of the newspaper. Having been a bit of a gypsy with all the moving when I was younger had helped me to not become overly attached to any place.

When I told the kids, I kept a brightness to my tone and convinced them that it would be exciting and somewhat of an adventure. They were surprisingly okay, my sales skills working brilliantly, especially when they saw how positive I was about the idea.

"I want my room to be bigger – and can I paint it any colour?" from Charlie, being a princess.

"Do I get my own room, and will it be as big as Max's room?" from Eddie, always competing with his older brother for a sense of fairness. Max and Eddie hadn't been sharing a room for a while now, as Max had moved into the small front sitting room to have his own space.

"It has to be close to the station and shops," Max insisted, as he needed to be able to walk home from the station, meet up with his mates, and flirt with girls.

Priorities! I just wanted to get us out of debt.

Anyway, with my decision made to free up some more capital, real estate was the easiest way for me to do just that. Now that the kids were sort of on board, I put our house on the market.

Enquiries started as soon as it was listed, and it wasn't long before I accepted an offer. We made an excellent profit, and I was able to buy a townhouse that I'd been looking at not too far away. We were all going to be sad to leave our little home that we had decorated in our own tastes, but the kids understood that it was necessary. There was a spa out on the back deck of the new house, which was a huge bonus for the kids, as they'd grown up with an enormous pool in the big house and we all loved anything to do with the water. This was a decent compromise now that they all had much smaller rooms and not as much space to play outside as they'd been used to. It still wasn't too far away from the kids' schools and transport, and it meant that we would have some cash in the bank and the ability to pay off at least one of my credit cards.

Not long after we moved in, I decided to have a party for some of the school parents from the three different schools my kids were attending. After the kids went to bed, we all upped the drinking and someone suggested going into the spa. I was nearly tempted until Gizelle, this gorgeous French woman who was the mother of one of Eddie's friends, unashamedly stripped off completely and went in. There was a collective jaw drop, especially by the men. She had the most perfect body – no stretch marks or cellulite to be seen anywhere!

"Well, that's me keeping my clothes on for the rest of the night!" I said, and everyone agreed with me.

We entertained quite a lot in our new home; I encouraged the kids to have friends over all the time and I did too, to ease the loneliness I often felt at night when the kids were in bed and I was by myself. Many of my friends were still married, and even though I knew many of them weren't overly happy and that their marriages were far from perfect, it was still tough at times. It was great that I had managed to meet quite a few single mums as well; they got what it was like and understood the fact that we so often felt like a different species from our married counterparts.

I definitely needed some hobbies if I was going to stay single: something for myself that wasn't about work or kids or the home and drinking with friends when they were free. I had always thought that I was the best singer ever; there was a local singing teacher I'd seen advertising through the school newsletter, and I decided that I should have some singing lessons.

It was exciting to be giving something different a go. However, after my third lesson, as I was desperately trying to master the singing exercises that were part of the lesson (I had thought we would be just singing my favourite songs and that she would tell me how good I was), it was hard for me coming to the realisation that I really wasn't as good as I had thought I was – even though the teacher tried to keep encouraging me to come.

"Keep it up, Jacquie. You'll improve," she said to me. Sincerity was severely lacking in her words, and not being a patient person by nature, I thanked her and never went back.

I remembered how famous Tom and I had thought that we were going to be all those years ago. As disappointed as I was initially, it didn't stop me from singing along to every song I heard.

Bugger the lessons, I thought to myself. *I still think that I'm talented and sound amazing in the car and the shower!*

Next hobby. I enrolled in a Reiki course that a friend had recommended, as I was so alternative, with my Tarot and my Buddhist tendencies. I enjoyed it and managed to complete my level 1. I practiced it for a while with great enthusiasm, but then it became boring and my certificate made its way, along with the song sheets from my singing lessons, to the 'room of failures', which was now a cupboard. I didn't have a spare room anymore, and I'd sold all my other stuff to Cash Converters a long time ago now. I learned a useful affirmation from my instructor, though, that I still sometimes use:

Stop worrying
Don't be angry
Give thanks
Work hard
Be kind to others

So, apart from these often insightful words, I just didn't have the perseverance to practice as much as I needed to. I found it interesting that I had always been searching for something to make my life complete, never being totally satisfied with myself the way that I was.

Max was now in year nine at school, and growing up so fast. He loved playing sport, where he excelled much more than academically. While he had started acting out a bit, being rather rebellious, I wasn't too worried; it wasn't anything that I hadn't done myself at his age. His attitude towards me, while very much muscle-flexing, was never rude or nasty. He was going to a lot of parties and generally having an absolute ball. Sadly, this didn't include a focus on his studies. He had had many girlfriends already, and had developed a great group of like-minded friends who liked to call me their 'second mum'. His sense of freedom away from the abuse that he had suffered was such a huge relief to me that I tended to let a lot of things slide by without nagging him or worrying unnecessarily. He was happy; the rest would take care of itself.

His friends were always at our place, in my fridge or cupboards, asleep on the lounge of the floor if Max's room was too crowded. There'd be a 'Hi, Mum' on the way in or out, masculine voices growing deeper, replacing the little-boy voices that were now disappearing.

Max had also managed to obtain a part-time job at a local café, which helped in terms of his own living expenses at least.

"So, your shout is it, honey?" I used to joke with him whenever we ate out. This was followed by an extreme eye roll, of course, and something like, "Mum! So funny... not." Apparently, I wasn't as amusing as I thought I was.

Charlie continued to struggle with her work throughout the final year of primary school, but still didn't want any help. I felt that the break-up was still proving to be the hardest on her, and had encouraged her to talk to someone about it. She said she didn't care as long as she could do her art and her dancing, now that netball had gone by the wayside. She flatly refused to see any of the therapists that I suggested and particularly couldn't stand the school counsellors on the rare occasions that I had managed to get her to see anyone or when the school had suggested it. I decided that I would respect her wishes and let her be who she wanted to be.

"She's a stupid old cow!" was her summary of the last visit to one of the school counsellors. "All she cares about is how smart you are and telling you to work harder. I'm not seeing her again, no matter what anyone says."

"Come on, Charlie." I tried to reason with her. "She can't be that bad." This was met with a defiant glare and silence. Subject obviously now closed in Charlie's mind, I said, "Well, will you at least talk to me about anything that's bothering you?"

"I'm fine, Mum," she replied. "Everyone just has to leave me alone." And so I did; after all, I couldn't force her to talk to or see anyone, and she wasn't miserable, or at least she didn't appear to be.

Simon and I rarely spoke, but we had somehow managed to agree that Charlie would go to the posh private school around the corner from her primary school. As hesitant as I was, I knew that many of the girls from her school were going there and I thought that it would be best for her to have a potential circle of friends. However, I did worry that more snobbery and more expectations of having to be smart might be an issue for Charlie. It was a dilemma, so I decided that I would keep an open mind and a watchful eye on her progress.

From the very first day that she started, she struggled to fit in – the main issue being that she much preferred hanging out with boys, having two brothers whom she adored. She found it difficult to cope with the ongoing snobbiness and overt bitchiness that apparently was part of her everyday school life at a girls' school. The girls that she had known from primary were rapidly changing and seemed destined to morph into their linen-wearing mothers in the not-too-distant future. There was a lot of 'you can't sit with us'-type of behaviour, from the little that Charlie did tell me. Was I actually the problem? I wondered. After all, these weren't evil people and neither were their daughters, really. Was it just that I didn't fit and that I had passed this 'nonfitability' on to Charlie?

By her second year, I thought about moving her as she came home most days terribly unhappy, but I was fearful that she might struggle even further somewhere else. I spent as much time as I could with her and encouraged her to ask any of the girls that she even remotely liked to come and hang out with her. There was one girl she really liked called Mandy, but neither of them seemed to be able to gain acceptance into the cliques that had rapidly started forming from the first year. There were the 'nerds' who would have them in their groups, but Charlie didn't want to hang out with them as they were too smart for her, she felt; the cool groups wouldn't have them, as they weren't considered cool enough. So, a bit like the movie *Romy and Michelle's High School Reunion,* they were a group of two, begging the other one to come to school even if she was feeling sick.

Eddie was okay, still quite easy-going and self-contained, in his own world. He managed to always have a few friends and enjoyed his own company. He stopped seeing Simon as much.

"I just want to stay home, Mum," he'd say. "Dad's place is boring."

Smiling to myself, I thought that it was nice to know that I had been able to provide a non-boring environment – that was a plus on my side. Simon never fought to see his kids, as he had started to focus on his new family.

Eddie's happiest times were when he could meet up with Patrick on the weekends. Nellie and her husband had sent their kids to a different school, as they had had to buy a house out of area from the school where my kids had gone to prior to them going away.

"But I need you in the playground with me. No one gets me like you do," I whined.

"We have no choice, babe. Our place is too far away for us to get in."

"At least I'm pleased to see that living overseas with all of your servants hasn't made you a totally spoiled little snob!" I added, trying to sound less pathetic.

"You've noticed that I'm back in the uniform, have you?" she said, doing a spin in her leggings and rugby jumper that looked much like mine and what I'd been wearing as an anti-linen statement for many years now. We spent a lot of our spare time together comparing notes, as her two boys were not fitting in at all at their new school, also on the North Shore, and she needed a friendly, understanding ear. *Are we both doing something wrong?* I asked myself.

Eddie was due to start high school the next year, and only knew one person well who was going to be going there. We had had his name down to go there from before he was born – such was the custom on the North Shore. If I'd only realised back then that the public schools did just as well, if not better, academically, in sport and in nurturing their students, then I would never have sent my kids to private schools in the first place. I guess the North Shore treadmill had become part of my psyche, sadly. *It works for many, so why not me and my kids?*

Even after all this time, my marriage was still taking its toll on me. I often felt like a failure. Sometimes I would question myself as to the part that I had played in the problems between Simon and me and the eventual break-up. It was hard knowing that he had moved on so completely with someone else. I found myself wondering how he was treating her and wondering whether there was something wrong with me. Luckily, I still had my 'happy pills' and I didn't go too far into the depths of despair. My decision was the right one; I simply had to continue to believe that for my own sanity. Niggling worries and doubts weren't helpful.

I enjoyed catching up with my family as much as possible. It wasn't always easy to coordinate times, though, with my parents living outside of Sydney still, Annie and Jo being extremely busy, and Tom, Jen and the girls living in Canberra. We all tried to get together at least three or four times a year, mostly in the school holidays. When we were all with each other, the laughter and fun were so worth it. The kids adored each other and Annie and Jo were such fabulous aunties, giving me a much-needed break from being in charge all of the time. And, best of all, Tom and I could sing our hearts out with everyone joining in – no judgement in terms of our talent; just the joy of being together.

Dad was getting older and sicker each time I saw him. His years of smoking had finally caught up with him, and he was struggling to breathe properly. Over a very short timeframe, he started spending more and more time in hospital. Mum told me one day when I phoned to say hi that he was getting worse and that the doctors had said that it was only a matter of time. I found it hard to believe that my funny, whistling, smoking, beer-drinking father would be gone from my life. I wasn't ready to lose him.

The last time I saw him, he said to me breathlessly, "The doctor's given me a death sentence, bubs. Look after Mum, won't you?"

I held his hand and kissed the top of his head.

"You're a great dad. Love you," I told him. Not able to meet his eyes, I couldn't stop the tears from falling.

He passed away peacefully in a daze of morphine with Mum dutifully by his side not long afterwards. He was eighty-six and had lived longer than the doctors had thought that he would. I felt like a piece of my heart had been ripped out of my chest. Mum, Annie, Tom and I busied ourselves with arrangements for the funeral. The three kids had prepared something to say; the grandchildren also said a few words each, tears running down their faces. They loved their Poppy so much. Tom and I sang *In My Life* by The Beatles. Someone even came up to me after the service and told me that I had a beautiful voice. *So there, singing teacher!*

The next few months consisted of one foot in front of the other, kids, work, seeing Mum and trying to sort out where she would live, as she no longer wanted to stay in the house where she had been living with Dad on the lower North Coast of NSW. It was hard for her to contemplate leaving, and yet she knew that it was time to settle somewhere there would be ongoing support for her in the future. She had never wanted to burden any of us by moving into one of our homes, even though I had offered.

We all ended up agreeing on a beautiful retirement village on the outskirts of Sydney, surrounded by lush bushland. She was going to be able to have her own little villa and live completely independently while knowing that help was only the push of a button away if she needed it. It was also a relatively short drive from my house, which meant that I would be able to see her more often than I had been. As sad as it was to see her leave the home that she had lived in with Dad, it was also so good to see her in a place where we all felt that she could be happy and comfortable.

After helping to settle Mum, Tom returned to Canberra and we left her to adjust to the new and unfamiliar surroundings. She was smiling bravely.

"Stop worrying – I'll be fine," she tried to reassure me. I wasn't entirely convinced.

"Call me any time if you need anything." I left her reluctantly, worried, and with a final hug there was a sense of the mother-daughter roles clearly being reversed.

"Jacq, come on. We have to go. She's going to be okay," from Annie, her usual calm and confident self, and from Tom nothing, which was in itself unusual for him. I had noticed that he was distracted and wondered why.

We all left her, waving at us madly until we turned the corner.

As I was driving away, I started to think about my kids. *Did I smell alcohol on Max's breath? Is Charlie too thin? Will Eddie fit in at his new school?* There was no time to explore the answers until I had Mum settled.

Chapter Twenty-Four
Eyes Wide Open

Not long after moving in, Mum started to make friends quite quickly and we all felt relieved that she was coping so well. I noticed her laughter returning more and more with each of my regular visits, and knew that she was starting the next chapter of her life with a positive attitude and a determination to make the best of her life as a widow. Her sadness crept up many times as we talked, laughed and cried about how much we missed Dad; but she was a moving-forward kind of woman, much like her daughter, trying not to dwell too much on the past however painful it was.

Tom called about a month after we had Mum sorted to tell me that he and Jen had separated.

"We've been having awful arguments and we're both worried about the impact on the kids," he told me. "I don't want it to end but it has to." He was crying and couldn't continue. I could hear how devastated he was. It surprised me, as they had always seemed to be so absolutely right for each other. What goes on behind closed doors is a mystery to us all, I guess.

We made a time to catch up with all of the kids and for me to give him the big hug that he so clearly needed. It was hard to hear him so down and defeated when I called him on a regular basis, as he lived his life between denial and anger for quite some time. Also, because Jen and I had always got along so well, I felt that I was losing a friend and hoped that once things had settled we could still be in contact. As much as he was my brother and I loved him, I did know from my own divorce that it takes two to tango.

"I'm here for you, whenever you need to talk. It's tough but you'll be okay. We all love you," was all I could manage to say to try to reassure him that he wasn't alone.

Now, Mum was sorted out and Tom knew that I would be here for him anytime he needed a shoulder: back to worrying about the kids.

While I was busily trying to help Mum settle into her new life after Dad had passed away, I had temporarily failed to fully notice that Charlie's ongoing desire to fit in with the cool group at school had reached epic proportions. She had started wearing baggy clothes, very unlike her usual tight-fitting, up-to-the-minute fashion choices. Also, perhaps in an attempt to control one aspect of her life that she was able to, over a period of time I was noticing that she had stopped eating with the family as much. She managed to hide it from me for a while, eating breakfast in her room while she was dressing for school, or saying that she would take her dinner into her room as well so that she could do some homework (alarm bells, as she didn't ever really do much homework!). Monty would usually accompany her and look very satisfied when he came out after being in there with her. I was suspicious, watchful and worried, but she assured me that she was fine. She kept playing sport and didn't take days off school.

"Charlie, you're getting too thin. I'm worried that you're not eating enough." I tried for a neutral, non-threatening tone to talk to her about my worries.

"For God's sake," came the angry reply, eyes blazing. "I'm fine. Leave me alone!" Subject closed, she stormed off, leaving me to fret even more.

One day I was talking to her in the kitchen, yet again trying to discuss her eating as I prepared a dinner that she probably wouldn't touch or would take to her room. When she didn't answer me, I looked over at her just in time to grab her as she slid down to the floor.

I screamed "Charlie!", and Max and Eddie came running. They had both been talking to me about how worried they were and when they saw her collapsed on the floor, we all knew that it was time to intervene. As we always did, we tackled the problem together.

When she opened her eyes, Max started yelling at her.

"For God's sake, Charlie, what the fuck are you doing to yourself?" I didn't say anything about his foul mouth as I usually would have; I could see how terribly upset the boys were. Eddie had tears in his eyes and Max was shaking. With the absence of a father figure in the house, Max often took on the role himself to try to help me out. The other two always listened to him, even more than they did to me much of the time. I didn't know what to say; I was shocked and felt so helpless, even though realistically I had been waiting for this very moment.

"I need you to weigh yourself, and I want you to get on the scales right now," I said firmly, pulling myself together and trying my best not to break down. I had to stay strong right now and not fall apart like

I wanted to. Reluctantly, she agreed as the boys both backed me up, taking turns in begging her and yelling at her to "Wake up! Can't you see what you're doing to yourself?"

She didn't argue; she did as she was told. We all followed her to the bathroom. Her height was one hundred and sixty centimetres, and she weighed thirty-four kilos.

"I'm sorry, Mum," she said, looking up at me, eyes pleading with me to try to understand. I think she was genuinely shocked by the number that we could all clearly see. "I didn't know that it would be that bad. I just wanted to be a little bit thinner. I promise I'll eat more. Can you please make me some toast and vegemite?" This was our go-to comfort food for the whole family in a time of sickness or a crisis, a bit like the English cup of tea remedy.

If there was to be a bright, almost comical side to this horrible experience, it was watching me run like a madwoman into the kitchen only to find that we were out of bread.

"What the hell?" I yelled out in frustration. "We always have bread!" I started rummaging around in the freezer and thankfully found that half a baguette that we always tossed up about keeping or throwing out. God, I was glad that I hadn't thrown it out. I started frantically sawing through it with a bread knife, taking what felt like forever. The unevenly hacked pieces certainly didn't look too appetising, but I toasted the whole lot.

Charlie ate it painfully slowly, but she did eat it all as we watched, willing her to keep going. It was obviously not easy for her to be on show after successfully hiding the problem for so long.

This was to be the beginning of a steady but long recovery for her, thankfully, and for me a massive wake-up call to keep my eyes wide open.

So, now to tackle Max and the knowledge that he had been drinking.

"Honey, I've smelled alcohol on your breath and we need to talk about it."

At first looking away from me, his eyes came back to meet mine. "Mum, you don't have to worry. I'm not like Dad!" he said, initially a bit harsh, and then he went on. "Sorry, but all my mates drink heaps more than me. I just want you to trust me. I will never end up like him." He hugged me, and I believed him.

As for Eddie, he assured me that he was fine about high school. He knew Mitch from his primary school, who was also going, and he would continue to see Patrick whenever they were both free.

"You're such a worrier, Ma," as the kids had started calling me. His big grin reassured me that I needed to just let him do the best that he could, as he had always done.

Motherhood is tough. The guilt, worry, and love is ongoing and endless.

Chapter Twenty-Five
Time for Me?

Max was really happy socially. With a great group of friends and many girls who were attracted to him, the next step was career options. He decided that he would like to start a career in sports coaching when he finished school, which suited his love of sport and wouldn't involve too much study – not his strong suit. I had spoken to the gym where I went as often as I could, and they suggested a course that they thought might interest him. I made a call and asked to have some information sent out to us.

"What do you think of this course, honey?" I asked, showing him the material that had just arrived in the mail. The course was local and not overly expensive.

His face lit up as he read through it. "It looks amazing. Exactly what I want to do." His eyes were shining, and he was positively beaming. That was all I needed to know.

"Would you like me to book you into it?" I asked, not wanting to be too pushy but sensing that he might need some gentle guidance.

"Please, Ma. That would be great." His enthusiasm was obvious, so I went ahead and booked it for him. As I was teaching him to drive, much to the detriment of our usually loving relationship, I would also be looking to help him buy a cheap car in the not-too-distant future, so the reasonable price of the course was definitely a bonus.

He was still partying a lot with his friends, but didn't appear to be out of control. Even after discussing it with him, I was always that bit overly vigilant and fearful of what I had seen alcohol do to our family. But whereas Simon had often been an aggressive man with a nasty temper, Max was a gentle soul with a happy, loving nature. Whenever I noticed that he had been drinking, I saw no evidence of his father's behaviour coming out at all.

Charlie was eating more normally, despite declaring that she was now a vegetarian, and she had managed to find a few more friends, even though they still weren't the cool group. She had discovered boys in a big way, along with makeup and a penchant for the more expensive style of clothes. Her recovery from anorexia, I realised, was going to be an ongoing battle. Sometimes it triggered memories of the many diets that I had tried over the years in an effort to be perfect.

One day she brought the, as she put it, 'love of her life' around to meet me, and I could see that she was completely besotted. It reminded me of how I had felt when I fell madly in love with 'heartbreaker Harry'. He had big, dark brown eyes, curly black hair and quite a swagger when he walked – he was gorgeous, and equally besotted with her from what I could tell when he looked at her adoringly. She seemed to be happy and that was all that mattered to me – that and the fact that he was really into food!

My only real concern for her now was that I had also smelled alcohol on her breath a few times, and it worried me just as it had with Max. I had to believe that with my love and the way the boys adored her, she would not become an alcoholic like her father. Max wasn't, even though he was drinking at parties, so hopefully she would be the same.

Peter, the boyfriend, introduced me to his mother and another friend of hers, who – unbeknownst to me at the time – were to become great lifelong friends. We all talked about how much we loved singing and dancing. I could just tell that we would all have fun together as, in my view, not only was I a great singer, but also a fabulous dancer.

It was time for Eddie to start high school just as Max was about to finish school and start his course. Even though he had reassured me and told me to stop being a worrier, I could tell that he was nervous, particularly because of the fact that he would only know Mitch when he started. Mitch's mother Alice was a woman I liked a great deal. She had a laugh that was infectious and a caring nature, and was happily married to a wonderful man. I sincerely hoped that Eddie's experience of school wouldn't be like the experience that Charlie had been through – just another posh North Shore private school with one of my kids trying and failing to fit in.

Since Eddie was usually so good at adapting to any situation he found himself in, I wasn't as worried about him as I had been with Charlie. As long as he could still see Patrick on the weekends, he continued to reassure me that he would try his absolute best to fit in. He was the only one of the three kids who still wanted to see his father, but it had been only occasionally for some time, now as Simon was always busy with his own life and new family – apart from which Eddie still found it more 'boring' to be with him than with us.

Simon had recently developed an almost irrationally deep hatred of me. We had managed to speak civilly at times since our separation when needed, but not anymore. There was a deep smugness and condescension to his tone whenever he did bother to actually speak to me. And if I ever needed to speak to him about the kids, he would often refuse, preferring to send me a text or an email instead. *Suits me, arsehole!* was my thinking.

So, as the kids appeared to be relatively okay for the most part, I thought I'd give the single scenes a go. One of the mothers I had met at Charlie's school, Tilly, had spoken to me about going to some singles events together. As most of my closest friends were either still married or not interested in doing something so supposedly tacky, one night we got all dressed up and bravely went out by ourselves.

Our first night out together was an absolute scream. It was on a boat (never a good idea when you don't have an escape route)! I turned to Tilly after the first five minutes, giggling like a little school-girl after a few glasses of cheap, nasty champagne: "There's more leopard print on this boat than you'd see in a jungle!" We both became hysterical, causing many people to stare at the two crazy ladies who weren't wearing the apparently compulsory jungle costume. The men were sleazy, continually propositioning us using tired old worn-out pick-up lines, and no one appeared to be my type – whatever that was these days.

We went to many other events together with equally depressing results, so I thought it might be better to give it a miss and try internet dating instead.

"What do you reckon, Tilly?" I asked. "Worth a shot?"

"Well, it can't be worse than what we've been subjecting ourselves to lately," she replied. So we both set about creating our profiles in the hope that we would attract someone suitable. This was where the fun really started.

The number of liars and weirdoes that I met convinced me not long after I'd started that I was better off giving it a miss. There were the obviously-marrieds – "I'm not married". *Then why the sunburn mark around your wedding finger?* Then there were the ones who were a minimum of ten years older than their profile pictures. Their photos were usually pictures of them climbing a mountain or cycling up a hill to assure prospective partners that they were in peak physical condition. And, of course, then there were the ones that spent the entire night trying to invent something, anything, that would get you back to their house for a quick bonk. I almost succumbed a couple of times for the hell of it, but it felt too soulless and empty to even bother.

Surely I would meet someone when the time was right, I kept reassuring myself, and yet not really sure that I even did want to meet someone. There was some loneliness for sure, but there was also my freedom. *Give it a break, Jacq,* I said to myself.

It wasn't long before I did give up on this as a dating option for me, having at least made a few great male friends who were excellent company when I wasn't hanging out with one of my girlfriends. My favourite was Danny – my new 'best boyfriend', as I liked to call him. We could have a drink, a coffee, or dinner and there was never anything creepy – we just enjoyed being together without fancying each other. I found that I liked these uncomplicated relationships, once we had established the appropriate boundaries. Between working, friends and still looking after the kids, or at least being there as much as I could, I was simply too tired to give any of these guys enough of my energy, so internet dating was over for me – for now, at least.

Max's course ended up being perfect for him, and he was able to set up a small business. He started with Nellie and me as his only clients, training us in her garage. Nellie called it his 'L-plates' and we loved it, doing a small amount of exercise and talking too much, according to Max. He moved on very quickly to a small client base and working part-time for a gym close by. It felt like he was truly off and running in the right direction.

Charlie finished school with way lower than the results that she would need if she wanted to study. Not caring one bit, she happily began her career in fashion, straight away securing a position in a trendy men's clothing store. It suited her better than putting her through the torture of more study anyway, when she had struggled and hated it so much. She took to it straight away and loved having her own money, rapidly becoming rather extravagant and even more glamorous. She was so incredibly beautiful, with her huge green eyes, her slightly olive skin and her gorgeous figure (still too thin for her mother's liking!): absolutely magazine-perfect. She had completely disconnected from her father and was enjoying the ongoing attention from a large number of boys, the 'love of her life' now just one in an already long line.

"Are you sure you're happy doing this? You don't want to do a course or something?" I sounded a bit pushy, but simply wanted what was best for her.

"God, no!" she eye-rolled back at me. "No more study! I like what I'm doing. It's fun." Subject closed. There never was much point arguing with Charlie. If it was what she wanted, then I would just leave her to it.

The only real new blip on my horizon, now that I didn't really care about a romantic (or even purely physical) relationship, was that Eddie had developed a hatred of school. He was doing okay academically and with the compulsory sports that he had to play every Saturday. He had found the social side of things a lot more of a challenge. Alice's son Mitch was still on the scene, but there were very few other boys who truly understood his quirkiness.

His father and I, on a rare moment when we spoke not via text, agreed to keep an eye on him (meaning that I would keep an eye on him and report back!) and re-evaluate towards the end of the academic year. I could see that making the decision not to send Max there had been the right one for him, but for Eddie I had hoped that it might be different and work out to be the right choice. The boys at this school all came from extremely wealthy families, and there were very few divorced couples.

Eddie never wanted me to be sad or upset. "It's okay, Mum. I'll be fine. Stop worrying." He hated me being upset, but not convinced, I continued to worry.

"Love you, honey. I just want you to be happy," I said, searching his eyes for a sign that he was okay.

"Love you too, Mum." So much flatter than how my gorgeous boy used to sound.

It was fortunate that the school counsellor adored him (not in a creepy way), and, unlike Charlie, Eddie enjoyed seeing him. He was determined to fit in and make it work. So, very gradually, with a lot of support from the school, Nellie and Patrick and his siblings, he started to find his niche over time. I like to think that he wore the other boys down with his individuality until they finally really got him for the unique, funny person that he was. His wit, when people took the time to listen, was razor-sharp and so clever. There were times when I'd be floored by one of his comments, and I had always thought that I was the funny one. So, once again, I began to think that surely my kids were okay now.

Next hobby! For many years, I had thought that I would like to write a book; there certainly was a lot that I wanted to say, and if truth be told, needed to tell – call it catharsis, I guess. In my spare time, which was somewhat limited, I began to write the story of my life. It felt good to get some of it down on paper – well, computer – but I stopped after rereading it for the second time, thinking that nobody would really be interested anyway. It was too bloody serious and sad, a tale of self-pity and a real sob story. I called it my 'sooky lala' book. I saved it, stopped writing and was not to revisit this particular project till many years later. With my job, my friends and my kids, for now that was enough. *Stop with the hobbies, Jacquie. They rarely end well!*

Chapter Twenty-Six
Seven Years a Virgin

The kids and I caught up with Tom and the girls one weekend when he brought them to Sydney. He told me about a woman called Lena whom he had recently met. He said it felt like she might become a long-term girlfriend, and that they shared a mutual love of music and photography. I was happy for him, but couldn't help wondering why I hadn't been able to meet anyone in all this time. Jen and I remained great friends, and I tried not to question her about any of the details. After all, divorce is complex, and there are two sides to any story that will be told as to the ultimate reason for the breakdown. She had had one boyfriend since their separation, but had been on her own for a long time now.

Annie and Jo were still as happy as ever, planning holidays all the time, doing up their house and having heaps of fun with all of their friends. Mum was happy and healthy too. It was great to see that all of my family was in a good place.

Max was succeeding in his business with a solid client base at last. He was making a pretty decent income and felt challenged by the thrill of running his own business. It hadn't been easy for him initially, but now that it was expanding as his reputation grew, he was a lot more secure and confident. I felt such pride as I watched him grow from a boy to a young man, still so sensitive and sweet whilst developing as an independent individual.

Charlie was still working full-time in her second position in fashion. She was now in a management role in high-end women's fashion, after becoming furious with a touchy-feely senior manager from her last job.

"He waits till there's no one around and then tries to grope me. It's so gross!" she had told me when she had finally had enough of it. "I love my job, but I can't do it any longer."

"Honey, you should report him." I encouraged her to do what I hadn't had the courage to do with Derek the Arsehole.

"I can't, Mum. It's his word against mine. He'll say that I flirted with him; I know he will."

"It's up to you, babe, but I'll support you if you want to fight it."

"It's not worth it. They won't sack him." Her mind was made up; she resigned and walked straight into her new job. While the girls she worked with were the 'Oh my God!' types, at least they weren't hitting on her.

Eddie had taken on a part-time job at the local movie theatre. He thought he was so grown up, with his own income and independence.

"I'm proud of you, honey," I said to him. He just grinned and hugged me.

I could work more now the kids were a bit more independent, although it was hard to obtain a permanent job where I worked – the tendency was to employ mostly casual trainers. Money was still often a bit tight and I always had to try to be careful to be able to afford the bills, but we were all pretty much okay. I had become rapidly accustomed to living on a budget after so many years of having everything that I wanted – everything, that is, except for a happy marriage. It was important to keep reminding myself of that fact, whenever I would sink into the 'woe is me' or the 'did I try hard enough?' self-talk. I was breathing much easier these days, with many, if not all, of my worries about money and the kids lessened. I gradually came off the 'happy pills' and even considered stopping smoking. Everything finally felt like just maybe it was moving in the right direction.

Next, I wanted to consider my virginal state, having counted up the time since my last encounter and realised that I had had no sex for seven years! I felt positive about myself, and even thought about perhaps trying internet dating again. Tilly and Lucy had met a lot of guys and appeared to be having fun.

"What have you got to lose?" said Tilly. "At least it's a bit of company, even if you want to stay a virgin!"

"But it's such an effort when they turn out to be duds," I whined.

"Just try it. You never know. You met Danny last time, so maybe you'll find some new friends, at least."

I had enough friends! But, with a huge sigh and an accompanying eye-roll, I decided to give it a go.

As I was contemplating this potential new life, redoing my online profile and pondering the possibilities for my future to be brighter, my phone rang. It was Max.

"Hi, honey. How are you?" I asked, chirpy and positive, still smiling to myself after my conversation with Tilly.

"Mum, I'm really sick," he said, sounding breathless and weak. He started to cry, which was very unusual for him. Having had to deal with so much from his father, he had managed to toughen up and roll with life's punches. Worry snaked its way into my gut, settling there uncomfortably.

And just like that, in that very moment, all thoughts of the possibilities for my new life went out the window. Max was my priority. My kids would always come first, and motherhood would always win.

"I'm coming to get you now," I said, grabbing my keys. Patting the devoted, tail-wagging, ageing Monty, I walked out the door. As I drove to Max's unit, in amongst my overwhelming concern, I felt a surge of purpose. Nothing and no one could ever fill me with such a feeling.

My worries were confirmed when he opened the door. His pale, drawn face greeted me as he fell into my arms.

Chapter Twenty-Seven
A Need Greater Than My Own

Max had moved out of home and was buying a unit; his business was great, and I had thought that his life was well and truly on track. I couldn't believe that this was happening to him. As I tried to comfort him, it struck me that he was simply too ill to continue working as much.

"Honey, you're going to have to cut down – I think coming back home for a while might be a good idea, don't you?"

"I just don't know what to do, Mum. I don't want to feel like a loser, running back home when things get a bit tough."

"Let's just look at it as temporary until you get better. If you rent the apartment out on a short-term lease that will cover the mortgage so at least you won't have to worry about that. I'll take care of you until you're back on your feet again."

"Ok, but I'm going to fight this, whatever it is." At this point tears were sliding down his face.

After going to the doctor and my favourite naturopath, we received the diagnosis that he was suffering from Chronic Fatigue Syndrome. Neither of us knew anything about it. He was terribly weak and lethargic, with little or no energy, and severely depressed.

His current girlfriend broke up with him when she found out about his condition, not being able to or knowing how to help him, according to what she told him. Not very long afterwards, she started going out with one of his friends. For him this was the last straw. I watched him completely fall to pieces, going from having scary panic attacks to bouts of the deepest sadness that I had ever seen him go through. It seemed like everything was going from bad to worse.

There was no official cure that anyone could offer, and so I wasted no time before starting to madly Google (one of my new favourite pastimes), determined to find the answers myself. I ended up buying a massive amount of herbs and vitamins based on my extensive research, and we were recommended by one alternative practitioner to put him on the Paleo diet. I would do whatever it took to see my beautiful boy smile again.

"Honey, this website says that you should take these vitamins,"

I said, holding my phone in front of his face. "And apparently you shouldn't eat dairy and gluten," I said with some authority, having read yet another article. He smiled indulgently, with a Mum-can-you-please-stop-stressing, pleading look.

My life was now officially on hold, and I knew that I would have to cut down my working hours rather than increase them to look after him. I didn't know how long it would take for him to improve, but I was going to be there whenever he needed me. The problem with my job was that when you said no to training work, it was a whole semester before there would be more hours on offer. That didn't bother me; there was nothing in the world that I wouldn't do for my kids.

As I always lived pretty much hand to mouth, it didn't take long for the bills to start mounting up; once more the outgoings exceeded the incomings and we were struggling yet again, with my two credit cards creeping up to their limits. There was no choice but to consider another move to free up some capital until Max was better and able to work again.

Charlie was amazing, giving as much of her pay as she could to help out. Eddie also helped out more around the house and we all just rallied around Max until finally, slowly, he started to feel a little bit better. He didn't want to go out at all for a long time, as he had no energy to do much apart from the basics to keep his business afloat. He had taken someone on to keep working with his clients until his health returned.

Many of his friends found it difficult to understand his condition and avoided him; some rallied around him – not too many. Apart from the devastating effects of his physical illness, his self-esteem and confidence had taken a severe beating.

We sold our town house, making once again a reasonable profit, and moved to a very cute, very tiny house on an extremely busy road. We loved it from the very first day. It had been built in the late eighteen-hundreds and had a lot of the original features: beautiful wrought iron around the bottom edges of the bullnose tin roof and pretty leadlight windows. Inside was deceptively spacious with a large, open-plan lounge-dining area. The wall that had used to create a hallway between these rooms and the bedrooms had been removed to give it even more space. Everything was freshly painted white and it was so inviting.

Being on top of each other, tripping over the dog and sharing one very small bathroom was a small price to pay for our family to still be together all under one roof, the love and bond between us stronger than ever. Max was recovering with each passing day and I was gradually able to take on some more work. It looked like we might once again be back on track. *Do I dare to breathe out,* I wondered?

Max went back to work after a long period of resting, slowly, week by week, increasing his workload. Not long after he was well enough to settle back into his old routine, he agreed to go to a party that he really wasn't quite ready for. With the CFS, he had developed quite a high level of social anxiety, mostly preferring to stay with the family or hang out with one or two of the friends that he had remained closest to during his illness.

"Come on, mate," said one of his friends to him. "You need to get out and have some fun."

I was thinking, as mother hens do, *He shouldn't be drinking. He's still not one hundred percent.*

"I just don't think I'm ready to go out yet," he told his friend. But I could hear that his resistance was weakening; I guess he figured that maybe he needed to get out of the state that he'd been in once and for all. And so, anxious and apprehensive, he agreed and went, while I stayed home worrying.

Going to the party ended up being a very good decision for Max, as he met a great girl that night who seemed to relate to him straight away and who understood his sensitivity, from what he told me – smiling broadly – the next day. It had been a while since I had seen him smile like that; I was happy for him and equally concerned, as I couldn't bear to see him hurt again.

"She's amazing, Mum. You'll love her," he told me, his face animated.

"Don't rush into anything," I begged, caution in my voice.

"I won't – promise. But it just feels right," he reassured me.

Her name was Chloe; they formed an instant connection and after that night, they started hanging out together all the time. He was able to talk to her about Simon's treatment of him, and it took very little time for them to fall completely in love.

He had risen from the depths of physical and emotional despair to start to live his life once again, and I was over the moon for him. Not long afterwards, he moved back to his apartment and continued to keep up his vitamins and healthy-eating regime. He was now not under my watchful mother-hen eye, but I trusted that he would continue to look after himself. It had been so devastating for our whole family.

Charlie had developed an addiction to smoking and excessive drinking and was still always obsessed about her weight (who does that sound like?). On the surface she appeared to be happy enough – flitting from relationship to relationship, party to party, very beautiful but never thinking that she was beautiful enough, no matter how much I told her. I still worried that I had passed on my weight obsession, and though I did not know that she had inherited the genetic predisposition to alcoholism – and had no idea at that point that it could be hereditary – I worried that her father had passed on his alcohol addiction too. Whenever I'd try to talk to her, she'd become angry and say something like, "I'm not like my father. Back off and stop worrying. I'm just having fun!"

I tried to back off, but knew without a doubt that I would need to keep a watchful eye on her yet again.

Eddie finished school and was more than a bit rudderless as to what he wanted his future to look like. He went to university, continuing to work part-time and enjoying the friends that he had managed to accumulate – people who really got him now for the quirky individual that he was, as I had hoped throughout his time at school. He had his first real girlfriend and was overall enjoying his life.

I wondered, yet again, if I could take my life off the on-hold position while still trying to support my kids through their ups and downs. Being a mother of three was always going to have its challenges; I did really need to let them learn from their own mistakes, and to be there for them if and when they needed me. I could now take on more work again, we wouldn't have to move, and although things definitely weren't perfect, the kids were okay, relatively speaking. *Surely Charlie's drinking is just normal for someone her age,* I kept telling myself. I started to think that maybe the fog that had been a huge part of my life for so long could be finally lifting once and for all yet again.

And so entered into my life the man who we would all come to call 'Mr. 50-Shades-of-Grey Nomad'. He was thus named after the recently very popular trilogy called 50 Shades of Grey. Charlie and I had recently seen the movie together and when I had told her that

I was going on a date, she was very quick to come up with his new name.

"But he isn't old, and he doesn't have grey hair!" I protested. "Apart from which – it isn't going to be like that. He's just a friend."

"Yeah right, Mum, we know," from my smart-arse daughter.

Mr. 50 (I thought that the abbreviated version was a better name for him) and I had worked together in the corporate world, which seemed like a whole lifetime ago. On a whim, he told me later, he had called me to see if I would like to have dinner with him. I knew that he had been in a long-term relationship, and when I questioned him, he said that he had recently broken up with her. I hadn't been on a date in a very long time and in my current virginal state, I thought *Why the hell not?*

The kids teased me mercilessly as I dressed up in my best clothes from the singles-scene days and applied a lot more makeup than I usually did.

"Whoa, Mumma, looking hot," from Max, who had popped in for a visit.

"Don't do anything too naughty," from Charlie, smiling cheekily at me.

"Make sure you're not home late, young lady," from my resident clown, Eddie.

Apparently, I must have done a good job because when I opened the door, Mr. 50 looked me up and down, smiling a slow, sexy smile, and took my hand, holding it as he led me to his car. I felt quite nervous and excited for the night ahead.

"You look absolutely gorgeous," he said.

He was a perfect gentleman right up until we left the restaurant and were about to get back into the car for him to drop me home. He suggested a nightcap at his place, and after a long, lingering kiss I once again thought *Why the hell not?* He was, after all, a very good kisser. His hand wandered further up my skirt as we drove rapidly back to his house, a five-minute drive away.

We didn't waste any time; it was the wildest sex that I had experienced in many, many years. It certainly broke the drought and initially I quite enjoyed it, although I could have done without all the dirty talk that he felt needed to accompany the actual act. I stopped enjoying it after a while, as it was too porno and raunchy for me; the name that Charlie had given him was well and truly earned, I felt. After forty-five minutes with no break, lots of moaning, dirty words and spanking, I felt like I'd been in a pump class, and I don't do pump classes. I'd had enough, but he sure hadn't. We finally stopped for a while, thankfully, me wanting a cup of tea and to go home to my own bed, and him wanting to go back for round two after a short glass of wine break. *Get me out of here quick,* I thought.

He was such a nice guy in so many ways that I wondered if I was actually the one who had become a total prude. Was this normal? I had just thought that with my advancing years, sex would be, while still passionate, not quite so... acrobatic. Reflecting back on my younger days, this would have been the norm, but not for a divorced mother of three. I told him that I would call a taxi to take me home, as I had an early start in the morning, even though he protested, wanting to do the right thing and take me home himself.

"But, babe, don't you want to fuck me again?" *Do people our age say that now?* I wondered. *I guess lovemaking must be out of the question!* I quickly threw my clothes back on.

"I had a great time, but I really have to go. We'll talk soon," I said, wondering if he'd picked up on my insincerity. The taxi arrived and I made a hasty exit.

On the way home I gave myself a big talking to. *Come on, Jacq, this could be fun. Uncomplicated, and a great workout!* But then the Mum in me replied to the newly sexually liberated me, *No – you're not twenty-one!*

I went home and had a cup of tea; the Mum voice had won.

Chapter Twenty-Eight
The Needle, the Knife or Me

After 'losing my virginity' again and thinking that I wasn't ready or inclined to revisit sex anytime soon, one day I took a good, long, hard look at myself in the mirror. I wondered if it was time to try to look a bit better – maybe younger, even. A few of my friends were having 'work done' and I wasn't keen on the idea of the knife. I remember my dad once saying that he never wanted to go under the knife and that if it came to that, "Just take me now!"

My diets were still working, so my body felt okay, even though there were saggy, flabby bits that had replaced the younger body I had worked so hard on. There were still traces and memories of Simon's cruel taunts about my weight, which kept me somewhat paranoid about ever getting even the slightest bit chubby. The gym that I had joined was dead boring, but I did enjoy the workouts that I did from time to time with Max, and I loved regular brisk walks with Nellie and Sara in particular.

A rather frank friend of mine, also an ex-smoker (which I now considered myself to be, at around five per week), looked at my face one day and said, "You have the same lines as I used to have. I got laser around my lips and Botox injections to get rid of my frown lines. You should give it a go; you have such a pretty face apart from the lines."

And despite what she said, yes, she is still a friend. I looked in the mirror again and had to agree with her.

So off I went to her beautician and had some needles stuck into my face. It hurt, and I wasn't too keen on the process. It seemed so barbaric – but it sure as hell worked. People started saying to me that I looked 'really fresh' or that I must be sleeping well because I didn't look as tired as I usually did. As much as I knew that some would judge me for being so vain, it temporarily helped me feel better about myself, even though I still didn't want to have sex with anyone. It was simply a small amount of artificial confidence.

Around this time, I was starting to really dislike my job. There were a lot of funding cuts and changes I didn't agree with that came from senior management and to be perfectly honest, I just wanted to do something different. At this point, I had been there for close to twenty years. What I really thought I wanted to do was to improve my Tarot reading skills and to read for people as a job. I still practiced on my friends and family and was apparently, according to what everyone told me at least, really accurate with my readings. So I started studying online and practicing even more, using anyone who was willing as a guinea pig. Having recently done a supposedly spot-on reading for Danny, he told me afterwards, "You should be doing this for a living, honey."

"Get out! I'm not that good," I replied, hoping that he'd insist that I was.

I had always had the spiritually-seeking side to my nature and always loved having readings from various clairvoyants and psychics. I decided to act on Danny's advice and that I would charge a very small fee, once I was confident enough to feel a bit more professional. There was no way that I was going to give up my job until I would be able to make enough money to support myself and still help out the kids as they needed it.

The other thing that was now driving me was the need to satisfy my thirst to write again. *Maybe I should go back to my book,* I thought. I reread what I had written all those years ago and realised that a lot of what I had written wasn't half bad – the main issue being that it was so damn serious and it was still, as I had labelled it before, too 'sooky lala'. It would be great to introduce some of the funnier and lighter sides of my life, before the descent into a darker time with Simon, and then to talk about the potential for a better life that had become my reality. Life was in fact improving for me day by day. There were always going to be dramas to face: my kids, my financial status and the dilemma of facing the possibility of living a life without a relationship. However, I was doing just fine and the absolute best that I could. With the amazing friends and family that I had, being alone no longer held the fear for me that it used to.

And then – in the midst of my *Should I quit my job? Should I write a book? Should I read Tarot for a living?* – way too soon for all of us, it was time to say goodbye to our beloved Monty. He was thirteen years old and had been deteriorating slowly but surely over the past year. The vet had suggested that it would be kinder to put him down, as his back legs were failing him and he was no longer the happy dog that we had all loved so dearly. The four of us were a pitiful sight, hugging each other and sobbing noisily as the vet did what he had to do.

"Goodbye, old boy," I sniffled.

"I love you, mate," said Max.

"You're the best dog in the world," from Charlie.

"I hope you have lots of fun in dog heaven," put in Eddie.

Take-away Thai food and quite a few beers were the best way for the four of us to cope with our loss, the sadness always less when we could handle things together.

Not long after having to say goodbye to Monty, an amazing opportunity came my way which precipitated my decision to leave work and venture out on a new path. As much as I knew that I would probably have to do some part-time teaching to augment what I could earn for reading Tarot and the fabulous wealth that my book was undoubtedly going to bring me, I couldn't stay working at a place where I was becoming increasingly unhappy with the environment.

Anyway, one night I was out with Becca at my still-favourite pub on the lower North Shore, having a drink and dinner. We started talking about how much I wanted to write my book and she mentioned to me in passing that she had heard of a writers' festival in Ubud, Bali that apparently was amazing.

"Why don't we go together?" I asked her, bright-eyed and enthusiastic.

"I can't afford it at the moment, Jacq, but you should definitely go."

"But I won't know anyone!" I did my best pleading puppy-dog face.

"I can't, babe, sorry. But you meet people easily. Why not treat yourself?"

I knew that Becca and her husband Dan were not in a great financial position and that he was extravagant with what little money they did have. Becca had told me on many occasions how it was their biggest argument. But could I be so frivolous with my money? I wondered, already knowing that I so wanted to go. On the other hand, apart from the Botox that had become a semi-regular treat for my 'fresh' look, I certainly didn't spend much money on myself or do anything else that could have been considered to be frivolous.

I resigned and booked the ticket to Bali before I could think too much about it. This decision was going to turn out to be one of the most pivotal moments in my entire life.

The kids were excited for me. They were now fairly independent, Eddie the only one at home, Max living with a group of friends and still very much in love with Chloe, and Charlie living way beyond her means with one girlfriend quite close to the tiny house where we had all lived together. I did believe that it was time for me to make some changes and to live outside of my role as a mother just for a brief moment in time – ten days, to be exact.

I hadn't been overseas since my honeymoon in Fiji and was nervous and excited as the kids all drove me out to the airport, hugging me and wishing me a wonderful holiday.

As I waved to them just before I went by myself through the departures gate, I looked back at them full of love and, of course, my ongoing motherly worry. Was Max really well enough to run his business? Was Charlie still too thin and drinking too much? Would Eddie cope without me mothering him and fussing over him so much?

"For God's sake, Jacquie. They'll be fine. Just go!" I muttered to myself, much to the concern of other passengers around me, and after one last wave, off I went.

I landed in Bali and from the moment I arrived, I just loved it. The people were friendly, the place where I stayed was gorgeous and the writers that I listened to and met were nothing short of inspirational. I met a beautiful American man who lived there at breakfast one morning and after talking for over an hour, we swapped details, promising to keep in touch after I returned to Sydney. I found the place to have such a relaxing, intensely spiritual vibe and I felt at peace, relaxed and content. I meditated, went to yoga, ate super healthy food, swam every day and generally had one of the best times of my life.

Initially the only negative was that I was there on my own, and so I set about getting to know as many people as I could. Nearly everyone had at least one other travel companion with them, but a few people were happy to include me in their arrangements, dinners and tours, etc. A lot of the people I met reminded me very much of the North Shore snobs I had spent so much time avoiding in Sydney. They were definitely the socially elite, with terribly posh speaking voices – and of course some of them even wore linen. Others dressed like ageing hippies and spoke in hushed tones, using big words to illustrate their literary knowledge. As politely as possible, I attempted to detach myself from those people and to seek out the company of some travellers who were more down-to-earth.

On my third night in Ubud, I was at my new favourite bar, now that I wasn't on the lower North Shore. I started talking to two Australians, a man and a woman who were great friends and had travelled to the festival together. The first thing that had attracted me to them was their laughter and the more I spoke to them, the more I found them to be genuine, intelligent, not at all snobby and absolutely hilarious. We made plans to go to some of the events together and to meet for dinner the next night. I had arranged to do a cooking course the next day and was not going to be free until later in the day.

At the cooking course, I met a lovely woman from country Victoria and asked if she would like to join my new friends for dinner as well. She happily agreed and from that moment on, for the rest of my holiday, we were hardly ever out of each other's sight.

While we were at one of the many literary talks with my three new best friends, I happened to start talking to a publisher who expressed interest in the concept of my book as I described it to her, should I actually manage to finish writing it. We exchanged details and I found myself wondering if perhaps I could seriously become a writer. I discussed it over breakfast with my new American friend.

"Well, I'm renting a place for a year if you want to come over and do some writing," he said. "You could have your own room, if that's what you want, and see how it goes." His smile said otherwise about the separate rooms.

"Are you serious?" I never wanted to leave this magical place. "Let me go home and see the kids and I'll work out how I can afford to come back." Funny how when you're on holidays everything seems possible; the barriers drop and reality plays a distant second to fantasy.

Very sad to leave all of my new friends and my potential new boyfriend - *Settle down, Jacquie, you hardly know the man!* - I returned home feeling like I had experienced more than just a holiday. For me it had been a lesson of independence, self-acceptance, reflection and being open to something new. I felt unbelievably happy as well as knowing that I would definitely go back and that there were new exciting things on the horizon for me. I'd met new people who were destined to become lifelong friends and damn it, I was going to finish my book! And it wasn't going to be all 'sooky lala'.

When I landed and collected my bags, there they were again, smiling lovingly. My three beautiful babies had all come out to the airport to pick me up. If hearts could actually melt, then mine would have right there and then. I loved them more than ever: their ups and downs and many dramas and challenges. Looking at these amazingly complex individuals as I walked towards them, I gave myself a virtual pat on the back and smiled back, eyes glistening.

"Mum, I missed you so much," said Charlie hugging me tightly. *God, she's even thinner,* I thought as I returned her hug, feeling the gloss of the moment and my magical holiday dimming. Willing myself to stop being a Negative Nancy (apologies to anyone called Nancy!), I smiled at them all, determined to keep my positive vibe alive. We drove home and had breakfast together, laughing and happy just to be the four of us for this moment in time.

The next day I wanted to have a good think about my next step career-wise. Having resigned from my old job before Bali, I'd been getting slowly but surely even better at my Tarot readings. I thought that I would continue to try to build up my business and put the prices up while I continued with my new love of writing.

The people whose cards I read loved it and I felt that I was adding value to their lives. One of my clients suggested that I could consider running small parties as well as doing the individual readings. I loved the idea and created a Facebook page (yep, I was actually by now that tech-savvy), to promote the idea. It took off rather well and generated a decent, if not huge, income for me.

I had also heard of a Theta healing course from one of the new friends I had met in Bali, which really appealed to me as I wanted to go further with the spiritual side of my search. I happened to find one locally that weirdly, coincidentally (is there such a thing?), was starting the next day – a week after I had come back from Bali. It was yet another great decision, as I met some wonderful people who encouraged me to continue with my Tarot readings and to add some of the Theta practice into my business as well. I completed the first level and felt like I was invincible. After years of struggling, I was writing, practicing Theta and incredibly grateful for everything that I had.

Considering all of these crazy and somewhat destructive phases in my life up until this point, here I was, meditating most days, thanks to the practice that I had started in Bali – and it was working. Mind you, life wasn't currently throwing any curveballs at me. I was finally feeling like it wasn't something or someone that would fix me and that any problems I might face could be handled and dealt with more easily than before. Learning to slow down and be at peace, grateful for all that I had, seemed to be doing the trick.

I had a beautiful friendship and ongoing daily communication with my new American friend, Bill, from Bali and I was hopeful that just maybe we might have something worth pursuing. Based on the limited time that we had had together, I had found that he was a deep thinker with concern for the planet and a love of nature. Each time we spoke, he was so supportive of my writing and excited for the time that we could share together in Bali if and when I decided to go to and see him.

"Mum, you're so Zen!" Eddie said to me one day. "But are you going to go back to work ever?" he continued, concern and confusion not at all well disguised in his voice. I guess he was trying (as was I, truth be known) to figure out this new Mum who had emerged from the plane after such a short holiday, dramatically different to the one who had left.

"Nah," I replied in my new-found dreamy, don't-give-a-damn voice. "I'm happy with my Tarot and something else will turn up." This new, nonchalant me was wonderful. I absolutely loved her. Ever since I had come back from Bali, the new me was smiling back at me daily in the mirror. Bill made me smile, writing made me smile, reading Tarot made me smile. *What the fuck? Am I taking drugs and nobody has told me?*

Having realised over a long period of time that I rarely if ever finished anything, the one thing that I was determined to finish in my Zen state was writing this book. I had given up on my singing lessons; my counselling was just a Certificate when I really needed a Diploma to be able to practice any sort of meaningful counselling; I had given up speaking French when I had spent three years at university studying it; my Reiki course was only a level one, not the Level two that I had wanted to do. And let's not forget the typewriter, the guitar, the sewing machine and the folk-art. Even my Theta course was only the basic one, and I should have continued on with doing the advanced. As much as I had tried and in many ways succeeded, it felt like nothing was ever quite enough or really complete. The book was different; this was going to be a success and completed to the very best of my ability.

I spoke to Tilly, who had a friend who had written a few books, and she gave the best advice ever.

"You should join a writers' group," she said, and so I did. As nervous as I was, thinking that perhaps my book wasn't as good as I had hoped and dreamed, I found a group that sounded like it could be just the one that I was looking for. They were called 'Open Genre', which sounded right. I didn't want to be with a whole bunch of people who were just writing memoirs or kids' books or science fiction; I wanted variety, and more than that, I was hoping for a lack of judgement.

I went along on a Thursday night, hating being the new girl. Fortunately, on the first night you weren't expected to read; I was able to critique if I wanted to, or I could just figure out if the group was going to be the right fit for me. It was and I knew it from the very first night. On the second night I read my prologue and cried (so bloody embarrassing), but they weren't fazed at all; they were immediately interested in my work and encouraged me to keep going.

I was feeling so at peace, with any anxiety almost gone. I read my *Buddhism for Busy People* book from cover to cover. There were awesome words that made so much sense to me. I kept writing, and booked my flight to go and see my friend in Bali so that I could explore the possibility of a romance with him and work on my book in a beautiful environment. The kids were happy as far as my floaty, hear-no-negative brain could figure out. I was purely and simply content with my life.

Chapter Twenty-Nine
Happy Ending?

So, if you're after a happy ending, that's exactly what you're going to get. Well – not so much an ending as an exciting new beginning. I now had the possibility of getting my book finished in paradise, published by the Australian publisher whom I had spoken to in Bali and who had really encouraged me. I even started to think about the possibility of a book launch. I had a new friend offering me a potential romance after all this time with only 'Mr. 50-Shades' who had broken the drought, and I had a brand-new outlook.

I was seeing so clearly that meditation could actually work when you kept practicing it and I was never going to give it up, thanks to my experience with Theta. I was practicing being kind and generous to others, and trying my absolute best not to bitch about or be negative about anyone. I was being positive about every aspect of my life and it was working. God, I was feeling so damn new age.

At last, the battle with my beloved ciggies had ended due to a slight pain in my left lung, signalling that perhaps this smoking thing really was a bad idea after all. My last cigarette was at fifty-five years of age – there was simply no choice, so with no patches, no gum, I just quit cold turkey. The demon nicotine had lost its control, but gravity was happily taking its toll. Now that my lungs were so healthy, I even contemplated joining a gym again to deal with the impact that gravity's pull was having on my now not-so-firm body. The sex with the new boyfriend and all the yoga that I was bound to be doing in Bali would be enough, surely!

Is it my time now? Can I really leave them for so long? Do I deserve to find happiness? I wondered.

I already really knew the answer to those questions. My kids were starting to forge lives of their own, and it really was time to check out the possibility that this new connection might have some substance for me and bring me the loving partnership that I had craved deep down for so long. My life since marrying and leaving Simon had been dedicated to making the best possible life for my children, and I had mostly put myself in the background or as second best for many years. Max was progressing well with his new business and his girlfriend

Chloe, who really loved him. I thought at the time that Charlie had woken up to her ongoing battle with her addictions and was focusing on her health; that was what she kept telling me. Eddie was growing up; he had good friends, an amazing girlfriend, and a part-time job and was looking at full-time working opportunities.

Then, taking a deep breath, looking in the mirror at a happy me, I recited my latest mantra: "They're fine just the way they are. They are adults now. I have always done my best. I love them and I trust them to live their own lives." I picked up my suitcase, knowing that they supported my decision; I opened the front door, and walked with hope and purpose to the awaiting taxi. I knew that I would be back, but not until I knew for sure. I paused briefly, looking back to reflect on the moments upon moments that had brought me to this moment. The future was bright. I had the tools to move ahead with my life, never backwards, positive and strong. I had a sense of peace, confidence and gratitude for the lessons that I had learned. My faith in myself and the wisdom of the universe was strong. I felt the possibilities, and I kept walking forward.

Well, that's how it was supposed to end.

Chapter Thirty
My Purpose

My ticket was booked and paid for, and after two months of "I miss you so much!" from Bill, I was ready to go. Our calls had been slightly less frequent over the past ten days or so, and there was a little niggle forming in my gut; whereas we had Skyped before, we were now mostly chatting on WhatsApp, but he was still flirting and sounded keen to see me. I'd had coffee with Nellie and Clara and told them that I was worried about going, but we all agreed (as I needed their approval) that it was worth a shot and that this way I wouldn't die wondering if I had the courage to take this chance. If it didn't work out with Bill, I'd still be visiting my beautiful Bali and doing some writing – not such a bad outcome. One week before I was due to leave, I had a call from him.

"Listen, babe, I really need to talk to you. It's important and I don't quite know how to say this." Hesitating before he continued, as I panicked, he went on to say that he had met someone else. The excuse was that she lived there too and that... blah, blah, blah. I tuned out the rest. It hurt me so much; I had really thought that we had something worth trying.

I said something very grown-up like "You're a complete arsehole!" or "Fuck you!" – I can't really remember. All I know is that I felt like I was about twelve and I wanted to cry my eyes out. When I told the kids, Charlie was furious. She always was, and is to this day, in my corner if anyone ever dares to mess with her Mumma.

"Well, fuck him; I hate him and he was ugly anyway. You deserve better!" she said. Just as well that he was in Bali and not Sydney – I think he may have suffered a serious battering otherwise, if not physical then certainly verbal. The boys hugged me and also reassured me that I would find someone who would be right for me.

Disillusioned, I was tempted to turn to my old friend, nicotine, but resisted. And so I started drinking instead and I let meditation and my Theta practice lapse. I realised that, once again, just when I had thought I had it all together, I was still relying on someone or something to be my answer. As we didn't really know each other that well, my reaction was possibly a tad over the top, but that's the way it was. My writing stopped, self-doubt reappeared, and that damn fog was threatening to make an unwelcome return.

I had received a message on Facebook from a dear old friend of mine, Nicole, when I was first in Bali, to say that she was going to be there later in the year and she wanted me to join her if there was any chance that I could manage it. She was living in Spain and I hadn't seen her, apart from our infrequent Skype sessions, for over ten years. I decided to change the ticket immediately so that at least I would have something to look forward to among the disappointment and sadness that I was currently experiencing.

The next thing to face up to was that there was a definite need to earn some money, now that I had realised that being Zen (and occasional Tarot readings) simply does not pay the bills. There was some part-time training available where I had been working before, and I started straight away.

From the moment that I started, I didn't enjoy it one bit; it felt soulless as I made myself go through the paces. I continued to read Tarot cards spasmodically, but found it too demanding and it did not provide enough income for the effort involved. While the people that I read for were impressed with my ability to interpret a pack of cards and give what they considered to be insightful advice, I was once again lost and afraid of my uncertain future. *Watch out for that old self-pity, Jacq,* was my ongoing concern. *Oh, shut up, sensible voice. I need to wallow for a while.* And so I did just that; I wallowed big-time. I took to lying on my bed, reading books and avoiding the world, when I wasn't working. The hole in my gut was reopened, like an old, tired, unhealed wound returning to haunt me, while the fog in my brain blurred my path, causing confusion and disorientation.

When I would get sick of the wallowing, not wanting to slip any further into depression, I would will myself to do even small amounts of writing as often as possible. There was a lot more 'sooky lala', some 'woe is me', many deletions and changes, and some quite small yet encouraging amounts of progress.

For the third time (or was it the fourth or fifth time?), I revisited the principles of Buddhism that I had read in my now rather tatty-looking *Buddhism for Busy People* book and decided it was time to start again, again. As I had always understood and agreed with the attraction/aversion/karma concepts from every attempt that I had made to read the whole book, I wondered, *Can I reopen that door? And will I this time find the answers to the meaning of life?* Having abandoned my Theta practice and not having a lot of faith in God or the universe delivering any much-needed answers to my never-ending questions, maybe trying to be a Buddhist was my best shot at figuring out life.

I received a phone call out of the blue one day when I was in my *what's it all about?* continual search from a work colleague, asking me if I might possibly be interested in coming for an interview for a full-time job. It was in the HR section of the college, where I had been doing a small amount of part-time training. *Is this the answer that I've been seeking,* I wondered? Well, I figured that I wouldn't have time to think or ask pointless questions anymore if I was to be working full-time, so I took a punt and said yes. My overwhelming feeling was that it could lead me away from the path of despondency and depression where I was currently headed. There would be a regular income for a change, and a sense of purpose, even if it was the wrong purpose long-term. They agreed to the time off that I would need to see my friend Nicole in Bali, so it was all systems go.

It was such a shock to be getting up early, not grabbing a cup of tea and going back to bed, trying to figure out how I was going to fill in my day – *the gym? Coffee with a friend? See one of my kids? Pretend to write? Or just lie here doing bugger all?* That was all solved, with the six o'clock alarm telling me that it was time to go and join the daily grind.

When I first caught the bus into the city, part of me enjoyed the prospect of the structure that this new chapter would bring to my life, knowing that I would follow the same routine for five days a week, and yet another part of me felt completely out of my body, questioning, *Surely this is not my purpose? Aren't I supposed to be doing something spiritual? Aren't I meant to be enlightened by now? Shouldn't I have all the answers to the meaning of life?*

With some trepidation, I threw myself into my new role, boots and all. Working long hours under enormous pressure was the expectation from senior management, in an environment where it quickly became evident that poor communication standards and lack of a work/life balance culture were at toxic levels. I worked hard, seeking praise and appreciation for my efforts, only to be hit with a never-ending supply of extra tasks to perform. It wasn't long before I started to have an extreme stress response to my environment, waking up with my hands shaking and my heart pounding loudly in my chest.

I knew with absolute certainty that things couldn't go on like this. I felt like I was making mistakes, too afraid to ask other equally stressed and busy staff members for assistance. While knowing that I was trying my best, it was like butting my head against a brick wall. After only two months, it was clear to me that the decision came down to leave or potentially end up being carted off to the psychiatric ward or carried out in a box.

"Mum, you look so tired and stressed," said Charlie, who for once was the one worrying. "You have to leave that job before it kills you."

"I know I should, honey, but I feel like such a failure for not being tough enough to handle it."

"You're not a failure." She put her arms around me. "We all love you too much to see you this upset."

She was right. Without any more over-analysing, I resigned just before I was due to go on my trip, and could feel the pressure start to ease immediately. I didn't want to fail, but also didn't want to kill myself in the process of trying to be a success. Perhaps after my trip more part-time training could be an option again, but no longer working in a pressure-cooker like this was an imperative.

On a whim, just before I left the job, I had accepted an invitation to a work dinner. One of my colleagues, seeing how down I was, talked to me at length about what she was doing to sort out her life. She suggested that I might like to speak to her life coach. UGGH – I had always hated that title for a job. Facebook was full of supposed 'life coaches' who could teach you to set goals – *don't I know all of that already? Did I need a twenty-five-year-old who hadn't experienced the pain and dramas that I have to tell me to how to live? What the hell is she going to say that I couldn't figure out by myself?* 'Get a life', perhaps. *Oh well,* I thought. *I'm struggling big-time, yet again, so I may as well give it a go.*

I made the appointment and drove to the other side of Sydney to see her. My negativity was back at such a critical level that it was hard for me to leave my car, walk across the road and through her door, but I did.

"Hi," she said. "It's so good to meet you, and from what you've told me over the phone, I truly believe that I can help you." *Yeah right,* I was thinking. *Knock yourself out.*

As it turned out, she was amazing, and coincidentally told me that she worked in partnership with another woman who ran writing courses to help you polish and get ready to publish your book. *What? Hey universe, are you messing with me again? Did this mean that I just might finally finish something? Is it possible that my book will never enter 'the room of failures'?*

I had never really liked being in a group situation, the thought of group work being a scary and fairly foreign concept. I had always preferred to catch up with friends one-on-one, always questioning whether I was talking too much or too little, or being too loud, and whether people genuinely liked me. I was always able to get a read on it when there was just one or even two people, but otherwise found it to be rather tricky. My writers' group was working out well; they seemed to like me, or at least I hoped that they did, so maybe this new group could work out too. It turned out that I would be able to go to the first weekend of the course before my trip to Bali.

Walking in on the first and second days, I felt nervous and shaky, and wanted to do a runner. This was prevented by my handbag being in a cube at the back of the room, which would mean making a scene if I tried to grab it and leave. Everyone in the group had a story to tell, and had all experienced varying degrees of childhood and/or relationship pain. What I hadn't realised was that the course was all about healing your past through writing. *This could actually work for me,* I thought. After all, that was exactly what I was attempting to do –
   get it out of my system and onto paper.

As it came to my turn to speak, my mouth was dry and my hands were trembling. Everyone in the room heard me, I could tell by the way that they looked at me; some of them cried with me and some laughed with me. As I continued to read a short excerpt from my still very-much-a-work-in-progress, I felt supported, and it gave me the courage that was needed to continue writing this book, just as my writers' group was doing, week after week.

I left work for the last time, partly still feeling a sense of failure, but mostly relieved to be escaping an environment where it was impossible to ever win. Now to pack my bags to go and see my gorgeous friend, regroup, and begin again. Having this adventure to look forward to was exactly the antidote that I craved to a toxic work culture.

Another trip to the airport, this time just with Charlie coming to say goodbye, and another trip that I was excited about, now that I had managed to get over the love that never was with Bill.

"Have a ball, Mumma. You deserve this. Love to Nic," she said, hugging me goodbye.

"I will, honey. Now you look after yourself," I replied a little too sternly, always overly concerned for her health and well-being. "I love you." I headed off to the departure gate, willing myself not to say anything else about her weight. I simply had to trust her.

When I arrived and saw Nicole after so long, it was as if time had stood still since the last time that we had been together. We immediately got stuck into making plans for our holiday, feeling the same strong connection that had always existed between us.

We laughed, we hugged, we shopped, we swam, we drank, and we talked well into the night, both of us eventually too tired to utter another word, until the next day! Ten blissfully wonderful days like this, and my sense of humour would definitely be back. I knew that I would feel totally refreshed.

I remember one night, after an early dinner and way too many cocktails, Nic and I decided to do some late shopping. She had told me that she wanted to buy these painted wooden statues. They were supposed to be made for wedding ceremonies with one male and one female, but as they were both heavily painted in similar colours, the same height and with very little difference in the clothing, it was hard to tell them apart. She kept talking about the need that she had to buy these 'men' and had been going from shop to shop, trying to find just the right size and colours to suit a specific spot in her home.

As we were walking along, I spied some at the back of a window display in one of the shops and called out rather too loudly, "Look, Nic, men!!" The looks we received, as we doubled over with laughter, were priceless. We quickly scurried into the shop before we made even further fools of ourselves.

There was another time when Nic was scouring a particular stall down a little side street looking at silver jewellery. I happened to glance up to see a huge number of colourful carved penises hanging from the top of the stall. She was totally oblivious until I said, "Hey, Nic, look up." I managed to take a photo of her before we made a rather hasty retreat, giggling like naughty little girls.

Way too soon, it was time to say goodbye to my dear friend and head back home, to reality, normality and the fear of what next. *Writing and finishing my book, perhaps?* I honestly wrestled with the idea that people were never going to part with their money to read the story of my life, as self-doubt crept in. At times, I'd read something that I had written, and say to myself "Jacq, that is awesome!"; and then voice number two would say about something else that I'd written, "What a load of crap!" It also concerned me that some people might feel offended if I said too much or too little, and that others might be shocked as they read the often sordid details of my life. Writing was great in theory, until lethargy started to take over and I felt the dangerous pull of having no structure.

Hello, bed, hello, old life; I remember you, I moaned when I climbed the stairs with my bags, heavy from overindulging in some delightful bargains at the local markets. Collapsing on my bed, I proceeded to sleep off an overnight/no-sleep flight, avoiding thinking too much about anything just yet.

Within twenty-four hours, I was back to exactly where I had been before I had started my job — on the bed, reading, drinking cups of tea, playing word scrabble and crosswords on my phone, checking Facebook and Instagram for meaningless posts, and wondering what to do with my day and my life in general.

Feeling the threat of darkness potentially descending once again, I kept going to the gym with my 'best boyfriend' Danny. He was in between jobs and an absolute godsend as we spent hours chatting, drinking coffee and doing a little bit of token gym work. Ours was a relationship where we could talk about our lovers or lack thereof, our job trials and anything else that was happening in our lives.

My friends and family meant the world to me and were what kept me moving forward when I felt like I was heading backwards. Apart from the ongoing confusion about my future, I refused to allow myself too much whining, still determined to be grateful for all that I had. I'd be damned if I would return to doom and gloom, and I didn't want to go back on the 'happy pills'. I was surrounded by loyal people who adored me; not everyone can say that.

The Negative Nancy side of me started saying, "For God's sake, Jacquie, you can't write. You're actually just not that good." And what we'll call the Positive Penny side of me replied, "I think the book is pretty good. Keep going." The joys of being a Gemini, with a constant two-way conversation going on in my head!

It was time to get some reinforcements, and that meant calling Nellie and Clara to meet me for a coffee.

"You have to finish it. What you've read to me so far is great!" – from a Non-Negative Nellie.

"I agree, honey. You've worked so hard. Just get it done!" from Non-Negative Clara.

Needing more convincing, I called Becca and asked her to meet me for a drink at my still-favourite pub. She asked if her friend Molly, an avid reader and also very pro me writing, could join us.

"Do it and stop procrastinating. It will be brilliant." Becca was always in my corner.

"You need bum glue. Sit down and do it!" agreed Molly.

"Bum glue? What the hell is that?" I asked, amused, after my second glass of champers.

"Stick some glue on your bum and sit in your chair at the computer and write." Molly smiled at me, as if it was obvious.

I knew that they were all right. It was time to stop procrastinating and finish this book.

Max came around to tell me that he had asked his girlfriend, Chloe, to marry him. They had just found out that she was pregnant and he told me that they were so happy. While he was still struggling occasionally with his illness, Chloe was supportive and by his side, loving him at all times. It was now time for me to back off and let him live his own life.

Charlie was still battling with being underweight, and even ended up in hospital not long after I came back from Bali, just after Max had announced that he was getting married. I honestly felt like I'd failed as a mother when I saw how desperately thin she was, but when she went back to her apartment she reassured me that she would stop doing this to herself. She was an adult now; I couldn't force her to make the changes that she so desperately needed. I had done a great deal of crazy things when I was younger, like throwing out my lunch in a bid to be thin. As much as I was worried out of my mind for her health, all I could do was to continue to love her unconditionally.

Eddie was in his third different course with no real idea as to what he wanted to do, but at least he was happy with the same girlfriend and still doing some part-time work to pay for his own expenses. He wasn't making much money and was a drain on me financially, but so funny in his quirky little way and great company when I needed someone for a light-hearted chat.

I reflected yet again on motherhood – that same old love, guilt and worry was never-ending. I had to be there for them while trusting that they could sort out their own lives for themselves.

I was feeling a mixture of anxiety and excitement in equal measure that I would be returning to my writers' group and my writing course in a few days. *Will I be able to find my purpose there?* I wondered. I loved writing so much, and I felt driven to keep going with my book. I didn't appear to be able to rekindle my love of Theta and meditation. God, I had felt so good for a while there. One thing was for damn sure; I was not going to return to the way that I felt before I went to Bali the first time. Feeling that good was not an illusion; no man or job was going to beat me or bring me down ever again.

I went along to my writers' group with the latest writing that I had done; once again their critiquing was insightful and spot-on in terms of helping me improve and polish what I had written. The first day back at my writing course, I met one-on-one with the two fabulous women who ran it. As I'd missed one class while I was away, they wanted to help me catch up. As I spoke to them and they encouraged me even more than before, I knew once and for all that it was time to put all the pieces together and that my writing was going to be the key for me to do this. They truly believed in me – both groups did – so it was important to stop the negativity and believe in myself.

Chapter Thirty-One
What Next?

I was starting to feel pretty good about life again and the possibilities that might lie ahead for me now that I was writing and loving it.

Max rang me one day. "Hey, Ma, do you want to grab a coffee?"

I was out walking, and needed an excuse to stop for a caffeine hit anyway.

"Sure, honey," I replied. "Fifteen minutes?"

We met up, and he wanted to chat about the possibility of taking on a business partner. Having loved recruitment for many years, I felt excited by the prospect of helping out with some suggestions, and thrilled that he wanted my advice. I suggested that we go back to my place and work on some ideas together.

As we were productively throwing around ideas, the phone rang. It was Charlie. When I picked up, the first thing that I heard were her tears.

"Mum, I'm so depressed. I don't know what I'm doing with my life."

We talked for a long time as I heard her start to breathe a little better, clearly relieved to get things off her chest.

"Thanks, Ma – I'm okay really. I just needed to talk," she said, before going to get ready for work. I sincerely hoped so.

Eddie had come into my room while I was talking to her.

"Hey, Ma. Hey, Charlie. Get off the phone. I need to talk to you."

Once I was reassured that Charlie was okay, I turned around to deal with child number three.

"What's wrong, babe?" I looked at him, hoping dearly that it wasn't a major problem.

"I just wanted to give you a big cuddle," he said, accompanied by a cheeky grin.

A major aspect of my life that I had started to see even more clearly now was that I needed to lovingly disentangle myself from my kids' lives, allowing and trusting them to live their own lives. I would be there if they needed me, just as I had been today, but not as a permanent fixer. I knew they really were okay. Max had his own family and business now, Charlie – even though she had many ups and downs – had a job which, while not perfect, mostly suited her, and Eddie was working full-time at last. *So now what about me?* I wondered yet again.

I was reflecting more and more on just how grateful I was to have so many loving friends and for my family. Mostly I was now eating well, drinking less, still having no ciggies and exercising (nothing too excessive of course!) whenever I could. In fact, nothing I was doing was excessive or addictive anymore. I deeply loved my writers' group and also loved my writing course, where I was able to speak with like-minded people and actually get a lot of writing done. The main constant with both groups was to just get it down, to stop editing too much until the end, and to stop being side-tracked with ideas for other books apart from my main one.

My primary issue now was that I needed an income so that I could survive financially, and I hadn't as yet finished one single book, let alone sold one. Also, I continually wondered if I would ever have a relationship again. But all I really wanted to do was to write. That was my ongoing dilemma. I had now started writing five books, and was worried that they might end up in the 'room of failures' if I didn't actually finish one. So I took the advice that Becca's friend Molly, who had a lot of experience in writing herself, had given me when we had parted ways at the pub not so long ago.

"Finish one book. Remember to get out your bum glue and stay stuck to your chair!"

The phone rang one day, dragging me from my reverie about completion and potential failure once again. It was Mr. 50!

Uh oh, I have a chandelier in my house and I am definitely not going to be swinging from it! I chuckled to myself.

"Hi, Jacq, I've recently started working in your area and was wondering if you would like to meet for a walk and a coffee?" he asked – friendly, polite.

Is that a euphemism, I wondered? Nothing sexy about a coffee and a walk, I thought, so somewhat hesitantly I replied, "Well, hi," rather coolly to shut down any hint that I might be up for another round of his brand of exercise. He was friendly and I agreed, thinking with my new non-judgmental attitude that I should give him a chance.

When we met up, I was rather distant initially, until he apologised for how he had behaved when I had last seen him and asked if we could be friends. He explained that he had been a bit crazy after splitting from his long-term partner, admitting that their relationship had been an extremely physical one and that his behaviour had been that of a crazy, sex-starved creep and totally inappropriate.

We met up quite regularly after that and quickly became good friends, going for walks and hanging out for coffee or dinner. He was actually quite nice, calmer, and less sexually demanding. In fact, he didn't even suggest it, thank God. I definitely was not up to that sort of work-out. *A possibility?* I thought. *We'll see, no rush.*

Chapter Thirty-Two
Clarity, Communication and Judgement

As I have grown up and experienced challenge and change, so have my relationships with many of the people in my life changed. My gorgeous mum and I have evolved and developed our relationship to be closer than ever. Looking back on everything that we have shared, we have always known a beautiful, loving bond. We dumped Christianity and enjoyed cardboard meals together; we survived the *Bex*-taking phase and the many diets. There is now a whole new depth to our understanding and appreciation of each other. With the pressures of raising kids and constant moving having been removed, we are just able to really talk, adult to adult.

I find that I am really listening to her and she is hearing me, seeing me not as 'bubs' but as a mature woman with solid values and a confidence that is not about having to be the funny one, the drama queen or the shallow little flirt. Whenever we catch up, I talk happily to her, fascinated by the stories that have shaped her life and made her who she is today. We laugh a lot as we go shopping together, especially when we read all of the knock-off names that Aldi gives to its products. We buy *Protane* shampoo rather than the usual *Pantene*, *Hedafen* instead of *Nurofen*, *Cart Wheels* not *Wagon Wheels* – the long list that amuses us so much goes on. Often, we find that we are hugging in the middle of the supermarket, loving being so much closer to each other in more ways than just distance alone.

She is also unbelievably supportive of my writing and encourages me to keep changing the direction ever so slightly from a totally 'sooky lala' story to one in which I am able to portray the lighter side of the life that I have led. We reminisce and look at old photos in a photo album (not on my phone!) and I am able to see the true nature of a loving, caring family.

The more we spend time together as just the two of us, the more I can accept that there have been some somewhat delusional aspects to my memory. In my efforts to blame others for my mistakes, failures and sorrows, I have rarely stopped to see clearly enough and to ask the questions that needed to be asked. After all, why should the truth get in the way of a good story, or the story that I had believed it to be at the time?

I have come to realise that Tom was never the favourite really, and his sometimes seemingly mean treatment of me was about the fact that he just didn't want to be replaced. As I had such a flair for the dramatic, I did manage to frequently steal the limelight, and as a young child that must have been quite a struggle for him. Mum was just trying to cope with raising three kids, constant moving and insecurity; she wasn't really favouring anyone, and I can now empathise with just how difficult it was to raise three kids with such different personalities and needs.

Annie was just so much easier to handle and fitted neatly into the background, while I had an urge to be heard, to be noticed and to not be 'self-contained'. Annie and I have talked many, many times throughout the years and especially in more recent times about how growing up was for her: the struggle and ultimate acceptance of her sexuality, her bid to fit in and then her joy to find true, lasting love.

Apart from my wonderful relationship with Mum, I have learned a lot about forgiveness, even though there are many things that I will never forget. I have learned so much about the patterns that have ruled my life and the communication that I didn't manage to have with people that could have led me to finding the truth. I chose to cut and run much of the time without exploring the reasons for failure or possibilities for resolution.

I have forced myself to closely examine a failed, abusive marriage and have realised that Simon, along with us all, suffered from patterns and childhood issues. His father could often be a control freak, a hard taskmaster and sarcastic towards others, as well as being a borderline alcoholic. While it is difficult to take my mind back to those awful times, I can see more clearly that Simon had carried that relationship and attitudes into his relationship with me and his treatment of Max. I am able to see that, even though Simon's drinking was worse than his father's, he was in fact a product of his upbringing, mirroring the environment that he had come from. Expectations from his father were often incredibly and unreasonably high.

Knowing all of this will never excuse the behaviour, but it helps me to understand and to let it go. He is now married to someone whom, from all accounts, he treats well. Apparently, he is happy, and I am happy for him; I choose not to pass judgement and hold on to the past. It is too toxic and damaging for my soul to do that.

One of my greatest epiphanies in my continual search for meaning is that putting others down never ultimately makes you feel better about yourself. I think back to the 'linen ladies' and can see so clearly that I was just afraid of not fitting in, so if I put them down, I could temporarily feel like I wasn't on the outside and not as good as them. That being said, I'm afraid that I do still hate linen!

I remain grateful for the family humour, my 'gift of the gab' and my dramatic flair, as they have all helped me get that job and win people over, as well as sustaining me through many a tough situation. In fact, I am now at last happy with the person that I am as a daughter, mother and friend.

Epilogue
Aha??

Well, I have finally finished my first book. I love it, it is going to be published, and there are people who have already told me that they do want to buy it. It is my hope that there are some insights that may be helpful to others – but at the very least, I would be happy if people simply feel that it is a good read. *Will it make me rich?* I couldn't care less. It was something that I so badly wanted and needed to do. I guess this is what catharsis is all about.

Now, I feel free to write more. I'm thinking of writing something trashy and flashy just for fun after pouring out my heart for so many pages. *Do I see myself as a North Shore Buddhist?* Partly I do, as I continue to review the concepts of karma, attraction and aversion, but I'm more of a dabbler who is interested in all religions, philosophies and ways of life. I remain curious, open and searching, as I always have been. I rarely read Tarot cards anymore, being more content to just let what will be – be.

As I think about the reasons that anyone writes a book, whether for catharsis, a message or just a good read, I know that for me it was a necessity. The questions about should I stay or should I go are easy to answer. Yes, I should have stayed; the evidence is there every time I look at the three people whom I love more than anything in this world. Yes, I should have left, to save myself and to save my children from seeing any more damage and abuse.

Maybe having Mr. 50 back in my life has inspired me. Upon reflection, he is more than I initially thought him to be – much like many of the people who have come and gone, flitting through my life for a reason or a season and some even staying for a lifetime. What he has taught me is that there may still be a possibility for romance and that I am able to clear my communication barriers when I actually take the time to communicate. Above all, we have become great friends who truly care about each other. I have talked to him openly, patiently, about how he made me feel, and about the relationships in my past that have failed so dismally for so many different reasons, the main one being my inability and fear to communicate effectively, to speak my truth and honour my feelings.

One day we went for a walk by a river near my house, me at my usual crippling pace: things to do, busy, busy. There is still a part of me that hasn't quite let go of the past, that feels fear and great sadness for the abuse I lived with and the struggle that sapped my energy for so many years. We arrived at a part of the river where there were no trees, just an overhanging rock ledge. I glanced and went to move on.

"Can we slow down? I'd like to stop for a while and just look at the river."

I turned around, ready to give him one of my best eye rolls. As I saw him gazing peacefully, I stopped and looked myself, glancing back at him, calm and relaxed.

I felt edgy for a while, not used to relaxing completely apart from my few mediations that were gradually making a reappearance. I joined him in the water-gazing experience, the trees from the opposite bank perfectly mirrored, two ducks gently skimming through the scene, creating the slightest of ripples.

I breathed out, turned back towards him and reached for his hand. "Ok," I said, "I'll slow down."

We smiled and started walking again at a calmer pace. I had a sense that slightly, slowly, the fog may just be finally lifting for good.

Will I stay with Mr. 50? For the moment, it is easy and I am able to just be myself. We are close and there is some level of attraction, that's for sure; however, without that real depth that I have always craved. The friendship is special but there is a certain something missing, if I was to call what we have the forever kind of love. I'm not looking to be with someone on a permanent basis just for the sake of it. We are simply happy to have each other as company.

Every day I am grateful for all that I have, and every day I try to live without regret and fear, content with just being present in each moment in time. I have been in contact with Chad through Facebook and plan to make a visit to see him. He is also divorced with three children, and still living in Boston. Our communications have been friendly, funny and positive.

Of all the relationships that I have had, Chad was the one who didn't cheat on me or abuse me in any way. I need to see him, if for nothing else than to make peace and to talk to him openly, face to face. Mr. 50 – his name is Steve (doesn't sound so glamorous, does it?) – knows that I am going and understands the need that I have. He and I are so good as friends that it's probably how we'll keep it.

There is no longer a need to have the relationship to end all relationships, although there does seem to be a flutter of some sort each time that we have spoken or emailed recently. It is more than anything, a step towards healing another aspect of my past. There is certainly no desperation or expectation and no more whirlwinds. At this stage of my life, I would much prefer a gentle breeze. I guess it's a case now of 'watch this space'.

Above everything in this complex life of mine, I have learned a lot about addiction. Nothing and no one can fix us: not God, not men, not drugs and alcohol. While I do still enjoy my wake-up coffee, a glass of wine or two and of course the odd mid-afternoon chocolate hit, I try not to let these simple pleasures rule my life.

I went to a few Alcoholics Anonymous meetings just after I left Simon in an attempt to understand the disease and the impact that it had on other people. I was deeply moved, and I learned so much from the people that I heard and met there. If I have learned nothing else than the words that were spoken at every meeting, then that is enough wisdom for anyone to live their life by.

The Serenity Prayer

God, grant me the serenity to accept the things I cannot change,
Courage to change the things I can,
And the wisdom to know the difference.

About the author

The author was born on the north coast of N.S.W. She moved to several different towns throughout her childhood until she ultimately settled in Sydney in the late seventies. Her life has taken her on many adventures and taught her many valuable lessons. The more painful lessons that have become an integral part of her have also strengthened her love of life and her gratitude for all that she has. She now loves to write at her desk overlooking Sydney's magnificent Harbour Bridge, to walk up the road for coffee in one of the area's fabulous cafes, or to have a drink at her favourite pub, a mere five minutes away.

Millie writes short stories and novels which feature honest exploration of contemporary issues. When she is not writing, she attends her two writers' groups and spends time with her many friends, her three wonderful adult children and her precious grandchildren. She lives a vibrant and full life, travelling when she can, exploring the many varied markets around Sydney and walking anywhere where she can see even a glimpse of water. She has surrounded herself with a community of writers who inspire and encourage her to pursue her passion for the written word.